THE
MERMAID'S
SECRET

FORGE BOOKS BY KATIE SCHICKEL

Housewitch
The Mermaid's Secret

KATIE SCHICKEL

~~~~~~~~~~~~~~~~

THE MERMAID'S SECRET

A TOM DOHERTY ASSOCIATES BOOK
NEW YORK

THE MERMAID'S SECRET

Copyright © 2016 by Katherine Schickel

All rights reserved.

Mermaid art by Heretic Templar

A Forge Book
Published by Tom Doherty Associates, LLC
175 Fifth Avenue
New York, NY 10010

www.tor-forge.com

Forge® is a registered trademark of Tom Doherty Associates, LLC.

The Library of Congress Cataloging-in-Publication Data is available upon request.

ISBN 978-0-7653-8130-9 (hardcover)
ISBN 978-0-7653-8131-6 (trade paperback)
ISBN 978-1-4668-7966-9 (e-book)

Our books may be purchased in bulk for promotional, educational, or business use. Please contact your local bookseller or the Macmillan Corporate and Premium Sales Department at 1-800-221-7945, extension 5442, or by e-mail at MacmillanSpecialMarkets@macmillan.com.

First Edition: June 2016

Printed in the United States of America

0 9 8 7 6 5 4 3 2 1

For Finn and Bridget

ACKNOWLEDGMENTS

Once again I am indebted to Kristin Sevick, who helped give this story legs (and fins), and Marlene Stringer for her sage advice and unflappable support. I am so thankful to the rock stars at Forge—Bess Cozby, Emily Mullen, Todd Manza, Tim Green for the amazing cover. Big thanks to the Newburyport Police Department for giving me a window into their world. Meg Mitchell Moore, what would I do without you? Lise Goddard, thank you for ferreting out the underwater details with me (next time I'll use the predatory nudibranch as a plot twist—no one will see it coming!). Mom and Dad, your encouragement is endless and always appreciated. Finn and Bridget, with whom I've spent many a low-tide to high-tide beach day, you make it all worthwhile. And, of course, my love and gratitude to Michael, my first reader.

NE'HWAS, THE MERMAID

A long time ago there was an Indian, with his wife and two daughters. They lived by a great lake, or the sea, and the mother told her girls never to go into the water there, for that, if they did, something would happen to them.

They, however, deceived her repeatedly. When swimming is prohibited it becomes delightful. The shore of this lake sands away out or slopes to an island. One day they went to it, leaving their clothes on the beach. The parents missed them.

The father went to seek them . . . The girls swam up to the sand, but could get no further. Their father asked them why they could not. They cried that they had grown to be so heavy that it was impossible. They were all slimy; they grew to be snakes from below the waist. After sinking a few times in this strange slime they became very handsome, with long black hair and large, bright black eyes, with silver bands on their neck and arms.

—Charles G. Leland, *The Algonquin Legends of New England or Myths and Folk Lore of the Micmac, Passamaquoddy, and Penobscot Tribes,* 1884

THE
MERMAID'S
SECRET

ONE

Out the windows of Kotoki-Pun Diner, I squint into the morning sun toward the Atlantic and watch a set roll in. The last wave spikes into a perfect peak and peels right. If I close my eyes, I can imagine myself in that little pocket of power, ripping down the face.

"More coffee, Jess?" Anne-Marie asks, walking up to my table with a glass carafe smudged in fingerprints. Her eyes aren't on me; they're watching the ocean as well.

"I'm good," I say. I haven't even touched my first cup.

"Got a lobster omelet for the special. Side of coleslaw." She straightens her apron.

"Lobster? For breakfast?" I pick at my nails, flaking black polish onto my bare legs.

"Honey, it's summer. We'd put lobster in the brownies if *they'd* buy it." She points her chin toward the sea, the waves, the distant ferries under sail somewhere between the mainland and our island.

A breeze blows in and I can smell the salt water. "Did you know that lobsters are part of the cockroach family? It's literally like eating bugs."

Anne-Marie doesn't flinch. "Then they're in good company in our kitchen." She taps her pencil against her notepad. "So, what'll it be? Haven't got all day."

"I'm waiting for someone. Can you give me a few minutes?"

She looks down at me. Her hard eyes soften. "Sure thing, honey." Waitresses at Kotoki-Pun Diner are supposed to be prickly and tough. They're always telling customers to "Hurry it up" or "Get your own damn ketchup." If you talk back, they skimp on your order or eighty-six the fries on you, even when you know that places like Kotoki-Pun Diner have at least five years' worth of frozen french fries stored in their walk-ins. For some reason, tourists love the abuse. I guess it's because people are always trying so hard to say the right thing that no one ever says what they're really thinking. Hearing the truth—for example, that you have no business ordering a strawberry sundae after chowing down a half-pound burger and side order of onion rings—takes people off guard. And being taken off guard is what makes people laugh. Wakes them up to the moment.

But I get special treatment. Special, awful treatment. With a side of pity.

Outside, a police siren wails. I lift my hoodie over my head and slink into the booth, the skin on the back of my legs sticking to red vinyl. Blue lights flash across the tin ceiling.

The diner door swings open and Sheriff walks in. There's a slouch in his shoulders, which makes him look old and broken, like a schooner with a snapped mast.

All the locals in the diner know him and look up with reverence, or else sympathy. Hard to tell the difference. They nod, greet him with "Sheriff." He knows them all and nods back. "Gary." "Jean." "Louise."

The line cook looks up, wipes his glistening forehead with the back of a sleeve, and gives him a "Morning, Sheriff." He swats at something I can't see behind the grill. Probably a cockroach.

The woman called Louise keeps looking at him long after he's passed her table. She has a smile on her face like she's just been crowned Miss Ne'Hwas, Queen of the Lobster Parade. It gives me the creeps. Not just because it's unnerving to see old people flirt, but because he's not available. Look at the wedding ring, Louise. I want to tell her to go fish in some other pond.

But I resist.

He stops at my booth. Everyone's eyes are on me—the line cook, that Louise lady. I know what they're thinking. The delinquent with the hoodie and the black eye makeup, busted before breakfast. Must be serious. Drugs. Solicitation. Grand theft.

"You had to use the siren?" I say.

"I was running late."

"It's embarrassing."

He sits down, pulls off his hat, and places it on the seat next to him. "For you," he says, and slides a box with a pink ribbon across the table. "Happy birthday, Jess."

I try to smile, but I've forgotten how. I feel the muscles in my cheeks draw my lips toward my ears. The skin tightens across my forehead. But my eyes don't change. It's a cartoon smile drawn by a big cartoonist hand in the sky.

"Next time, can you just pick up a phone to let me know you're running late? Like a normal person?"

"I don't trust mobile phones," he says. "Reception's spotty on the island."

You'd think we live on the moon. But it's not quite the moon. It's Ne'Hwas—pronounced nuh-*he*-wuz, as all tourist brochures by the cash register point out. According to the plethora of marketing materials designed to drum up summer business, we are "a quaint island in the Gulf of Maine with lush mountains and glorious beaches . . . a charming retreat for the whole family . . . a world-class fishing destination . . . a perfect mix of rugged nature and refined living." If I were to write my own brochure, I might add "isolated, suffocating, and haunted."

I pull off the ribbon and open the box. Inside is a comb carved of bone, its prongs sharp and buffed to a polish. On the handle, four concentric spirals swirl outward from a star inlaid with black onyx.

"It's the Passamaquoddy symbol for strength," Sheriff says.

"I got it at a strange little shop downtown. Right near your apartment, actually. Lady in the shop told me it's made out of sperm whalebone."

I turn it over, admiring the intricate carving, the burnished bone. It's a unique piece. Very cool. Very me. I'm thankful it's not something girly that I'd never wear, like a pair of pewter sand dollar earrings from the Anchor's Away gift shop downtown.

"It's legal," Sheriff says. "I checked. The tribe gets special dispensation for collecting whalebones under the Marine Mammal Protection Act."

I fumble through a series of responses, trying to find an appropriate way to express my feelings. Finally, I mumble out, "Thanks, Dad."

He smiles.

I never call him Dad. He's always been Sheriff. He earned that nickname when he was a kid, and it stuck. Apparently, he was always keeping other kids in the neighborhood safe, facing off against bullies, rescuing people from rip currents and rising tides. He was the sheriff in town, there to protect and serve all.

Well, almost all.

I pull off my hood and let my hair fall down to my shoulders. I twist it into a bun, and stick the comb in. "What do you think?"

"It's very becoming on you," Sheriff says. "She had one with the symbol for harmony, but I thought this suited you better."

"Yeah, harmony isn't exactly my thing."

"I was going to get you a pretty little sand dollar bracelet," he says.

I smirk.

"But that old woman was quite insistent on this comb. She's Passamaquoddy, just like you. Figured she probably knew more about it than I do."

"Sometimes I think you're more interested in my Passamaquoddy roots than Mom," I say.

"It's who you are, Jess. You have to honor that. Your heritage is as old as the rocks that line Kotoki-Pun Point."

"I'm half Creary, too," I say, but as I look into Sheriff's blue eyes and freckled Irish skin, I don't see any of me in him. I inherited my mom's dark skin, high cheekbones, and golden eyes. I definitely look more Native American than Irish cop.

"Did you hear from her?" he asks, cradling the cup of coffee Anne-Marie has set down for him.

"Not even a card."

"Well," Sheriff says, blowing into his cup, "don't hold it against her if she doesn't call you today. She's hurting."

"We're all hurting."

The first year after you lose someone, there are no birthday parties, because celebrating doesn't even enter your mind. Holidays only serve as reminders of what you've lost—the first Thanksgiving Kay and I won't stay up all night watching a *Godfather* marathon; the first Christmas Kay and I won't crack ourselves up by sneaking chunks of coal into Sheriff's stocking. The birthday Kay would have turned twenty-four. These are days that are best left ignored. And people understand. By the second year, though, the world has moved on, and expects you to move along with it. Only, I haven't. And neither has Sheriff.

I look out at the waves again. A gust of wind churns the surface into a thousand whitecaps.

Not that suffering is a competitive sport, but if there were a family lottery on misery, today I'd be the winner. Today, I'm twenty-three and getting older every day. Kay will be twenty-three forever. From this day forward, I will be older than my older sister. From here on out, I'm the first. I'm the one who gets to experience adulthood, marriage, childbirth, and old age. I'm the one with my whole life in front of me, with all the shimmering hope that implies. I'm the lucky one who gets to do extraordinary things and make a difference in this world.

I'm also the one who gets to fail to live up to my potential, screw up everything I try, push away the people I love, and end up as a huge disappointment to everyone around me. Happy fucking birthday to me.

Sheriff changes the subject. "Are you working for Harold this summer?"

"Tips are good." I dump a packet of sugar into my coffee and swish it around.

"It's a little late, but I can get you an interview at the park. If you want."

I sigh. "To do what? Work as a ticket taker for minimum wage? I'll make triple that on the fishing boats."

"There are good benefits working for the state."

"Here it comes." I give him my petulant-child look. I'm good at that one. I've also got I-don't-give-a-crap-what-you-think un-grateful teenager and go-ahead-dare-me-and-see-what-I-do rebel girl down solid.

He's undeterred. "You have to think about the long term, Jess. Are you just going to stay on Ne'Hwas for the rest of your life? There's more opportunity on the mainland."

"You've been on Ne'Hwas *your* whole life."

"There's more for you out there." Instinctively, he points west. "The world is your oyster."

I rub my temples. "Do you know how corny that sounds?"

He tightens his jaw and he touches the bridge of his nose. "It's not too late to get your degree. You liked biology, remember? You were very good at it, if I recall."

"Yeah, I like biology, but you can't just take biology. You have to sit through all those other classes, too. I tried it, Sheriff. College wasn't for me."

"If you're not going to go back to school, you should at least build your résumé working for the state."

"I don't want a crappy job working at the park. I like working on boats. I like being out on the water. It's the only place I like to be."

He slaps the table. "It's not always about doing what you like. You can't just party your summer away and hope to get by all winter. You're not a kid anymore. You have to think about your future, Jess. If you put in your time working for the state, you can move through the ranks. It can be your ticket out of here."

I throw my hands up. "I'm not her, okay?"

His face falls. The very mention of my sister casts him somewhere far away. He puts his coffee down and wipes imaginary crumbs off the table. "I know you're not her."

Anne-Marie comes over to take our order. "You two ready?"

Sheriff pulls a menu out from behind the napkin dispenser.

"Got a lobster omelet for the special today," Anne-Marie says.

Sheriff shakes his head, his eyes still on the menu. The slouch in his shoulders has deepened since we've been sitting here.

"I'll have blueberry pancakes," I say.

"It's her birthday," Sheriff says, trying to sound cheery, but hitting a flat note instead.

Anne-Marie puts her hands on her hips. "Why didn't you tell me? How old are you now?"

I cringe. "Twenty-three."

Anne-Marie looks out the window, through all the birthdays that have come and gone. "Ah, to be twenty-three again. Well, happy birthday. Extra whipped cream for you."

Sheriff concentrates on the menu intently like it's a work by Shakespeare or something, but I can tell his mind is far away from breakfast combos.

Anne-Marie can tell, too. She takes the menu out of his hands. "OJ. Two eggs over easy, bacon, home fries, whole wheat toast. Buttered."

Sheriff nods. "Thank you."

I can't bear the weight of my father's grief for another minute.

It's like watching a pilot whale beach itself on the sand, giving up on any chance of rescue. Kay was twenty-three when she died in a boating accident two summers ago. She was heading to law school in the fall and had an amazing future ahead of her. Instead, she got in a boat with Trip Sinclair.

It's the tragedy that has come to define my family.

It didn't take long for my mom and Sheriff to start sabotaging their marriage after that. Every time they looked at each other, all they could think about was what they'd lost. Their gifted daughter, the scholarship student, the athlete, the most likely to succeed. The girl who was going somewhere. The good one. The pretty one. All that potential, splattered molecule by molecule into the sea.

My mom finally split after Christmas. Said she was going on a spirit journey. Packed up and caught the ferry west, where she couldn't be pulled anymore by tides or constant reminders of Kay. She hugged me for a long time at the ferry dock. She had a curious look on her face, one I didn't recognize. It seemed like she was holding so much back. She told me she loved me and that she'd see me soon, but that was six months ago. Soon never seems to come.

I don't fault her for taking a break. Believe me, I know what it's like to want to drop everything and run. To escape. That's another thing I inherited from her. But her absence is starting to eat away at both me and Sheriff.

We sit in silence.

"Any big birthday plans tonight?" he says finally.

"Sammy has a party planned. It's supposed to be a surprise, but you know Sammy."

He throws his head back. Yes, he's known Sammy her whole life. "What tipped you off?"

I think about this for a second. It was strange when she went on a cleaning rampage in the apartment, clearing the bathroom

vanity of all her hair products and lotions. She must have origi-
nally planned to have the party at our place. It was also very
un-Sammy-like to sneak into her bedroom to make phone calls
every time we were watching *The Bachelorette*. I mean, she's practically had phone sex with Spencer while sitting right next to me
on the couch. The girl doesn't keep secrets.

"She kept insisting that she didn't have plans. That was it,"
I say. "She'd bring up the lack of plans, even if I didn't ask."

"Rookie mistake," Sheriff says.

"Definitely."

"Well, have fun," he says. "No drinking and driving."

"I know."

"You can always call me if you find yourself in a situation."

I give him the you've-got-to-be-kidding look.

"I get it. I'd embarrass you. But season opens today. Things
are always chaotic the first week. You have to be extra cautious."

I look out at the waves again. Season. All of life on Ne'Hwas
revolves around that single word. "How many people do you
think are blowing chunks on the ferry right now?" I ask.

He looks out the window, too. "Onshore wind. East-southeast.
Perfect seasickness conditions. I'd say sixty percent."

I give him a conspiratorial laugh. "Seventy-five. At least."

"Now that's one seasonal job you definitely *don't* want."

"For sure."

TWO

It's my birthday and the world is my oyster. And all I want to do is run away.

By the time I get to the harbor, the ferries have just landed, and for the first time in ten months there's a traffic jam on Ne'Hwas. Seagulls circle overhead looking for handouts. Diesel chokes the air. The granite walls of the harbor are slick with seaweed.

Slowly, the crowd spills out from the steep gangplanks to the pier and onto the boardwalk—a sea of people dressed in jelly bean pastels and khaki shorts. Tourists hobbled with suitcases, coolers, fishing poles, tennis rackets, golf clubs, blow-up beach toys—instruments of leisure.

They're like a school of bluefish making their way down the docks, blocking sidewalks, slicing through summer, shopping, eating, drinking, playing in one giant whirl of activity.

I decide to wait and let the mob pass instead of fighting against the current.

At the Blue Lobster Grille, I peek at the menu. Same food. New prices. Everything jacked up for the season. Economic Darwinism. The ones most adaptable to change are the ones who survive. Not the strongest. Not even the smartest. The ones who charge twelve dollars for a two-dollar hot dog.

About fifteen years ago there was a red tide that rolled in, shutting down all the beaches. The ferries were empty. Half the restaurants closed shop. Stores folded. People lost their retirements. I was eight, and I still remember how it changed everyone that summer. You could feel the tension in the air. Streets were quiet.

Our dependence on tourism was crystallized. All because a tiny change in ocean currents thousands of miles off shore sent a colony of microscopic phytoplankton to Ne'Hwas.

Once the ferry is off-loaded and the crowd thins, I make my way down to Buster's Wharf. I cross a crumbling asphalt lot to the Slack Tide headquarters to pick up my work schedule, since Harold Stantos, my boss, doesn't believe in modern conveniences like e-mail or phones—or health insurance, for that matter.

When I get to the office, Harold is hunched over his ledger, writing columns of numbers. He hands me my schedule for the week and I take a look.

"You've got me on mackerel trips three times this week." I hold the paper up for emphasis.

"What have you got against mackerel?" he asks.

"Tips suck on mackerel trips."

"Well, somebody has to run the galley on the *Mack King*. Burgers don't fry themselves," Harold says, his pen working on columns of numbers.

"Can you put me on the *Dauntless*, instead?" I ask. The *Dauntless* is the hundred-and-six-foot boat, fully outfitted with the newest fishing tackle, sonar, and weather systems. It runs all the way out to Jeffrey's Ledge for deepwater cod and haddock. The *Mack King* is a sixty-five-foot jalopy with a shorter range. It's slow and rusty and heads west into the gulf for the shallow mackerel fishing. *Dauntless* is built for long voyages and holds triple the passengers, thus bringing in triple the tips.

That, and, well, Matthew is the captain of the *Dauntless*.

"You and Jacqueline are the only galley girls. You split trips. If I give to you all the cod trips, Jacqueline will say I'm not fair to her. If I give to Jacqueline all the cod trips, you will complain. Always complaining. I have no choice. I split the schedule."

"I have more seniority, Harold. I should get the *Dauntless*," I insist.

"Seniority? Talk to me about seniority when you have fifty years of work on you. When I was your age, all I had was a dream and twenty dollars in my pocket. I left my country and everything I knew. I spoke no English, and you know what I did?"

I've heard this story so many times in the last five summers of working for Harold that I answer it with him: "I (*You*) worked like a dog. Pinched my (*your*) pennies. Kept my (*your*) head and wits about myself (*yourself*). And made my (*your*) own way in the world."

I finish the statement alone: "Thus proving that today's youth are a bunch of lazy, good-for-nothing slackers who don't know the value of hard work."

"That's right," Harold declares, shooting a finger into the air. He sets a box of fishing supplies on the counter, pulls the keys out of his pocket, and slices through the tape. "Stock these."

"I am *not* working in the shop," I say. "I'll prep the galley today, but that's it."

"Don't consider it work. If it's not work, I don't have to pay. Now, no more squabbling."

I dig into the assortment of bobbers. "It's my birthday, Harold."

"Congratulations. Stock these, too." He hands me another box of sinkers and then disappears into the back room.

Five summers of hearing about the shortcomings of America's youth from a grouchy old Greek man has made me fairly immune to insults. But I wouldn't give it up for anything. I love being on the boats. When I'm aboard the *Dauntless*, out of sight of land, in the rush of the Gulf Stream, I feel free. It's the only place where I can breathe without worrying about anything, where tomorrow doesn't matter. They should put that in the tourist brochures.

To appease Harold, I arrange the jigs, bobbers, and sinkers on a scratched Peg-Board, along with hooks, reels, and other tools of annihilation. "This is harassment, Harold," I yell.

"This is nothing compared to the harassment he gives me."

I turn to see Captain Matthew Weatherby. He's carrying an engine part in one hand and a greasy rag in the other. Wrenches and screwdrivers stick out of his back pocket. He smiles through his scruffy beard, and I can't help but notice how his eyes crinkle outward like rays of sunshine. I also can't help but notice the *way* he's smiling at me. Like I'm the only person in the room, which I am, but still. I fumble for a sinker and drop one on my foot. "Ouch."

Matthew sets down the hunk of black metal and runs a hand over my toes. "You okay?" Suddenly I wish I had bothered with a nail file.

"I'll survive," I say, tucking my unmanicured toes into the gritty floor. "When did you get on island?"

We both stand, and he seems taller than I remember. He's also tan for this early in the season. "Two days ago."

"Where was it this winter? Florida? Mexico? Jamaica?"

"Gulf of Mexico. Lots of shrimp down there. Lots of sunshine. Endless days at sea. You'd love it." He grins.

Matthew is like a big brother to me. We've worked together for the past five summers. In the winters, he takes off to run a commercial fishing boat down south, then returns to Ne'Hwas every summer out of some deranged sense of loyalty to Harold.

"Sounds great. I don't know why you keep coming back here," I say.

"I love it here." He's about to say something else but Harold marches back into the shop and bombards Matthew with a list of supplies and repairs that need to happen in the next twenty-four hours.

Harold turns to me. "And, Jess, don't forget to sweep out the forward hold. I found mice droppings down there. We need to get ahead of the vermin problem. I'm not about to waste good money on an exterminator when I have employees," he says, then heads back to his office.

"You heard the man. Better get ahead of those vermin, Creary," Matthew says.

"Seriously, why do you keep coming back here? I'd be gone in a heartbeat if I had a gig like you."

"I can't stay away." He looks at me with a smile that's too big for his face to contain. His eyes actually twinkle.

This embarrasses me, so I change the subject. "I'm stuck on mackerel trips three times this week."

He grabs a handful of jigs out of the box and helps me stock the display. "Don't worry. I'll get Harold to switch the schedule around."

If I have any hope of making good tips this summer, it'll be because of Matthew. Not only is he is the best fisherman on Ne'Hwas, and something of a local legend, he's also the youngest islander to ever get his hundred-ton license, and the only person Harold will listen to. A charter company depends on the captain's ability to find fish. And Matthew knows how to find the fish.

"Happy birthday, by the way," he says, lifting a box of lead sinkers effortlessly.

"How did you know?"

Matthew shrugs and opens the box of sinkers. The sleeves of his T-shirt hug his biceps, which are carved like rocks, from hauling nets and pulling anchors. I wonder if they were always like that or if it's just that I'm noticing for the first time.

"Doing anything special?" he asks.

"Sammy's planning a surprise party." I swing a jig in my hand, watching the sparkly tassels flop around the head. "I might just blow it off."

Matthew turns to me, his face pained. "Don't blow it off."

"So she *is* having a party!"

"Just pop in. Let everyone sing 'Happy Birthday,' then you can go home and mope."

"Did she invite the whole staff?"

He nods.

"Even Tony?"

"Even Tony."

"Ugh."

He moves closer to me. "You don't feel like celebrating. I get it. You probably just want to go surfing, then crawl into bed."

That's *exactly* what I want to do. I don't have to explain myself to him. He knows what it's like to lose someone. He lost his father without even knowing him, and his mother when he was a teenager.

I take a deep breath. "Wish I could, but I have to get on those vermin."

He grabs the tackle out of my hands and looks me in the eye. "I'll cover for you. Go get your surf in."

"But Harold will murder me. And then he'll cut me up for bait to save money."

Matthew laughs. "Nah. You wouldn't make good bait."

"Why not?"

"Too much salt and vinegar in you, Creary."

I fake punch him in the arm (which, for the record, is solid muscle). "Why don't you come with me? When's the last time you went surfing, anyway?"

"Can't. Got an engine to inspect, an ice maker to fix, and an oil change to finish." He takes the jigs and starts hanging them. "You go. Have fun."

My big brother, always watching out for me. My big brother with big biceps I've never noticed before.

THREE

The wind has kicked up since this morning, sending a dry rage over Nipon Beach. Sand stings my bare legs. Waves that were shoulder-high earlier are Mackers now, as in, big enough to drive a Mack truck through. It's a solid eight to ten feet, with the occasional twelve-footer slipping in.

I wax my board and push away the butterflies in my stomach. Most surfers will stay dry today. It's too big. Too heavy. Too messy. Waves are breaking too far out the back. It takes courage to get in the water in these conditions. *Cojones*, the surfer dudes would say.

Waves like this never used to bother me; I was fearless. But after Kay died, I didn't surf for a while. I kept thinking about her drowning, picturing it a thousand times in excruciating detail. I would imagine those final moments before she slipped silently under the waves, her lungs filling with water, the cold finally settling into her skin. I wonder what was she thinking about.

Did she think Trip would save her?

All we know for sure about the accident is that Trip Sinclair was driving the boat. It was late at night. It was high tide. The boat ran aground and sank on an unmarked shoal near Tutatquin Point. Trip made it to shore, alone. Five hours later, he called the police. Kay's body was found washed up on shore.

There was no reliable blood alcohol test, since it took him so long to report the accident.

And thanks to his extremely wealthy family, Trip was cleared of manslaughter charges. There was no jail time. We buried Kay. Trip went back to his life on the mainland.

There were no apologies.

I stayed out of the water for a whole year after that. When I got back on my board, I had lost my nerve. My cojones.

But today I'm twenty-three, and being twenty-three sucks, and I need to get away from it all. When you live on an island like I do, the ocean is your only escape.

I take a deep breath, tuck my board under my arm, and run into the water.

Paddling out, I stay close to the jetty, which provides some shelter. As soon as I cross the point, the waves are even more monstrous than they looked from shore.

Suddenly, I'm staring at a rising wall of water. It climbs higher and higher, steeper and steeper, changing its green face with every passing second. A moving mountain. My mind races. It calls on a million other images of waves I've faced before. Surfer brain kicks in. I judge the size, shape, speed, and wind all at once, trying to come up with an answer—*over* or *under*. Over, I decide.

But I misjudge.

The crest curls, then tumbles into a fierce white chute before I make it over the top. There's a thunderous crash around me. The nose of my board catches in the break and lifts out of my hands, sending me over the falls and down into the churning, furious mess. I kick hard against the force of water on top of me.

When I come up for air, my board is behind me, dragging in the whitewash toward the rocks. My mind goes blank. My body takes over. I pull on my leash, hop on my board, and paddle hard, hard, hard. *Get away from the rocks before the next wave.*

But the next wave's already here, a wall of water in front of me. This time, I'm ready. I don't think. I don't second-guess. I take in a deep breath and duck dive below the wave just as it breaks.

I make it out behind the wave and paddle like hell to put more space between me and the jetty. Every breath is a struggle as I paddle farther and farther out, duck diving on every wave, even when I think there's a chance I can clear the top.

Learn from your last mistake—one of the principal rules of surfing. I wonder if Trip Sinclair learned from his mistake. There'd be so many lessons from that night: Don't drink and drive. Don't be reckless with other people's lives. Don't leave innocent girls for dead.

Getting past the break zone takes forever with the onshore wind working against me. My body is a sail, driving me in the wrong direction. Every two feet forward is met with one foot back.

By the time I'm out the back, out of the crash zone, I'm completely spent.

Freddie and Josh Collins are the only other souls out here. If the waves were five feet smaller, the lineup would be mobbed. But today isn't for novices. Freddie and Josh sit on their boards, silently gazing at the horizon. They're old-school. Surfing is a religion to them, and you don't talk in church.

I lie on my board and recover, thankful for the quiet.

Once I catch my breath, I push myself up to the seated position and stare out at the waves. A kernel of fear builds deep inside of me until it has words: *too big*. I try to push it down deep.

Another two guys paddle to the lineup. Jay Delgado and Tyler Ferguson. They are the opposite of old-school; they're pricks. In addition to being a self-loathing misogynist with (I suspect) a small penis, Jay has a special hatred for me on account of the fact that Sheriff busted his alkie old man twice on DUIs. Now, Mr. Delgado has to ride a bicycle around town, even in the winter, one of the many aimless drunks of Ne'Hwas who can't be trusted to drive a car. They should put *that* in the brochures.

Jay's family tried to fight the charges, arguing police discrimination. The DUIs stood.

Jay looks at me, unable to hide the surprise in his eyes that I've made it out here. "Playing with the big boys today."

I keep my eyes on the horizon. "I'm just here to surf."

"You don't belong out here. You're out of your league."

"I made it out, didn't I?" I say. I can't let Jay get in my head. I need to focus on the waves.

"This isn't the kiddie pool, Dreary Creary. Don't expect me to pull you out when you get thrown down by one of these monsters," Jay says.

"Don't expect me to save your ass, either," I snap.

Jay laughs. "Right. Like that's ever going to happen."

I could point out that I'm the only one with a surfing championship under my belt, but I know how hollow that sounds. I was seventeen. My glory days of surfing are far behind me. I straighten up on my board and try to look tough.

"Where'd you pick up that sled—the Salvation Army? 1962?" Jay says.

I steal a glance at Jay's brand-new custom board. It's bright yellow and shaped by some famous surfer in Hawaii, or so I've heard. "That thing come with training wheels?" I say.

Tyler pipes in. "Dude, it's custom. Don't dis the sled."

"You're not on your period, are you, Jess?" Jay says. "You're not going to attract sharks, are you?"

Tyler howls. Almost falls off his board laughing.

"Screw you," I say. Back when I started surfing, I thought I was joining a special tribe. A great big, happy cult that shared in their mystical love of the ocean, but without the typical cult drawbacks like drinking acid-laced Kool-Aid or worshipping aliens. I quickly learned that Nipon surfers are more like a pack of wolves. You have to earn respect from the alpha male here, and then maybe, just maybe, you can earn a place in the lineup.

Freddie and Josh aren't part of the pack, but they don't exactly welcome you with open arms, either. Freddie looks our way, hands turned up on his board like a surfing Buddha. He rolls his eyes. Doesn't engage. Here to surf.

"Paddle home, girl," Jay says.

I ignore him. There's only one way to get him off my back, and that is to catch a wave.

When the next set appears, talking stops. All eyes are on the waves.

No one takes the first wave, or the second. I watch the third. Its crest forms a light pyramid, which means it's peaked, rather than closing out. This is the type of wave you want. I study it for another few seconds and realize I'm too far out. I'll have to paddle in fast to be in position.

I spin my board around so I'm facing shore and look over my shoulder. It's a behemoth. Bigger than any wave I've ever ridden. Double overhead. I start paddling.

After six or seven strokes, I feel myself rising and I put it into full gear, windmilling both arms. Paddle, paddle, paddle. The wave lifts me up, but it doesn't grab hold. It's faster than I am, and it passes below me before I can build enough speed to catch it.

Now I'm on the back side of the wave and my arms are like jelly, and another big wave is coming at me.

I either have to go for it or turn around and paddle to get behind it. In waves like this, you have to be all-in or go home.

All-in.

I paddle slowly at first, so I won't be too far inside when it breaks. I look over my shoulder and see that I'm in pretty good position. *This is it. This is my wave.*

Two hard strokes build my speed, and when I turn my head this time, Jay is barreling down the line toward me, his bright yellow board aimed my way. If I don't get off, he's going to hit me, and hit me hard. If I drop in on his wave, I'll be breaking the cardinal rule of surfing and I'll never hear the end of it. In this crowd, drop-ins find their tires slashed when they get back to the parking lot.

I have to put the brakes on. I slide my knees underneath me and pull up on the rails of my board to stop my momentum. The wave passes under me and Jay zips by.

Now I really am too far inside. I spin around on my board just in time to see the next wave head-on. It will break right on top of me. In the entire hundred million square miles of ocean, this is the worst place to be. I gulp some air, push down the nose of my board, and try to duck dive, but I don't have enough speed. The wave catches my board and flips it over. I'm spinning head over heels. I lose all sense of up and down.

I'm in an underwater cyclone. My ears pop.

I need air.

I open my eyes to a whirling mass of white water. The pain in my lungs rises to my head, my throat. I kick hard, but go nowhere. I need air so badly I open my mouth and suck in seawater. This is drowning.

Just when I don't think I'm going to survive another second, my head breaks the surface and I cough out water. I cough so hard my body convulses. But I'm still in danger. Thoughts pass without a beat between them. *Inside crash zone. Get on board. Get out.*

I rely on my hands to find my ankle, grab my leash, and pull my board to me. I slide on top of it as waves materialize before me. I paddle and duck dive through countless waves. Desperation drives me.

When I make it to the lineup this time, I'm panting from exhaustion. My nerves are shot.

Jay is the first one to return from his ride. "What's the matter? Set too small for you?" he says.

I don't speak because I don't trust my voice. I grab the rails of my board to steady my jittery hands.

Jay laughs. "Paddle home, girl."

Tyler gets to the lineup next. Then Freddie and Josh. They're all smiles and adrenaline from their amazing rides.

In the lull between sets, everyone's conserving energy, except Jay, who can't keep his mouth shut. Sick waves and hot girls are his only topics of conversation. Every once in a while he looks my way, just to make sure I can hear how he rates all the single girls on Ne'Hwas, based on body and face hotness. As if it's up to him.

"I'd give Jess a five. Five and a half, tops," he says.

Tyler laughs.

"I'd give you a ten, Jay," I say, casting him a fake smile. "As in, IQ points." I know it's not my best work, but my energy's low and I need to stay focused.

Now I'm in the primo spot in the lineup, which means I should have first dibs on the next set. In surfing, positioning is everything. You're constantly moving, paddling in for the smaller waves, out for the bigger ones. Keeping up with the tide. Traveling up or down the shore as the waves shift. A sandbar here, a dead spot there. It's a game of cat and mouse, always jockeying for the sweet spot, which is a small and elusive thing.

These guys don't give up the sweet spot for anyone. Especially a girl. They take the best waves for themselves. They're takers. Just like Trip Sinclair.

When the next set appears on the horizon, the chatter stops and everyone gets focused. I decide I'm going to take the first wave, no matter what. It's not the best strategy. The first wave is always the smallest, the least shaped, but no one else will go for it. I just need one wave, after all.

As the first sharp ridge comes closer, I spin my board, lie down, and start paddling. Out of the corner of my eye, I see Tyler paddling out from the shoulder toward me. He's cruising fast. I pick up my speed a little, but if I go too fast when the wave is this far out, I'll be too far inside, and I'm not going to let that happen again.

I check the wave. Tyler, having more upper body strength, has caught it from farther out, and he's riding down the line. *Damn.* It's his wave. Fair and square.

I pull back on my board and spin around. Josh has the next wave and is riding right in the shoulder. Either I have to slow down to get behind him, and get pummeled by white water, or speed up and cut in front of him, where the wave is still green. Since I don't trust my noodle arms, I opt for white water.

Freddie takes the next wave. I watch him make a beautiful bottom turn, then carve a sharp switchback off the lip.

At the lineup, it's just me and Jay now, and the set is petering out. We both start paddling for the last wave. Technically, I'm closer to the shoulder, so the wave is mine, but Jay doesn't back off. He paddles harder. I paddle harder. As the wave rises up behind me, my board accelerates with it, powered by its energy. This is the feeling I live for. I pop to my feet and drop down the face. Just as I turn my head, Jay drops right in front of me. Our boards hit and I lose my balance. I fall. This time I get knocked under the water with more force than before.

"Asshole," I scream when I resurface. Jay turns and salutes me with a smug smile across his lips. I'm so angry I could kill him. Why do the takers always come out on top? The Trip Sinclairs and Jay Delgados of the world?

The entire set goes by and I don't catch a wave. I don't even try on the next set. All the guys catch great rides again, except for Freddie, who paddles up next to me. "Tough day."

"Yeah."

"You'll get one," he says. Freddie's older. I couldn't say for sure whether he's in his thirties, forties, or possibly even fifties. He seems old to me in the way that anyone beyond their twenties is.

He's in those decades of life so impossibly far away from my own. "Clear your mind and commit to it," he says.

I let his words move through me. Out here, your thoughts can only be on the surf. Not on the guys taunting you, or the people on shore, or the people you've lost, or your shattered life.

As the next set comes through, the waves pass, each one getting bigger and better. The fourth wave is perfect.

"All yours," Freddie says.

I start paddling. The green face of the wave is rising fast and unbroken and I'm in the sweet spot. I take a few more hard strokes. My board accelerates with the energy of the wave. I pop up to my feet and take the drop down the face. *Perfect*.

Then, I pearl.

The nose of my board goes under water and the tail goes up. I lean backwards to correct it, but the nose dives farther. I tumble headfirst over my board, the force of the wave rolling me in somersaults. Once again, I'm sucked into an underwater tsunami, desperate for air.

Of all the rookie mistakes! I haven't pearled in years. That's what beginners do when they don't have a clue how to position their weight on the board. I was on the perfect wave and I pearled! *Stupid, stupid, stupid*. What is wrong with me? I can't even catch a wave anymore.

A few more surfers have arrived and are paddling out the back, passing me in the opposite direction. More competition in the lineup. More alpha males to push me out.

There's nothing left to do but paddle home. *Girl*.

I catch a wave of whitewash and ride it in, lying on my stomach the whole way.

As I walk up the beach, I turn around and see Jay, already sitting in the lineup, his yellow board making him stand out from the tiny, indecipherable row of surfers. He gives me an obnoxious wave.

I clench my right fist and raise it to the sky as I slap my bicep with my left hand. He can't mistake that for a friendly gesture.

What a waste of a session. All that exertion and not a wave to show for it. I sit on the sand and catch my breath while the Nipon gang catches killer rides.

A seagull lands at my feet, black eye searching, then takes off. It flies over the beach, past the jetty, toward Tutatquin Point at the park. The granite face of the point glows a magnificent orange in the afternoon slant of sun. That silhouette is so familiar to me I could draw it with my eyes closed. The peak where Sheriff and Mom took Kay and me every Memorial Day for a picnic, Mom yelling at us not to get too close to the edge. The spot where Kay and I stood, feeling the wind in our faces, throwing pine cones over the edge of the cliff, testing out the laws of physics. Does the heavier object fall faster?

Right below it is the spot where Kay's body was found.

What was she thinking in those last moments? Did she know she would die, or did she hang on to a morsel of hope? What did it feel like to take that last slide into the sea?

I need to get out of my head. I need a wave.

I pick up my board, tuck it under my arm, and walk down the beach. I walk past the parking lot, past the seawall, past the last of the houses on Nipon Beach, past the sign for Wabanaki State Park, past the NO SWIMMING signs, past the NO SURFING signs, until I get to the field of granite boulders, sharp with barnacles.

The waves here are even gnarlier, breaking past a boneyard of submerged rocks. I study the sea for a while and notice a spot where the shoulder lifts up consistently to a sharp, triangular peak, where a hidden sandbar meets the force of water and directs it upward. Everywhere else, the waves close out. I watch for a few more sets, just to be sure. And every time, the peak forms in the same spot. Am I really going to do this?

I take a land bearing. If I line myself up with the tallest spruce on shore and parallel to the last rock outcrop, I'll be in the spot. These two bits of information will be invaluable when I start paddling out and get cold and confused trying to muscle my way through the break. I repeat it to myself: tallest spruce, parallel to the last rock outcrop.

I must be crazy. No one surfs Tutatquin Point.

But I need to catch a wave today. Today, I'm twenty-three years old. The thought of heading back to town and pretending to celebrate is too much for me. Right now, I need to get away. I need to escape. I need to feel something other than failure.

I climb over the jagged rocks.

FOUR

It's low tide and Tutatquin Point bares her teeth like a rabid dog. Locals call it the boneyard because of all the ships that have run aground here over the centuries. Wooden schooners. Warships. Old steamboats. One luxury yacht with Trip Sinclair at the wheel.

It was high tide, Trip's lawyer said. He couldn't see the rocks. Not his fault, the lawyer argued. Head trauma. Couldn't be blamed for his actions, the lawyer spewed.

If you grow up on Ne'Hwas, you know the tides in your bones. They are the blood that pumps through your veins. We have the highest tidal range in the world—another highlight for the tourism brochures. They say that more water passes through the Gulf of Maine into the Bay of Fundy at every turn of the tide than the combined flow of all the freshwater lakes and rivers on earth. Twice a day, the water rises and falls over forty feet in the narrow end of the bay. Everyone here has a story of how the tide almost took them.

Mine happened when I was five, and Kay, eight. It was July. Hot as hell—I remember that. Sheriff and Kay were far down the beach, collecting shells in the tide pools—periwinkles, hermit crabs, urchins, that sort of thing. My mom and I were building a sand castle with a tall spire and a seaweed forest all around. I needed a shovel to dig a moat. My mom smiled and said that she would protect my castle from invaders. No, I said, I needed a moat. I was a willful child. She told me to stay put while she went to the car to find a shovel.

I didn't stay put, though. I walked down to the water to stomp in the wet sand. I loved how my feet would get swallowed by the sand whenever a wave receded. At first, I didn't know what was happening. The water swirled up around my knees, then my waist, then I was swimming in it. I watched a beach umbrella shrink into a tiny dot on the shore until it disappeared completely. I remember thinking, in my five-year-old mind, that the land was moving and I was staying still, and somehow that made everything feel safe.

I treaded water for as long as I could, and when my little arms and legs got too tired, I simply let go. Part of me knew I would sink and that it would be the end, but in fact, I didn't sink. I floated. The ocean cradled me. I felt like a cork, bobbing high on the surface, unable to sink. I was so comfortable floating in that clear blue water that I lay facedown and pretended I was a dolphin crossing the ocean to meet up with my dolphin family, twisting my mouth up to the sky when I needed to breathe.

By the time Sheriff reached me, I was half a mile off shore. I hadn't been scared the whole time, until I saw the fear in his eyes. I can only imagine what he must have been thinking as he swam toward me, adrenaline flooding his body, seeing his daughter facedown in the water. He later told me that position is called the dead man's float, that it's a survival skill and that he'd never heard of a five-year-old teaching it to herself.

He towed me back to shore. Kay wrapped her towel around me and gave me her prized shell from the day's tide pool treasures. When I saw my mother, her smile was gone. She hugged me for what seemed like hours, and later she fed me and Kay Popsicles that turned our tongues blue.

The next day, she disappeared for three whole nights—the first of her many spirit journeys. I always blamed myself for her disappearance. If only I'd stayed put like she said, instead of going into the water, everything would have been fine. She wouldn't have needed a spirit journey to wander away her sorrow, or guilt, or whatever it was that pushed her away that time.

I take one last look around before I hit the water. No one is here. No one to stop me. No one to rescue me if I get swept out to sea this time.

The water seems even colder now, but that can't be. It's the same ocean. I'm just chilled, my muscles fatigued and crying for rest. I should turn around, go home, let everyone sing me "Happy Birthday" like Matthew said. But I need to feel something other than disappointment today. I need to remember who I am. A survivor.

All-in, I tell myself.

On a receding wave, I grab my rails and ride the rush of water out to sea. Granite grinds against the bottom of my board, gouging into fiberglass. The next surge of white water comes, and I brace against it. The force swings like a pendulum, carrying me seaward.

I do my best to aim for the narrow passages between rocks, but my paddle power is nothing compared to the mighty force of water beneath me. Incoming waves break against rock in unpredictable ways. A shift in the current swings my board around and I hit a rock broadside, my board taking a beating. Then another shift in current, another swirling eddy, and I'm pointed in the right direction, darting through a clear channel. I'm the pinball. The ocean is the wizard.

Somehow, I make it out of the boneyard in one piece.

Paddling out to the sandbar is easy, by comparison. But beyond the bar, the waves are even bigger than the overhead monsters at Nipon. I paddle and duck dive, paddle and duck dive, paddle and duck dive, my body emptying its entire reserve of energy.

In between the breaking waves, I look up and check my bearings.

Tallest spruce. *Yes.*

Parallel to last rock outcrop. *Not yet.*

My arms are numb with exhaustion and the wind howls in my ears as I fight against the waves. Jay's voice pops into my head, *You're out of your league.* My heart pounds. My breath is frantic. *Paddle home, girl.*

Finally I make it past the break.

I sit upright on my board and relax. The water is a sparkling blue all the way out here, not green and cloudy like the shallows. The island is a million miles away and I have the ocean to myself. I made it. I paddled through the boneyard and the breakers, and that's not something just anyone can do. But the feeling of contentment doesn't last long. I feel a throbbing in my leg. I look down. Blood seeps from a gash on my knee, mixing with salt water in a zigzag down my leg. I must have knicked it in the boneyard.

Blood and ocean. *Bad combo.*

A dark shape rises and falls out of my peripheral vision. A fin? I turn and look. Nothing. Another dark shape appears for a split second, then vanishes. Shark? It can't be. Even if it is, sharks don't attack surfers in Maine. Never happens. Never has. *It's just a little chop*, I tell myself.

Paddle home, girl. Jay's voice in my head.

A gust of wind flips the surface of the ocean into a million flickering ripples. At least, I think it's wind. It could be a school of bait fish swimming by, churning up the water from below. And where there are bait fish there are . . .

No! I tell myself. I look left, right, and down, searching for dark shadows below as my blood trickles into the water. It's all a mind game out here—the sharks, the self-doubt. I know the panic it can lead to. I try to bury it, focus on the next set, double-check my bearings.

Tallest spruce. *Check.*

Parallel to the last rock outcrop. *Check.*

Another flicker of wind or wave or fin catches my eye. I could just head in now. Paddle to the sandbar, catch a smaller wave. Lie in bed tonight stewing on all the missed waves.

But I need to catch a wave. Just one. I need to give myself that. A birthday gift from me to me. If my five-year-old self could survive a riptide without panicking, my twenty-three-year-old self should be able ride one wave today.

As I watch the horizon (ignoring the shadows and flickers around me), a set works its way toward shore. Gorgeous rows of clean, unbroken lines.

The first wave is six feet, at least. Overhead. I'm too far out to catch it. The next wave is a little bigger, a little more organized. But a thousand lessons have taught me that if I paddle for an early wave and miss it, I'm screwed. I let it pass.

The next wave is seven or eight feet. It looks like it's going to break before it gets to me. I lie down and paddle like a maniac to get to the outside of this wave. It's peaked and is already breaking off to the right. I paddle, paddle, paddle, rising up its face to get over the unbroken shoulder.

As I make it over the peak, my board goes vertical and then slaps down against the back side of the wave. I keep paddling to get over the next one.

The last wave in the set is massive. Double overhead. The face is sheer and dark. A light green triangle at the top tells me where it will crest, where I need to be. I spin my board around. Three slow paddles. Wind drives a sharp spray into my eyes. Land disappears in the trough of the wave ahead.

All-in, my mind screams. Five more strokes, hard and fast.

And then I feel my board lift and accelerate as it rises along the face. *Now or never.* My muscles know what to do. I put my hands flat on the board, arch my back, and pop up to my feet.

Nothing but air below the nose. Then, the drop. Fast and terrifying. Instinctively, I lower my right knee, swing my weight left, and trim.

I feel the immense power of the wave beneath me.

Knees bent, one hand over each rail, I take the most perfect ride of my life. I look down the line at Tutatquin Point, its graywhite veneer towering into the sky. My position and speed are perfect. I am a rocket. I am a goddess.

Suddenly, the point gets smaller as the wave curls ahead of me. But instead of breaking down the face into a fury of white water, it curls like a Slinky. The sea is all around me, above me, below me, circling me. I crouch down into a ball. For the first time in my life, I'm inside a barrel. They call this the green room, and only a handful of people on earth have been here.

I run my fingers along the glassy face of the wave. All is silent, except the swoosh of fiberglass skimming the surface. Sun lights the water from the outside in, an emerald green, and it's oddly still inside, like the eye of a storm. It's the most beautiful thing I've ever seen.

I crouch lower. But instead of shrinking, the barrel gets taller and broader and opens up inside. I stand up straight. My head remains clear of the ceiling of water.

This is wrong, I think. Barrels don't expand; they contract.

I wobble slightly, get my footing back, and focus down the line again, savoring every moment, knowing that this ride will end any second.

But it doesn't.

I'm still rocketing down the line, the hollow barrel of water holding its shape.

This can't be right. Barrels don't last this long.

Suddenly I think of the sandbar. I must be getting really close to it. What if I break on the shallow bar? I'll do a face-plant into sand.

I ride for five more seconds. Ten. Fifteen. How is this possible? Twenty. Thirty. Ne'Hwas surfing isn't like this. Forty.

I still am encased in water.

A small aperture appears in the end of the barrel. The light there appears bright green instead of white. It's an optical illusion, like the way blood looks black when you're deep under water.

The tunnel opens more. The ceiling peels back, releasing me, letting in sun. When I look toward shore, I am past the tallest spruce, heading toward rock. The sandbar is behind me.

But that's not possible. How could I have made it over the sandbar? Waves break on the sandbar every time. Unless I was out there so long that the tide came in and I lost track of time.

The wave continues to carry me through the boneyard until I'm on a soft spot of sand. I walk over to the stand of pine trees and set my board down. Then I sit against a boulder on the shore.

My eyes sting with the salt and my head feels dizzy.

I'm totally confused. Did I pass out? Did I hit my head and get a concussion? How else can I explain riding one wave from out the back, over the sandbar, past the boneyard, all the way to shore? I look out and watch the break, noticing every wave rise and crash long before it hits the sandbar. How did my wave sneak past? Impossible. What did they teach us about concussions in the mandatory Red Cross classes at school? Lay the victim down, or keep them upright? One or the other.

I take in a long breath and exhale, pain crossing my chest. The next breath is shallow, like I can't get enough air into my lungs, so I inhale deeply through my mouth, but my lungs don't feel full.

A seagull on a nearby rock eyes me, then flies away.

I try to breathe, but I can't. I gasp for air. There isn't enough air on earth. I feel like I'm drowning on dry land. I push my hands into the rock and try to get to my feet, but my feet have stopped working. I can't feel my legs. I can't wiggle my toes. I'm paralyzed. Maybe I bumped my head, got a concussion, *and* broke my spinal column. I'm going to be a paraplegic. I'll have to live the rest of my life in a wheelchair.

Thoughts come rapidly as I try to figure out what happened, but then they disappear and the only thought in my mind is *Breathe.* I try to suck air into my lungs. Nothing.

Something deep within me knows what to do.

Get in the water!

Now!

I drag myself on hands and knees over rocks to the ocean's edge. Then I keep going. A force I can't name is taking me to the water.

The next wave rolls in and the white froth covers my lower body. My goddamn paralyzed lower body.

I keep crawling farther and farther into the water, my legs drifting uselessly behind me. As it gets deeper, I swim on the surface, trying to keep afloat. I'm going to die. Right here. Alone.

The next couple seconds are inexplicably peaceful as I feel my head and my body sinking below the surface. I close my eyes. I need to just let go. I will die here, and my body will wash up on shore where Kay's did.

I think about Kay, and how I will see her very soon. Do I believe in heaven? Maybe. Will I get in? Maybe not.

I sink lower and lower into the water. My chin goes under. My mouth and nose go under. My forehead. I close my eyes and try the dead man's float, but my body sinks.

Feeling the last desperate need for air, I inhale.

Cold water rushes into my mouth, down my throat, into my lungs. I feel a sharp pain and then I feel my lungs fill with . . .

Air?

I inhale again, open my eyes. I'm completely submerged, but the water is like air. I suck it in and feel it surge through my lungs.

I'm not drowning. I'm breathing water. It's the most fantastic sensation I've ever felt.

But this can't be real.

This is the opposite of real.

I kick my legs, only they're stuck together. Instead of scissoring back and forth, they move up and down in a dolphin kick. I feel my knee, where the scrape is, and it feels hard. I look back at my legs, but it's all a blur.

Something flashes in the haze of water. I look toward the flash, and a little fish comes into focus. They're lit up in neon blue, like one of those black lights that Sammy had in grade school, where you turn off the lights and the whites seem extra white, while everything else is pitch-black.

I kick my legs and look behind me. There's a huge fish following me.

I stop kicking and all goes blurry again. I pull my legs in front of me and feel around.

My legs are gone. In their place is a fish tail. The fish that's following me is *me*. I feel scales, and beneath the scales, bone and muscle.

I feel around my upper body—my arms, chest, neck, back. My bikini is gone and I'm naked. I move my hands over my face and head. They feel unchanged, and at same time, completely different. I'm acutely aware of my tongue, nose, and eyes. They are all on overdrive. My nostrils are not exactly smelling, and my tongue isn't quite tasting, but they are sensing.

And right now, they're telling me to *move*.

FIVE

ove! The word isn't coming from my brain. I don't think it; I feel it.

I kick my tail, which stirs up a blizzard of bubbles and propels me like a torpedo. I am flying through the water. The rocky bottom races beneath me.

Vibrations pulse through my body, along my sides, and down my nerve endings.

I taste danger on my tongue.

Danger from what, though? I need to make sense of this. *Think.* I am swimming faster than humans can possibly swim. I am breathing water. I am a mermaid. I'm running from a danger I cannot see.

Ahead of me, the sandbar rises up to the surface, so I slow down. The vibrations intensify. Each shock wave delivers information, a piece of the puzzle. This one, a heartbeat. That one, a change in water pressure. The next, a spike in temperature.

Something is after me. The deep, primal part of my brain knows one immediate truth: *vibrations=danger.*

A million sensations bombard me at once, garbling my senses—I can see with the nerves along my spine. Taste and smell come at me from every direction. Sound is something I can touch with my fingers. They all add up to one thing.

Go deeper!

I scurry to the sandbar and claw my way over it, fighting against the force of waves crashing from above.

On the other side of the sandbar, I aim myself downward and swim. Down, down, down, into the deep space of ocean where light barely penetrates. I swim low and fast against the sandy floor, something telling me it's safer against the bottom, even though I can't see a thing. My eyes are blind down here. Up ahead, there's a movement. A fish is lit up in pixels of neon light. I make out the shape of a striped bass. Its fast-moving body is crystal clear.

Things in motion come into focus. An eel. A dogfish. A rock crab skittering along the sand. I see them all clearly just before they scatter to get out of my way.

My human brain can't wrap around what's happening. It's screaming, *This is too deep. This is not safe. Turn back.*

I stop swimming and look up through the darkness to a pinprick of sun sending rays of white light through the water. I want to be in that light. I want to be in that human world. I swim toward it.

As I swim up into open water, the vibrations grow stronger, pricking my sides right into my spinal cord.

Stay down.

Instinct and logic are pulling me in opposite directions. My mind keeps telling me, *This cannot be happening*, but my body knows differently. My body knows where to go and what to do. It's being driven by something other than *me*. Instinct takes over. All other thoughts shut down, except the one that keeps whispering, *This cannot be happening.*

But the voice of instinct is louder. *Stay down. Find shelter.*

Yes, shelter. Now that makes sense. I swim back down into the dark, inhuman depth.

In the distance, a large mass appears through the hazy water. Visibility is poor, and the shape drifts in and out of my vision like a mirage. As I get closer, I see it's a huge rock formation. Fish of all kinds scurry around the rocks, appearing in pixels of light.

I slow down and swim along the bottom of the ledge, looking for a place to hide.

The vibrations sharpen.

A hollow space in the rock appears in my blurry vision. I squeeze inside, my tail sticking out of the opening. Awkwardly, I pull my tail in and press my back against the farthest wall of the shallow cave. I try to slow down my breathing and calm myself. Think of yoga class. The hot instructor in the tiny shorts and perfect abs. Remember his words, his mantra: *In through the nose. Out through the . . .*

Armpits? Water is coming out of my armpits. I reach underneath my arms and feel the feathery folds of gills. *This cannot be happening.* I have gills like a fish. Somehow the gills seem even more disturbing than my tail. *Get a grip. Hold it together.*

I wish I could see better, but my eyes can't focus on anything unless it's moving.

A blast of vibrations surges down my spine and I tense up. At the mouth of the cave, the tip of a pectoral fin drifts by, lit up in a thousand dots of ultraviolet light. A heartbeat pumps through the water, telling me it's here. Telling me *it* is actually a *she.*

She is a predator.

I am prey.

A minute goes by. Then another. I can feel the electrical current in the water, but my eyes don't detect any movement. On fingertips, I creep over sandy floor to the opening of the cave.

Suddenly, the shark dives at me. I shimmy backwards into the cave. My head slams against rock.

She thrashes her tail and jams her snout into the cave opening. Her eyes are like pools of oil, her jaws open. Hundreds of gleaming white teeth poke out from pink flesh. I can see down her throat, which is a black, pulsing crater.

She jerks back and forth violently, her motions lighting the water in brilliant neon blue. I'm so close I can see the texture of her skin, the scars cut into her face. Black spots crisscross her skin. The words *ampullae of Lorenzini* flash in my mind. Intro to Marine Biology. Professor Sherwood. Freshman year, Ne'Hwas Community College. "*These special sensing organs found in carti-laginous fish help detect electromagnetic fields as tiny as one millionth of a volt.*" Like Sheriff said, I always was good in biology. Then again, Ne'Hwas Community College isn't exactly Harvard. It's practically like an extra year of high school.

Not to mention, Professor Sherwood never described what to do when you come face-to-face with ampullae of Lorenzini inches above the gaping jaw of a killer shark.

I squeeze farther back into the cave, but I'm not familiar with my new dimensions and my tail juts out into biting range. I pull it back, kicking up a plume of silt. The taste of chalky, ancient sand fills my lungs.

Terror paralyzes me as the shark lashes forward again. I can't imagine a worse way to die than being eaten alive. She must be eighteen feet long and weigh a few thousand pounds. Bigger than the dinghies that ferry sailors out to their moorings. Definitely a great white.

She pushes into the cave, my safe haven getting smaller and smaller with each thrust.

I look around for something, anything, to defend myself. There are tiny shards of coral on the sand. Useless. I try to pry a rock loose from above. Nothing budges. I am defenseless against those glowing white teeth.

She thrashes her tail. I can feel tremors coursing through her body, her raw intent to kill me. I try to think back to everything I've ever read or seen about shark attacks and shark behavior, every episode of *Shark Week* running through my mind. *Don't swim at dusk. Avoid swimming or surfing in colonies of sea lions. Try not to move erratically. Don't play dead.*

Nothing prepares me for this situation. Great whites are

supposed to strike in open water, from below. They don't burrow into caves. They eat other fish, and birds, and fat sea lions; humans are too bony for their taste. Then again, I'm not human anymore, am I?

Why is this happening to me? How is this even possible? How did I go from eating pancakes and arguing with Sheriff this morning to becoming a mermaid hunted by a great white this afternoon?

Then, I remember. I reach into my hair and feel around until my fingers land on the comb that Sheriff gave me for my birthday. From all the swimming and surfing, my hair has become a tangled nest around it. I yank and twist, ripping out hair, until I free the comb. Five sharp prongs run down from the carved bone handle.

The Passamaquoddy symbol for *strength*.

I clasp the handle of the comb in one hand. *Aim for the eye.* When the shark lurches toward me again, I plunge the prongs into her flesh, missing the eye but puncturing a big cluster of ampullae of Lorenzini.

Immediately, she retreats. I lie still, blind in a cloud of silt. I brace myself for the next attack, my comb positioned. A faint smell enters my skin. Blood in the water. An infinitesimal drop. And then it's gone.

Slowly, the silt drifts down, particle by particle, and the water becomes clear. A fish swims by. A shad, I think. Another minute passes. No shark. I see a few more fish emerge from hiding spots. The vibrations running through my body simmer down.

I lie in the dark cave a few more minutes, willing myself to stay calm, to survive. *Sharks eat mermaids.* This is new information; this is important to know. It's not something Professor Sherwood ever tested us on. Not something they've ever mentioned on *Shark Week*. This is something you have to learn on your own.

Eventually, the vibrations disappear altogether.

By the time I swim out from my cave, the ocean has darkened. Feeling for vibrations around me, smelling with my skin, listening with my tongue, I swim upward.

My head breaks the surface, and I feel a flush of relief. *My world.* The sun is a low, orange luster on the horizon and the sea is rippled in waves.

As my eyes adjust to air again, everything comes into focus— the silhouette of Mount Wabanaki, the gray face of Tutatquin Point, the warm yellow lights from the homes at Nipon Beach. I'm about a mile from shore, by my rough estimate. *I can make it home. I can survive this.*

I take a deep breath of air, uncertain what will happen. At first, my lungs feel heavy and sore. Then the water flushes out and air rushes in. I breathe like normal. Like human.

But am I human? Can I change back? What if a boat came up to me right now? Would I terrify them? Would they spear me and roast me up with some lemon and dill? Would they take pictures to sell to *Weekly World News*? Would I be featured alongside the monkey-faced boy or the bat-eared grandmother? Am I a mermaid forever?

What if I showed up at County Hospital with this tail? That wouldn't go well. They once amputated the wrong leg on a diabetic patient. It was such a major hack job, it made national news and everything. What would they do with something like me?

What would my friends say if they saw me like this? Sheriff would have a heart attack. What would Matthew think? *"Maybe you're good bait fish after all, Creary."*

I lift my tail in front of me. It shimmers in the fading sunlight. Magically, my scales oscillate from blue to green to purple to pink as I twist around. Colors so brilliant, they appear to be made of pure light. My tail sparkles like veins of mica in granite, like cut crystal. Maybe I'm dreaming. Maybe I'll wake up any second in my bed, Sammy snoring in the next room.

A seagull squawks overhead. It dives down and plucks a small fish from the water near me. I watch it swallow the fish whole and fly back toward land.

I start giggling, and the giggling takes me off guard, so I start laughing, and then I laugh uncontrollably. I laugh as though I haven't laughed in a hundred years. I laugh as though all the laughter has been trapped inside of me, brewing and percolating, stewing and fermenting, and it's finally ready to be released. I shake with laughter. Hearing myself laugh like this makes me laugh even harder.

It occurs to me that I should be freezing by now, hypothermic even, but I'm not. I'm comfortable in my body, unfazed by the elements.

I look back at Ne'Hwas. Somewhere on the island Sammy is sitting around with a bunch of our friends, waiting for me to walk through the door to yell "Happy Birthday." I wonder if she's worried about me right now. I wonder if she's called Sheriff to tell him I never returned from surfing. I wonder if Sheriff is driving around the island, lights flashing, looking for my car, a sick, familiar dread in his gut. He'll think the worst. Cops always think the worst.

I need to get back to them.

I lie on my back and start swimming toward land, but it's slow going. Wind whips in my ears as I'm tossed around on the waves. So I slip under the surface. The shock of breathing water is gone now, and I tune in to my senses. There are no vibrations, no danger. I hang motionless in a state of neutral buoyancy—not floating, not sinking—watching faint streaks of sunlight dance around me. It is absolutely silent. Peaceful. Calm. So different from what's above.

Naked, my hair flowing behind me, I dolphin kick and glide through the water, feeling strong and free. A trail of bioluminescence appears in my wake. I stop and swish my hands around, watching the microscopic particles light up with the friction of my movements. I draw figure eights and swirls and happy faces, like trippy, underwater fireworks.

A thought flickers in front of me, so faint I have a hard time catching it: I could stay. Be a mermaid forever. Escape once and for all. I could live out here. Never return. It would be easy to slip away. It would be . . . wonderful. The thought vanishes and a more familiar voice chimes in: *Don't be stupid.*

I swim to shore, amazed by my speed and stamina. As I get close to land, the sandy bottom slopes upward. I break the surface to get my bearings. Nipon Beach is straight ahead. The sun is almost gone. Luckily, no one's at the beach at this time of night, this early in the season. I swim to shore.

I crawl on my hands up the sand, like some sort of sea monster. After my grace under water, I feel like a lumbering idiot. But I made it. I'm home. I'm safe.

Or am I? Without my legs, an entirely new danger sets in. I'm completely exposed and vulnerable—not to mention topless. Not far off in the distance, the summer sounds of Nipon Beach ring out—laughter and voices on the streets. Cars cruising by. Music blaring from speakers propped in windows.

I look up to the night sky. *Please don't let anyone see me. If someone does see me, please let it be someone who can handle this. Not some high-strung Nipon junkie or a deranged conspiracy theorist with a shotgun in his truck.*

My scales have changed color from the incandescent blues, greens, and pinks of the ocean to a dull gray. And they itch like crazy. I wiggle back and forth in the sand to relieve the itch, but that doesn't help, so I reach down to scratch, and scales come off in my hand.

Okay, think. I can breathe air. That's good. I can wiggle my fingers. Also good. Stripping off layers of tail. Probably not good.

But the itching sensation is killing me, like a thousand fire ants stinging at once. I rub my tail harder against the sand, which helps, but it only relieves the bottom portion. So I roll. I cross my arms against my chest and roll along the beach, the same way Kay and I used to race down the hill in our backyard when the first tufts of grass appeared in spring. I keep rolling until every inch of me is coated in sand and the itching subsides.

All the rolling makes me dizzy. I stop. I feel lighter, different somehow.

When I look down, two familiar legs are pressed into the sand.

SIX

I t's about time," Sammy says, when I get to the apartment. She slams the rest of her Corona and grabs her purse off the salvaged lobster trap that serves as a coffee table. "We are so-o-o late."

I shake sand out of my hair. "You're not going to believe what happened," I say, shivering. I'm wrapped in an old Mexican blanket I found in the trunk of my car. It's itchy and smells like cheese. My body temperature has plummeted since I left the water. Since I returned to warm-blooded.

Sammy squints in the hall mirror and runs pink gloss over her lips. "Oh my God, Jess, wait until you see the gorgeous crop of boys that came off the ferry today. Must be some college graduation trip. Out to sow their wild oats and all that. How old are college boys, anyway? Are they too young for me? Mm-mmm, these boys looked delicious. Like little Jujyfruits. Sweet and yummy." She primps her hair. "Remember how Mrs. Hopper always handed out Jujyfruits at Halloween and we loved them so much we'd switch costumes and sneak back for a second round and Kay would yell at us and tell us that's bad trick-or-treating etiquette? Do they still make Jujyfruits?" She looks up from her reflection to me. "Why are your lips blue?" Then she really sees me. "Holy shit. Where are your *clothes*?"

I wiggle my bare toes and feel the solid weight of my feet on the floor. I try to imagine a tail in their place. I still feel like I might be dreaming, but seeing Sammy in the flesh, hearing her yammer on about cute boys and Jujyfruits, snaps me back to reality. "Something happened to me," I say.

She collapses into the couch and pulls a pillow over her lap. "What?"

"I was surfing." I try to find the words to tell her. *I'm a mermaid. I have a tail and no legs. I breathe through my armpits. I'm an underwater torpedo. I have beautiful scales that shimmer like jewels. I faced off against a great white shark.*

"Was it a rip current? Did you lose your board? That happened to Spencer once. He tried to make it sound like no big thing, but I know it shook him."

"It wasn't a rip." Can I tell her? Will she believe me? Or will she laugh in my face? Would I tell Kay? Would she believe me? I'm not even sure I believe it myself. The words won't come. My stomach, however, won't shut up. It grumbles. Suddenly I'm aware of how ravenous I am.

In the kitchen, I pull out a box of leftover fish sticks and ziti marinara from the Lobster Corral. Chunks of fried fish crumble to the floor as I shovel fistfuls into my mouth, not even tasting it. My body screams for calories. All that swimming really emptied my tank.

Sammy looks horrified. "Hel-lo. It's *bikini* season."

"I turned into a mermaid," I blurt out, wiping marinara sauce off my chin.

"Huh?"

I explain the whole thing to her as best I can, from the barrel at Tutatquin Point to the great white shark chasing me. As the story pours out of me, I have the sensation that someone else is telling it. Nothing that extraordinary could happen to me.

"Right," Sammy says. "I think you must have hit your head on the rocks. Do you have a concussion? Let me see." She feels my head for lumps.

"I didn't hit my head," I say. "Although, come to think of it,

I did bang it pretty good against the ceiling of the cave. But that was after I'd already transformed."

She checks my eyes to see if my pupils are dilated. "Are you drowsy and lethargic? Are you dizzy? Do you have ringing in your ears? Do you feel nauseous? Do you have pain when you urinate?"

"Pain when I urinate? What kind of head injury causes that?"

She looks flustered. "I don't know. I get all those symptoms confused. Should we get you to the hospital?"

One thing about living on Ne'Hwas is that everyone knows basic first aid. It's a requirement, starting in fifth grade. So is passing a swim test. Some schools teach art or music or Spanish. But if you live on Ne'Hwas, treating near-drowning victims or swimming out of a riptide are as important as math and spelling.

So we all know about head trauma. We know there's a period called the lucid interval, when you seem totally fine, and then *bam!*, you drop dead from a hematoma or edema. No warning. No second chance.

"I didn't bang my head. It was real." The shark, the tail, the scrape on my knee, which is still tender to the touch.

Sammy digs into my hair, looking for bumps and blood. I pull away.

"Did anyone see you . . . turn into a mermaid?"

"You don't believe me." My teeth are suddenly chattering. I pull the blanket tight.

"I'm just asking," she says. "It seems a little far-fetched. Even for you."

"Jay and Tyler were there. Freddie and Josh Collins, too. But I was all the way down at Tutatquin Point. They couldn't have seen."

"Jess," Sammy says. She's talking to me the way you talk to a child, or a foreigner. "Tutatquin Point? The boneyard? Really? There's no way you caught a barrel there. It's not that I don't believe you. It's just that . . . well, I think you're confused."

But I don't feel confused. I'm completely clearheaded. Everything I see is saturated in color. The bright blue and pink of the tapestry on the wall is more vibrant than ever, the scent of the vanilla candle melted onto the windowsill is stronger. The sounds of the lobster boat riggings at White's Wharf behind the apartment are sharper. I feel alive. Outside, the moon is a great ball of white light. It didn't fall out of the sky. I became a mermaid and the world didn't implode.

At least, I *think* I became a mermaid. Even now, as I try to recall the details of what happened, the images fade away. Under water everything was a blur, and now my memory of it is slipping into the blue haze.

"Maybe I can do it again." I say. "Yes. That's it. I'll go again. You can come with me. I'll show you. I'll catch another barrel."

"Jess."

"You'll see what happens. It's weird, Sammy, but it's beautiful. My tail captures the full spectrum of light. You'll see how fast I can swim. Maybe you can become a mermaid, too."

"Jess."

"We could go now." I grab her wrist. "What if it's gone tomorrow?"

"What if what's gone?"

"The barrel. The . . . magic."

Sammy ignores me. She runs the shower and pulls me into the bathroom, "Get in. We can talk about this later all you want, but right now you've got to get ready." She takes the blanket from me, closes the curtain, instructs me on which conditioners will get the knots out of my hair and which will get rid of that godawful smell.

She slides the curtain aside and pokes her head in. "Do you see spots? Spots are bad. Like, brain damage bad."

"I didn't bang my head."

"Maybe we should go to the hospital, just in case. Skip the

party. Oh, and, by the way, everyone's going to be at the Rongo for your birthday. It was supposed to be a surprise."

I pull the shower curtain closed. "Today is full of surprises."

〰〰〰

Any plans for jumping out and yelling "Happy Birthday" evaporated hours ago, along with everyone's sobriety. It's 11:36 P.M. on the Budweiser clock with the missing neon *w*. No one even notices when Sammy and I walk into the bar.

"The birthday girl is here!" Sammy yells, but the music is loud, the bar is packed, and the moment for orchestrating a grand entrance has long passed.

"Son of a bitch," Sammy says. "I had a whole thing planned. The lights were supposed to go off and the candles were going to be lit, and we were going to sing to you. I wanted this to be special."

"It's okay. I'm still feeling a little woozy. You know," I say, "from before."

"But there's cake."

"Honestly, I'm fine without making my birthday into a production." I need time to process what happened to me.

"Well, I'm not! You need to have fun. When's the last time you had fun? You need to get back into the swing of things."

She sounds genuinely bummed and a little perturbed that no one is cooperating with her plan to make this My Special Day. I put an arm around her. "It's better this way. We can ease our way in." "Easing in" pretty much sums up my whole reentry-into-society process anyway. After we lost Kay, I didn't want to be around people.

Sammy grabs my hand and leads me to where the Slack Tide crew has a tiny patch of oak bar carved out.

"Look who's here," Sal says, eyes half-mast. "About time. Been waiting for you," he says. He puts an arm around me and one around Sammy. A girl on each side—yeah, that's Sal.

Ben (another Slack Tide captain), Jacqueline (galley girl), Tony (first mate), and Ian and Stefan (deckhands) give me hugs, and all insist on buying me drinks.

"How was the surf?" Matthew asks.

I turn toward his voice. "It was . . ." Magical. Terrifying. Something out of a dream. It was a dream. "I caught a barrel."

"No way." His black eyelashes curl at the ends. "I've never caught a barrel. What was it like?"

"Gorgeous." Somehow my word choice embarrasses me. "And weird," I add quickly.

"I always knew you were a better surfer than me," Matthew says.

"I am not," I object. "You're the one who taught me to surf."

"And the student surpasses the teacher," he says. This feels more like flirting than any other conversation I've ever had with Matthew. And, well, I have to admit I like it.

The chatter rises around us. Heavy metal blasts out of the speakers. Somewhere, a glass breaks. I want to tell Matthew that the barrel led me to a magical portal where I transformed into a mermaid, or at least, I think I did, even though Sammy thinks it was a concussion. Instead I opt for: "Thanks for covering for me. Was Harold mad?"

"No. I told him you were downtown passing out Slack Tide flyers to drum up business. He liked your initiative. Thought you probably saved him a bundle on advertising."

I smile. "Maybe I'll get a raise."

"Doubt it." He smiles. He tilts his head to the side. "There's something different about you."

Is it that obvious? Do I have scales stuck in my hair? "What do you mean?"

"I don't know. Maybe it's that you're actually smiling," he says.

"Who's ready for a drink?" Sammy screeches.

Next thing I know everyone's yelling, "Shot, shot, shot," and a row of tequila shots appears on the bar. I throw one back, a harsh burn shooting down my throat. I wince and stifle a gag. Someone hands me a slice of lime. I suck on it to wash away the flavor of the tequila, which is inexplicably replaced by the briny bite of seawater on my tongue. Suddenly I'm swaying in the current and I'm a mermaid. The glaring white teeth of the shark are in front of me.

I shut my eyes tightly. What if Sammy's right? What if I did get a concussion? I wouldn't be the first person to blame their behavior on a head injury.

There's more chanting. "Shot, shot, shot," and another round materializes before me.

"This is how we do birthdays around here," Tony says. He lifts me up so I'm looking over the tops of sun-bleached heads.

"Shot, shot, shot."

Someone hands me a shot glass. They won't leave me alone until I imbibe, so I slam the tequila and Tony lets me down and everything is a blur. It's summer and it's a party, and it's a party all summer long on Ne'Hwas.

Sal starts to sing "Happy Birthday," but it's so loud in the bar, no one can hear, so Tony starts the song all over, and they're all wonderfully drunk and singing and swaying, and everybody is off-key. Then someone hands me a drink. I take a sip. It tastes like soda, but I'm pretty sure it's a Long Island Iced Tea, and for a flash of a second I think about how much it will suck tomorrow to be hungover and working on a fishing boat, with the rocking motion and the cloud of diesel filling my lungs.

But it's my birthday. So I take the drink.

Ian and Stefan are beside me now. Brothers from Norway, they are Nordic giants, and the best deckhands of any fishing party boat on the island. They tower over me. They tower over everyone.

I can't hear what they're saying, but I'm tired of asking, "What'd you say?" so I just smile and drink my drink and they laugh and talk like we're carrying on an actual conversation.

Sammy is telling me about the latest drama between her and Spencer, but I can't follow. There's too much noise and the tequila is working its way through my body to my brain. My senses are garbled. My hearing shuts down, but my sense of smell is on overdrive. I can pinpoint the location of Jacqueline's perfume on the left collar of her shirt. Notes of fig and oak moss. I can smell Stefan's laundry detergent on his T-shirt, which was washed today. Ian's breath is a mix of onions, french fries, and Jägermeister.

I feel like I've gone from zero to drunk in five minutes. I have to lean against the bar. Suddenly there's a cake in front of me, with a forest of candles. Tony tries to light them, but he drops the match into a shot glass, igniting it instantly. "Whoa, check it out," he says. He tips over the glass and sends a streak of blue flame down the bar. The bartender smothers the fire with a dishtowel, tells Tony to go away, and lights the candles himself. The lights are dimmed and the cake burns bright. People I don't even know are hugging me and offering to buy me drinks.

I lean forward and blow out the candles. There's more hugging and toasting and everyone's talking at once and it all becomes a ringing in my head. The air is choked with smells. Cigarettes. Pool cue chalk. Sweat.

There's a smell in the air that steals my attention. It's a man's smell, intense and steeped in my memory. My brain tries to make sense of it, amid all the other, familiar scents in the room.

Before my mind can catch up with what's happening, my body is moving across the room toward the scent. It's like blood in the water.

Then I see him.

Trip Sinclair.

He's standing at the pool table, halfheartedly playing pool, wholeheartedly flirting with the flock of townie girls around him. He's dressed in khaki shorts, a preppy polo shirt, and a preppy Yale baseball cap. Even his name is preppy. In one of those truly aristocratic traditions, he's called Trip as the third of a namesake. It's really William Bennett Sinclair III.

I can't stop moving toward him. My eyes won't blink.

He looks right at me.

Those blue eyes are on me, searching. Recognition follows. His face changes. He smiles at me.

He smiles at me.

How can he smile at me? He has one of those faces that's fixed in a permanent smile, as if everything in his world were always A-OK, hunky-dory, put there for his satisfaction. Kay loved his smile. She said it made her feel like every day of the week was a Friday.

I wonder if he was smiling behind the wheel of the boat before he crashed it? I wonder if he was smiling when he climbed out of the sea and left my sister for dead?

I want to wipe the smile off his face.

He raises his glass to me. A toast. Like we're old buddies at a high school reunion.

My nostrils flare. Rage builds inside of me that feels too big to contain. I start to sweat. My hands tremble.

His buddy says something and Trip laughs, and I can feel my heart beating like a jackhammer. I am losing control of my body.

I'm vaguely aware that the floor is sticky beneath my flip-flops and that someone behind me is saying my name. But I can't stop myself; something inside me needs to get near Trip, to see into his eyes, to see what's in his soul. As Sheriff would say, see what I see.

As I cross the bar toward him, my sense of smell tunes in to Trip. He gives off a million little scents. Wax. Chrome. Canvas. Sweat. Alcohol. Anxiety. My body is moving without me. I am so close, I can feel the soft cotton of his polo shirt against my skin. I can hear his heart beating.

Suddenly I am being pulled away. Matthew has me by the arm, and he's leading me out the door. "What are you doing, Creary?" he keeps asking.

Before I know it, we are outside in the parking lot and my whole body is shaking.

"Are you okay?" Matthew asks.

"I can't believe he showed up on this island again." I wobble a little, trying to stand straight. I feel drunk and angry. The world starts to spin.

"Maybe you should call it a night," Matthew says.

"Why's he here? After two years? Why'd he come back? What makes him think he can just walk back into our lives like nothing ever happened?"

"Don't let him get to you," Matthew says. He frowns in a way that makes me think *he* thinks I have every right to give Trip Sinclair a piece of my tequila-soaked mind.

I look up at the stars and almost fall over. "I'm going back in," I say.

"That's a bad idea."

"He killed her, Matthew. Trip Sinclair. Rich. Perfect. Trip Sinclair. Drunk at the wheel. That's manslaughter. That's leaving the scene of an accident. That's prison time for anyone else. Why does he just get to walk away?" The ocean is near. I smell the salt air on the wind.

"We've got work tomorrow. First thing. You need some sleep."

"Motherfucking Trip Sinclair."

"Calm down, killer. You need to let go and get on with your life. I know what I'm talking about here."

A memory of Trip Sinclair standing in front of the police station with his lawyer, Grant le Carre, by his side flashes before me. Reporters asked questions: *"What was your relationship with the deceased?*" "*Had you been drinking the night of the accident?*" "*Did you attempt to resuscitate the victim?*" "*Why did it take you five hours to report the accident?*" Trip read a short statement, but his lawyer did all the talking. There was no hint of an apology in the statement. Not a whiff of culpability. Trip Sinclair had a wall of protection around him. And a smile hidden beneath the charade of condolence.

"It ruined us. All of us. My mom. My dad. Me."

Matthew puts his arm around me.

"I have something for you, Creary. Come here." We go to his pickup, my flip-flops dragging through the gravel.

I lean against the truck to stabilize myself. "Cops gave up too easy. My father gave up too easy. I'm not going to let my sister down. She deserves better."

Matthew pulls something out of his truck and hands it to me. "Happy Birthday."

It's wrapped in newsprint. A bow of twine tied on top. "Whyd'ya get me a prezent?" My tongue and my lips are on different speeds.

"It's nothing."

I unwrap it. "I'z a picture frame."

"Turn it over, Einstein."

Inside is a newspaper clipping of the day I won the Northeast Regional Surfing Championship in New Jersey. It's a picture of me standing on the winner's podium after the competition, holding a trophy high over my head. I have a look of pure exhilaration on my face. My eyes are turned up at the trophy and I'm letting out a terrific cheer. I was seventeen. It was the best day of my life.

"Read the caption," Matthew says.

I squint at it, try to read, but the Long Island Iced Tea and tequila aren't helping.

Matthew takes it out of my hands. "The title is 'All-In.'" He reads: "Jess Creary, of Ne'Hwas Island, swept the junior girls' amateur surfing competition at Beach Haven, NJ. Big waves and rough conditions narrowed the field of talented young surfers. Creary posted a perfect ten-point ride, taking the waves with unmatched determination. 'It's a dream come true,' Creary said of her first career win. When asked how she gets herself mentally prepared for tackling such rough conditions she said, 'I don't overthink it. As soon as I enter the water, I'm all-in.'"

I take the frame and look at the picture of my seventeen-year-old self, marveling at how dynamic and vibrant I seem, how completely content in the world. When did I lose that? When did my life become such a shit storm of disappointment?

"I know it's been a rough couple of years," Matthew says. "But that girl is still inside of you. You've just got to find her."

I hug him, and I feel tiny against his giant fisherman body, and I feel like I could spill my guts to him. Like I could tell him my deepest secret.

SEVEN

These are the things I remember about last night:

1. Matthew drove me home.
2. I puked once on the side of the road.
3. I tried to get in my car and drive back to the Rongo to give Trip Sinclair what was coming to him.
4. Matthew stopped me (thank God!).
5. I told Matthew I was a mermaid.

After that, nothing.

I'm still dressed in my clothes from last night, and my tongue feels like cotton balls and kitty litter. My birthday present—the framed clipping of my junior surfing championship—is on my nightstand next to the alarm clock, which Matthew must have set for me so I'd wake up in time for work.

I rub my aching head and catch a glimpse of myself in the mirror. My hair's stuck to the side of my face. Puffy skin lines my eyes. I have that sick feeling that I did or said something stupid in my drunken state last night. Something embarrassing. Something I can't quite remember, but that other people (namely Matthew) probably can. I vaguely remember going off on a tirade about what assholes great white sharks can be.

Ugh. I will never drink again.

I down a warm bottle of Gatorade and get dressed for work.

As I pull on my Slack Tide shirt and a pair of clean underwear, I look around for my other birthday present—the comb of whalebone that Sheriff gave me. I want to hold it in my hands. If it's here, then I didn't use it to stab the shark, which would confirm that I definitely imagined the whole mermaid thing and I'm officially losing my mind. On the other hand, if it's not here then maybe it is lying at the bottom of a cave in the ocean and I really did become a mermaid, in which case I'm officially losing my mind. Either way, I'm losing my marbles.

I dig through drawers, look underneath piles of bras and bathing suits on the floor. But I can't find it.

In the light of day, nothing makes sense. Did I really become a mermaid or was I dreaming? Sometimes dreams feel so real that it's impossible to tell the difference. Did I get a concussion, like Sammy thinks? I feel around my head for lumps. It makes me sick to think I would use a concussion to explain what happened.

Trip Sinclair blamed his behavior of the night Kay died on a concussion. His lawyer actually convinced a judge that Trip couldn't be held responsible for his actions (or lack thereof) in the hours after the accident because he had banged his head and didn't know what he was doing. *Obviously*, the lawyer argued, Trip was impaired by an injury because he would have jumped in to try and save Kay, being an experienced sailor and all. At the very least, he would have called for help instead of returning home and waiting five hours before picking up a phone.

Trip had suffered both physically and mentally from the accident, the lawyer claimed, and that was supposed to explain everything.

~~~~

It's high tide when I get to the boardwalk, lobster and scallop boats head out for the day. Restaurants are setting up for the breakfast crowd. My head throbs, the Long Island Iced Tea and tequila working their dark magic on the inside of my skull. Walking feels good and clears my head a little, which isn't good, because now all I can think about is how bonkers I must have sounded telling Matthew about sharks and mermaids.

He probably thought it was the tequila talking. The girl who spends so much time in the water she's part mermaid. *How cute.* There are cheesy T-shirts all over Spinnaker Street to that effect: "You know you're a mermaid if you drink like a fish and seas the day." "Keep calm and swim on."

The hull of the *Dauntless* shimmers like liquid where it catches the reflection of the rising sun on the water.

A handful of customers are already lined up at the shop to buy tickets for today's trip. Harold hands me the keys to the mess locker as he rings up a party of four guys on a bachelor weekend. Beneath their ball caps and scruff, they look like they partied as hard last night as I did. Chunk blowers, for sure.

I get a cart from the supply shed and load it up with cases of beer, soda, and water. Since this is the first trip of the season, I'll have to stock the galley with nonperishables like ketchup and candy bars, along with the daily ration of frozen burger patties, hot dogs, cheese, milk, and bacon.

When I get to the end of the pier, Ian pulls off his heavy rubber gloves and helps load food into the boat. Tony stands at the fillet table, cutting bait.

"Gonna be a good day, people. Let's make some money," Tony says in an excessively cheery voice. If he's hungover from last night, he doesn't let it show. He's here to make money, and he's not going to let a little headache cost him anything in tips.

"How are you not hungover?" I ask.

"Guys can hold their liquor better than chicks. Everyone knows that," Tony says.

Stefan is setting up tackle and stowing burlap bags for the customers to store their fish. "Norwegians don't get hungover," he says proudly.

Ian pounds his chest. "We are raised on aquavit and breast milk from when we are babies." The brothers high-five each other as I step onto the boat.

"Well, I'll be in the galley mainlining Advil if anyone needs me," I say.

"It was a good party," Tony says.

I wait for him to give me the business, to tell me what a fool I made of myself, but luckily I had enough sense not to do anything too stupid in front of Tony last night. I'd never hear the end of it.

"Hey, bring me a coffee, would you?" he says, chopping the head off a bait fish.

"Me too?" Ian says. "Black and sweet, please, just how I like my women."

"Coming right up," I say dryly.

Like the lineup at Nipon Beach, the universe of fishing boat charters on Ne'Hwas is a macho sport. Deep-sea fishing is very physical, and you have to be tough to make out here. Guys get injured all the time. They catch hooks in the hand and gaffs in the arms, and it takes a lot of strength to pull an anchor from two hundred feet below to the surface. Since Harold refuses to hire girls as deckhands, we get the lowly job of serving coffee and frying burgers. It's appallingly sexist and unfair, but I do it because I'd rather be here than stuck on land waiting tables or cleaning hotel rooms.

"How you feeling, Creary?" Matthew asks, popping his head into the galley.

"Like a million bucks," I say. I pour the ground coffee into the machine.

He pulls his sunglasses down and looks at me, and I feel like my insides might flutter away.

"Ready to go toe-to-toe with some great whites today?" he says, a smirk on his lips.

"So . . . I guess I did say that?"

"You had quite a story to tell."

"Did I embarrass myself?"

"Not at all. But I would like to learn more about your superhuman powers. Apparently you can swim like a rocket under water. You know, like a mermaid." He laughs.

I rub my temples. "Ugh. You must think I'm nuts."

"I've always thought that."

I think back to Matthew at Kay's funeral. I remember the moment the casket was lowered into the ground and I was trying so hard not to cry, and he knew I was trying. He held me up straight and told me to stand tall, and as soon as everyone turned to get back in the cars, I buried my face in his chest and cried for the first time. I remember thinking how crisp his shirt was, and that I was ruining it with my snot and tears. And I knew he wouldn't care, that he would offer up a thousand clean shirts for me.

"Can we just pretend I didn't make a fool of myself last night?"

"Hey, don't worry about it. You had a few drinks. You said some crazy stuff. Been there, done that."

He steps into the galley and grabs a Coke out of the fridge. It's a small gesture, but it means a lot to me. All the other guys would ask me to get it for them, instead of taking the two extra steps themselves. I want to talk to him some more, thank him for my present, ask him if he's ever had a dream so realistic that it makes him question his sanity. But now the passengers are entering the cabin and they all need something from me. They want to know where they should stow their bags, how long will it take to get to the fishing site, how much for a cup of coffee, where can they buy a Slack Tide angler's hat.

Matthew gives me a salute and heads up to the wheelhouse.

~~~~

The day is already hot, but as we make our way into the bay, a cool breeze sets in. One of the guys from the bachelor party walks up to the galley and orders a beer as I fry a slab of bacon.

"Sorry. Can't serve you 'til noon," I say.

"Aren't we in international waters or something?"

"Not quite."

The guy leans on the counter, puts on his best frat guy smile. "Ah, come one. Just a beer? Something to settle my stomach. I'm feeling a little queasy." He holds a twenty-dollar bill and winks at me. "You can bend the rules, right?"

"Sorry," I say, and go to work filling the salt and pepper shakers. As he walks away, I give him some friendly advice. "Keep your eyes on the horizon. It helps. And definitely stay out of the main cabin."

His face is already turning green and his eyes are glassy. He turns and walks away, but I can tell by the way he's moving that he's not going to make it through this trip in one piece. He teeters to the rail outside and leans against it, cradling his head in his arms.

Five minutes later, frat boy runs into the cabin, covering his mouth.

"*Out!*" I scream, but it's too late. He hurls all over the floor.

I get the mop and bucket and clean up frat boy's filth, which only makes me want to hurl myself. His friends are laughing hysterically, oblivious to the fact that they've only made my job harder.

"You think it's so funny? Get in here and clean it up yourself, assholes," I bark at them.

They cast their eyes away from me and move farther down the port side. I know I should be nicer to the customers. Service with a smile and all that. I can expect to be shortchanged in the tip jar from those guys today, but I can't help myself. I hate being at the mercy of others, of having to serve.

Once the cabin is clean, and the breakfast orders are done, and the galley is prepped for lunch, I step out to the back deck. I climb the steps to the upper deck, away from everyone. It's the only quiet place, since passengers aren't allowed here while the boat is under way.

Billows of diesel smoke circle in the updraft. I breathe the heavy air into my lungs. Seagulls chase after the boat, steely eyes peeled and watching the bait table.

I try to remember the feeling of breathing water. I close my eyes and imagine swimming through the sea, the effortless movement of my tail. It was so peaceful, so calm, so beautiful. So real. I try to envision the brilliant show of bioluminescence that enveloped me as I swam to shore, the pink and purple reflections in my scales.

I want to believe. I want to believe that I became a magical creature who doesn't just clean up after seasick frat boys and fetch coffee for her coworkers.

Below me, I watch the way the steel hull cuts through the water, breaking it into prisms off the stern. If I look at it just right, rainbows appear in the mist.

Was it only yesterday that I was under these waves, swimming faster than any human can, going places never explored before?

I think about the picture of my seventeen-year-old self on the winner's podium, standing tall, proud to be the best at something. I believed I could do anything, then. I felt invincible.

I look down at the dark blue water. What lies beneath? Dogfish and cod and haddock and wolf fish, whales bigger than any living thing on earth, and creatures so small and otherworldly they light up like fireworks in the dark of night. Great white sharks.

Do I belong down there, with those creatures? Was it just a concussion or was it real? Was it a dream? Or am I special? I used to feel special, once upon a time. All I ever feel now is loss. The things that were. The people I loved.

I need to remember the feeling of winning. Of being a champion. Of being happy. I need to believe in myself again. The sea chose me yesterday. I need to believe that it will choose me again.

"All-in," I whisper. I kick off my shoes, step over the railing, and dive.

Down, down, down I dive. The sea will remember me. I will breathe water and grow a fish tail, like I did before. I will transform into that magical creature I was yesterday.

The pressure in my ears forces me to slow my descent. I pinch my nose and blow. Any second now, I will find out if it was all a dream.

I swim deeper, the cold water hitting me like a sledgehammer. Behind me I reach to feel my tail, but instead I find feet and legs. I take a few more tentative strokes downward, then stop and wait.

The transformation is not happening. I'm still human. And I'm dangerously close to becoming a drowned human. I need air. The surface seems like it's a million miles away. My lungs are screaming. I swim straight up toward the sunlight, kicking hard against the weight of water.

~~~~

I'm in the wheelhouse with Matthew, dressed in a Slack Tide T-shirt from the ship store and a pair of board shorts Tony found in the bottom of his gear bag. I have to roll the waistband down so they won't slide off me.

"What happened exactly? I need to write this up in the log," Matthew says, his tone no longer playful.

I squeeze water out of my hair. "I slipped."

"You slipped?"

"Yeah, I slipped." Under Matthew's gaze, I feel as transparent as Scotch tape.

His jaw is tight. "Did you slip over the rail or under it?"

"Over," I say.

Matthew puts a hand at my waist at the point where the railing would hit me if I were standing against it. "Must have been a big slip."

I look out the window at the water, the endless energy of waves, the sun rippling against them making dark shadows and light peaks.

"I have to get down to the galley. It's lunchtime."

"This is more important. I should document what happened. You can't start jumping off boats in the middle of the ocean. As captain, I'm responsible for your safety."

Responsible for my safety. That's Matthew for you. Only a responsible person would save a newspaper article about a coworker and give it to her years later as a gift. Why was he holding on to it? Is he trying to tell me something? Does he think of me as more than just a coworker? A friend?

"I get it. I need to be more careful."

"You could have seriously injured yourself."

"It was a mistake."

"I know you're a free spirit and you like to do your own thing, and you don't always follow the rules, but I'm responsible for you out here."

I want to curl up and die. "I had too much to drink last night. That's all."

On the dashboard, the fish finder blinks with pixels of life under the sea.

"So," he pauses. "Going overboard has nothing to do with Trip Sinclair being back on the island."

I exhale. I'm actually relieved. As much as it kills me that Trip is back on Ne'Hwas, carrying on with his privileged life, I'm glad Matthew suspects Trip is the sole reason for my stunt. It sounds a lot more rational than trying to prove that I'm a half-human, half-fish creature that only exists in myths. "No, it doesn't."

"Then you're not having a psychotic break?"

"No."

"Good." He looks away. I notice a scar just beneath his eye, shaped like a crescent. It looks like it was put there long ago. By a stray fishing hook? A jammed winch? A gale wind? Given Matthew's years at sea, his face should be etched in scars.

I turn to leave, but linger at the doorway. "Hey Matthew, can I ask you something?"

"Sure."

"Why did you give me that old newspaper clipping? Why did you save it all these years?"

"I don't know." He looks down, embarrassed. "I thought you'd want it. You know, remind you what a cool, badass surfer you once were. Maybe it was wrong."

"It wasn't wrong. I really appreciate it."

Way off to the starboard side, a fish jumps into the air. In a flash, I see the rigid points of its fin, the great mass of its body. A bluefin tuna. And I wish I could be there, too.

EIGHT

After work, I go home, take a shower and wash the salt water out of my hair, scrubbing away any reminders of my stunt aboard the *Dauntless* today. I'm not a mermaid. I'm just a galley girl on a fishing boat, with a really active imagination. *Accept it,* I tell myself.

But I didn't imagine Trip Sinclair in the flesh at the Rongo, strutting around like nothing ever happened. Sheriff needs to know: Trip Sinclair is back on island.

Sheriff's truck is in the driveway when I get to his house. His house. *My* house? *Our* house? How old do you have to be before you no longer consider your parents' house "home"? When does home become the thing that *you* decide it is? I only moved out a year and a half ago, at the ripe age of twenty-one, but I don't think of it as home anymore. My apartment—with its stained furniture and cracked plaster, with the bathtub that's filled by Sammy's shampoo collection—that's home.

I don't visit as much as I should. In fact, seeing Sheriff twice in two days will probably send him into a coronary. He'll think I'm here to ask for money. Which I'm not.

I'm here to ask for much more than that.

As I walk up the porch, I can see him hunched over bills at the kitchen table. That's where he'd sit every Friday, to catch up on police reports or pay bills, when we were growing up. He used to give me and Kay the deposit slips from the back of the checkbook to play with. We felt so grown-up, so important, to have those little blue booklets in our possession.

"Hi, Sheriff," I say, letting myself in. The screen door squeaks shut behind me.

"Jess. What a pleasant surprise." He shuffles his paperwork into a neat stack and slides it to the side. A moment later his face is tangled with concern. "Everything all right?"

"Does something have to be wrong for me to come see you? Can't I just swing by to say hello?" The cop in him is always just below the surface, ready for the worst, prepared to spring into action.

He sighs. "Of course you can swing by. Have you eaten?"

I plop into a chair. "I'm not really in the mood for a ham sandwich."

"I think there's steaks in the freezer." He gets up, walks to the fridge.

"Did you put them there?" I ask, raising an eyebrow.

He pretends to think about for a minute. "Um, no."

"Did Mom?"

He doesn't look at me. "Yes. I suppose Barbara is the one who bought them."

"Then they've been there too long."

"They're frozen."

"Shelf life of six months, tops," I say.

He straightens the pictures stuck to the fridge with smiley-face magnets. There's one of me, Kay, and Mom at the beach. One of Kay in a graduation cap and gown. One of Sheriff getting a civil service award from the city marshal, which was so long ago he didn't have a single gray hair in the picture. All ancient history.

"The steaks are fine," Sheriff says.

"They'll have freezer burn."

He touches the bridge of his nose. "Are we going to argue about expiration dates?"

The question hangs in the air. We both know this fight isn't about steaks going bad, but about what's been left behind. It's about my mother walking out on us, leaving a freezer full of uneaten food, cutting us out of her life without any warning. It's about Kay. It's about him and me struggling to preserve the family we have left. And failing at it.

He opens the fridge and I can see that all he has inside is a six-pack of Pepsi, a jar of mayo, a carton of milk, and some soy sauce. It's like peeking into a bachelor's refrigerator. I know there are packages of sliced ham and cheese from the deli in the meat drawer, because that's the extent of his culinary skill. My mom is the cook.

He pulls out two Pepsis and sits back down, gives one to me. The aluminum is cold in my hand. "Let's not fight. I'm glad you're here. How was your birthday party?"

"It was white trash meets tequila."

I take a sip of my Pepsi and study my father for signs of depression. I know what to look for—anger or irritability, loss of energy, weight loss, reckless behavior, loss of interest in daily activities. I read a bunch of Web sites on depression, but it's hard to tell. It builds and creeps up on you. In my mind, I picture depression as the game Jenga, which we used to play with my mom on winter nights. Each small catastrophe is a wooden block taken out of your stack and piled on top, the stack getting more and more wobbly as the blocks get higher. Sheriff has so many holes in his stack that it's always on the verge of toppling over.

"It's important to celebrate milestones, Jess. We can't forget that," he says.

"Tony set the bar on fire," I say cheerfully.

He sips his soda. "Sounds like a good thing I wasn't there."

I twirl my hair, an old habit I developed as a kid, whenever I was hiding something. There were years when my hair was so knotted from the twisting that I had dreadlocks in the downy underlayers of hair around my neck.

I remember being in fourth grade and twisting my hair as

I sat on the wooden bench outside the principal's office, mud all the way up my legs, dripping on the checkered floor. My parents were called in for a meeting after I had snuck off during a field trip to the old lobster cannery. The lobster cannery was converted into a Native American educational center sometime in the 1980s, and since there isn't much in the way of culture on Ne'Hwas, it's a field trip hot spot for elementary schools, scouting troops, and senior citizen clubs.

We were there to learn Passamaquoddy history, but all they talked about was how canning lobsters was big business back before shipping was dependable, and how the local Native American families were hired to work at the lobster cannery, since their ancestors had been fishing the area for lobster for hundreds of years and were pretty much experts in anything that had to do with fishing or hunting. The tour guide showed us a birch bark canoe that had been made by some other Native American tribe on the mainland, and told us how important canoes were as a form of transportation for the Passamaquoddy. I raised my hand and told her I was Passamaquoddy and never canoed anywhere, and that I preferred to ride around in the back of my father's pickup truck when I needed to get someplace. She scowled and told me to hold all my questions until the end of the tour. Then she pulled a spear out of a closet and explained how the native people had fished for pollock with nothing but spears for hundreds of years. When I pointed out the Bass Pro Shops logo on the handle and made the other kids laugh, she told me I was a very disruptive young lady. The tour drudged on and I kept my mouth shut, even though there were a bunch of other so-called artifacts that had nothing to do with actual Passamaquoddy culture, like the whale skeleton hanging from the rafters.

The old lady giving the tour wasn't even Passamaquoddy. The whole thing was such a sham. Here I was, the only actual Native American in the whole place, and I had to listen to some bogus stories about a cannery that no one in my family had ever set foot in.

After a while, they marched us through the gift shop, where we could buy plastic toy lobsters made in Taiwan, Tootsie Rolls, and rock candy.

By the time we got to the part of the tour where they herded us into a windowless rec room and taught us how to weave sweetgrass baskets, I'd had enough.

I snuck out.

It was low tide, so I left the Native American educational center, walked down the beach to the mudflats, and went clamming. I used my hands to dig, and found a broken planter to use as a bucket. It was full of clams by the time they discovered I was missing. The teachers spent hours searching for me. "Tainted the cultural experience for the entire class," the principal said.

Sheriff was furious. He had to leave work early so the principal could tell my mom and him what a wild and unrepentant child I was. He sent me to my room for the rest of the day as punishment. But as soon as he went back to work, my mom called me down to the kitchen and we boiled up those clams with garlic, parsley, and wine. We made a chocolate cake and picked fiddlehead ferns from the creek bed behind our house.

When Sheriff came home from his shift that night, there was a beautiful feast on the table.

He wasn't impressed. He pulled my mom into the living room, as I hid in the coatrack, eavesdropping.

"She needs to be punished, Barbara. You can't reward her bad behavior. She'll never learn."

"Why should she get in trouble for bringing home dinner?" my mom asked.

"She needs to learn to respect authority."

"Why? So other people can tell her how to live her life? That's what my mother always did, and I ran away as soon as I could."

"She's too wild."

"She's adventurous."

"But she ditched school, Barbara. Don't you understand? She's going to end up in big trouble if we don't rein her in. I see kids every day on this island who end up in the wrong crowd. Kids who don't have any direction." Sheriff was whispering, but I could hear anyway.

"Maybe if school taught her something worthwhile, like how to dig for clams, then she'd want to go."

"Barbara, I'm worried about her."

"She's a strong girl. You never need to worry about strong girls."

He sighed, and then I heard them kiss, which is how all their conversations started and ended, and my mom said, "Now, let's be thankful and eat the food Jess has brought us."

She always understood me better than Sheriff.

~~~~

I look up from my hair twirling to find Sheriff's eyes on me. "What's up, Jess?"

I pause. Take a sip of my Pepsi. "He's on island."

Sheriff's face is blank for a minute. He's trying to figure out which "he" I'm referring to. Then it registers. "The Sinclair boy." It's a statement, not a question. He stands, puts his hands on his hips, and stares out the window to Mom's backyard garden, with its asparagus gone to seed and dead, dry patches where there once were zucchini and peppers of all kinds. "And?"

I stand, too. "And . . . how can he just come back here? How can he just walk around our island like nothing ever happened?"

"He's not breaking any laws."

"I don't care what the laws are. Trip Sinclair has no right to be on Ne'Hwas. What's he doing here, anyway?"

"Vacationing would be my guess."

"It's not right."

"I can't stop him."

"You can do *something*. You're a cop. You investigate crimes. You arrest bad people," I say.

He tightens his jaw. "What am I supposed to do, plant a crack pipe in his Corvette? Write him a citation for breathing?"

"Prove he's guilty. Charge him with murder. Manslaughter, at least." My voice is rising and I can feel the heat rise to my face.

"Jess, they went through all this. He was cleared."

My palms sweat. "How can you be so calm? I want to kill him. I want justice for what he did. How can you just stand there and not do anything?"

Sheriff rolls the kinks out of his neck. "You can't take the law into your own hands. Promise me that. Promise you won't do anything stupid."

The anger is taking over. I'm angry about Trip Sinclair killing my sister. I'm angry that Sheriff won't react. "Aren't you mad?"

"Of course I am. But Trip Sinclair isn't my problem. You are. And the only thing I care about is protecting the family I have left."

"We can't let him get away with it!" I say.

"There is no *we* in this. *You* need to stay out of trouble. *I* need to do my job, which is to protect and serve."

"Mom would freak if she knew he was here."

Sheriff's face drops. "I think Barbara would be more interested in keeping you out of trouble than getting revenge. If she comes back, that is."

"Mom is on a spirit journey. She'll come back," I say.

"I don't know about that. I looked into phone records, credit card statements, but the trail was cold from the start. She doesn't want to be found this time."

"She's coming back," I say. My mom is coming back. She's on a spirit journey, that's all. It's like an Australian aboriginal walkabout, a period of wandering. She used to disappear for days. No warning. No explanation. Wandering, she would tell me, was the best way for a person to get rid of sorrow. When you lose your-self, you set free anything locked up inside of you, she would say. Some people turn to Prozac or wine; my mother would wander.

They should have taught us about spirit journeys that day at the lobster cannery. I might have hung around.

Sheriff sits down at the table again. His shoulders are slumped. He's lethargic. He sighs constantly. All those signs of depression written across his body.

"I want you to stay away from Trip Sinclair."

"I want you to arrest him."

"Promise me you won't do anything stupid."

I get up and head for the door. "Like what?"

"I don't need to give you any ideas."

"What do you think I'm going to do? Track him down? Stake out his house?"

"The law only works if you follow it when it's hard, Jess."

"Sometimes it seems like you're more concerned with the law than with me."

"That's not true."

I can't stand how sad he sounds. How lonely. I can't stand how quiet the house is now, how overgrown and unkempt the garden is without my mom around to tend it. I can't stand how much Sheriff needs *me* now. I hate that I don't get to be the child any-more.

I'm twenty-three and the world is my oyster, but no one passed me the shucking knife. I want Kay here to help me out, to tell me what to do. To glue my family back together.

The screen door squeaks on my way out.

NINE

I take Sheriff's advice and manage to get through the next couple days without doing anything too stupid. I don't try to rip Trip Sinclair apart limb from limb with my bare hands. I don't jump off any fishing boats in the middle of the ocean. I don't yammer on to Matthew about being a mermaid and escaping the jaws of great white sharks. In fact, I try not to think too much about what happened to me out there.

Life goes on. Ferries continue to cart boatloads of people to the island. Parking spots become hard to find. Restaurants fill up. Tourists swim at the beach and sail their yachts and shop for tacky T-shirts along Spinnaker Street while locals tend bar, wait tables, and cater to their every whim.

On Wednesday, the sky is the color of pewter when I get down to the docks. Storm clouds roll in from the east, spreading a fine mist over the island. It's cold today, rain on the way.

At the Slack Tide shop, only a handful of people linger under the covered porch, waiting to buy tickets. I'm scheduled to work on the *Mack King,* but since there aren't enough passengers signed up for mackerel fishing to justify the price of gas, Harold cancels the trip. He sticks them on cod fishing instead. Running an empty boat puts the day in the red, and there's nothing that Harold hates more than a day in the red.

So I get the day off. Unpaid, of course.

The rain really picks up as the last passenger climbs aboard the *Dauntless.* I help Tony untie and coil the heavy lines from the dock as passengers huddle on deck tightening the hoods of their rain slickers. Matthew waves to me from the wheelhouse, flashing a broad, white smile as he drives into the harbor.

I'm completely drenched by the time I get back to Barefoot Lane.

"Good morning, kitty cat!" someone yells through the pounding rain.

Lady Victoria, the drag queen who rents the apartment across from mine, is sitting on her balcony smoking a cigarette. She's the main attraction at Club Ooh-la-la, the drag show revue down the street, and one of the many summer transients of Barefoot Lane. She's dressed like a man this morning, except for the black eyeliner. It always throws me for a loop when I see her as a man. She looks so plain. So ordinary. Only when she dons her drag queen regalia does she become her true, fabulous self. The Incomparable Lady Victoria. Not just plain Victor from Pennsylvania. It's a complete metamorphosis from the everyday to the extraordinary.

"Welcome back," I say, dodging the rain beneath the striped awning of Bob's Fishmonger.

"Aren't you fishing this morning, pork chop?" she says, sashaying over to the railing.

I crane my neck to look up at her. "No one wants to go out in weather like this."

She blows a smoke ring that floats over her balcony. "Do tell. Rain does terrible things to mascara. Wreaks havoc on stilettos, too. Simply isn't natural to be out in the rain."

I shrug. "Well, the plants seem to like it."

"You got yourself a nice man to curl up with on a day like today, sugarplum? Someone to rub your feet and warm your heart?"

I shake my head.

"A beautiful thing like you? Girl, you need to find yourself a man. Why don't you try a little harder. A little lipstick, perhaps.

Maybe a pink scarf to brighten up that gorgeous face of yours. A pop of color here, a sparkly brooch there. It's not so hard."

"Isn't inner beauty what's important?"

She waves her long red nails at me. "It's about letting the girl you are on the inside shine through on the outside."

I head up the narrow stairs to my apartment.

There's not much to do on a rainy day like this, so I strip out of my wet sweatshirt and watch the morning news. There are stories of war and natural disasters, political debates, stock market frauds, droughts, celebrities doing crazy things, fashion trends. I get bored with the news pretty fast, since all of it is happening someplace far, far away from Ne'Hwas. Another world.

I do laundry. I clean up my room. I mop the kitchen floor.

I go into my room and call my mother. I don't know if I'm really expecting her to pick up. I've called about a thousand times already. Like always, an automated message tells me that the number is no longer in service. So I sit down on my bed and write her a letter.

I tell her that Sheriff and I got into another fight, and that it was mostly about her, so she really should come back home so he's not so lonely anymore. I explain how my birthday was pretty much the worst birthday ever, since turning twenty-three only reminded me of Kay being twenty-three. I tell her that Trip Sinclair is back on the island. I tell her about the special present Matthew gave me and admit to her that I feel like melting every time I see him lately. And since I know I won't send the letter (seeing as I don't have an address for her), I tell her that I had the most incredible dream about turning into a mermaid. I explain the sensation of breathing water, of how beautiful it was, how liberating. I tell her I wish it were real. That maybe it was real.

Then again, it could have just been some kind of psychological wish-fulfillment thing. If only I'd paid better attention in psychology class. Maybe Freud could have helped me. Who wouldn't want to transform into something else? Who wouldn't want to escape to their own world as easily as Lady Victoria does with just some makeup, hair spray, and sequins? Oh, and a boa. Always a boa.

But my mind was always on the waves, not Freud.

I ask her how her spirit journey is going and whether she's managed to let go of her sorrow yet. I end the letter by saying that maybe I could join her, since I have a few things I need to let go of, too.

"What are *you* doing here?" Sammy asks, popping her head in my door.

"My boat got canceled."

"You okay?"

I must look pretty pathetic and waterlogged, writing a letter I'll never send to my absent mother. "I'm fine."

"Well, I'm off to work. Lunch shift. I'll see you tonight. Want to grab drinks at Schooner Wharf?"

"Sure."

I read through my letter one last time, then wad it into a ball and toss it in the garbage.

Outside, the rain is coming down in sideways sheets. I think about how rough it must be out on the boat today. Passengers will be cold and wet, miserable no matter how many fish they catch. I wonder if Matthew is wishing he had the day off.

I wonder about the waves, too. I always wonder about the waves. I once heard that Inuits have a hundred different words for snow. I must have at least that many ways of describing the waves—waves that sparkle in the sun, waves that slice through you, waves that welcome you, waves that trick you, waves that ride on bigger waves, waves that transform you.

〰〰〰

There's just one thing I have to do before I head back out there. I pull in to the lot at the Lobster Corral and double-park, since there isn't a free spot anywhere. Inside, it's packed with tourists wearing plastic bibs around their necks and bright red sunburns on their cheeks and noses.

Sammy is waiting on a table of ten for a very late lunch. She's taking their drink orders when I walk up.

"I'm going surfing," I say.

She looks at me while scribbling orders on a little notepad.

"Okay." Rain beats against the windows.

"I'm going surfing at Tutatquin Point." I raise my eyebrows.

"What do you want, a permission slip?"

A woman at the table orders two Shirley Temples for her kids and a margarita for herself.

"Rocks or blended?" Sammy asks.

"Rocks. No salt," the woman responds, wiping her son's nose with a napkin.

Sammy slides over to the next customer and I move with her.

I put a hand on her shoulder. "I want someone to know where I'm going. Understand?"

"What do you have on draft?" a man at the table asks.

Sammy lifts the drink menu off the table and shoves it into the guy's hand. She turns her back to him.

"You're not seriously still thinking you were a . . . you-know-what? You got a concussion. Or maybe not a concussion, but, well, I don't know what happened. You fell asleep and had a trippy dream. Probably one of those flashbacks they talk about from the time we dropped acid and went to the Stones concert in Portland."

"Excuse me, can I order?" the man says, glaring.

"Why did we go to the Rolling Stones anyway?" Sammy says. "They're, like, so lame. Couldn't we have found someone a little more current?"

"Sammy, focus. I need to go back there and figure out what happened to me. I need to see if I'm losing my mind."

"Losing your mind, for sure."

"Hello. Miss. I'm waiting," the man says.

"What do you want?" she asks him curtly. Good thing they automatically add a gratuity for big parties.

"I'll be back later. We'll get drinks at Schooner Wharf," I say. "I just wanted you to know where I'm going."

"Okay, fine. I'll be sure to call in the unicorns and leprechauns to run a search party if you don't come home tonight."

≈≈≈

No one's around when I park my car on the old utility road overgrown with sumac and sea oats. No one sees me walk through the spruce trees to the rocky edge of shore, looking for my board. No one hears me yelp for joy when I find it, unbroken and not stolen, nestled between rocks on the edge where woods meet shore.

If anyone had noticed me, they would have called for help by now. They'd guess I'm on a suicide mission. That's how wild the surf is today.

The crash of waves drowns out all other noise. Gray clouds hang low to the east, turning the water opaque and black in the distance. I stand on the shore, watching for patterns in the waves, trying to work up my nerve. The waves are sloppy and disorganized, breaking here, breaking there, breaking everywhere.

I grab my board, climb over the rocks, and wait for a rush of water to carry me out to sea. The tide is coming in and the rocks of the boneyard are partially submerged, making it appear deceptively clear between shore and the wild blue yonder. I get knocked around a bit by the swirling water and underwater forces, but this time I make it through the boneyard easily. My arms feel strong. My breathing is calm.

After you do the impossible once, it suddenly seems easy.

When I get past the sandbar, rain is shattering the surface into a million little pieces. The waves are peaking all over the place, like a washing machine on the heavy soil cycle. I watch for a while, trying to read the waves, looking for the calm amid the chaos. I look for fins, too, wondering if that was my imagination as well.

Then it comes. Through the mess, a set appears on the horizon. Sharp, perfect lines cut across the sea. It never fails to amaze me how sets roll in out of nowhere, as if the ocean is running out to greet me, yelling a glorious hello.

Hi there, old friend.

My surfer brain screams to move, that I'm too far inside. I lie down and paddle toward the oncoming set, furious to get past those massive waves before they break. It's hard to see where to go, with the rain stinging my eyes, but I make it over the peak of the first wave just in time. The next wave is even bigger, so I keep paddling. I'll paddle to Portugal to keep from getting caught in the white fury of these monsters again.

I make it over two more waves. The next one is the biggest of the set, and I'm in perfect position.

This is my wave.

I go for it. I feel myself rise up the face. Three more strokes, both arms tearing through water, and my board catches the power behind it. I pop up to my feet, the nose hovering over air, rain hitting fiberglass. I crouch low and take the drop.

Down the line, the lip of the wave begins to curl. Instinctively, I know I need more speed to move into the pocket. I dig my heels into the board, swing my upper body to the left to move up the wave, then reverse the motion and zip down the face.

I grab the rail as the wave curls over me. The sky darkens, the rain stops, and I'm inside the barrel.

Like before, the barrel gets taller and wider as I ride it. I haven't hit my head and gotten a concussion. I'm not dreaming. I am shooting the barrel at Tutatquin Point. And like before, the ride lasts longer than it should. Twenty seconds. I count: twenty-one

Mississippi, twenty-two Mississippi. Thirty seconds go by. Forty.
A minute. I'm still surrounded by water. When it finally peters
out, I'm far inside the sandbar, past the boneyard, skimming over
rocky bottom.

I hop off my board and run to shore. This time, I'm ready.
I stash my board in the pine trees and wait. Within a minute, my
breath gets shallow, my lungs feel heavy. Rain pelts my skin, the
sand, the rocks, the trees. I am not unconscious or asleep. I am
wide awake.

I take a breath, but the air won't come. The sea calls to me.

This time, I don't wait. I run into the waves and dive under.

My lungs fill with water. It's a shock, but I manage to stay
calm. I reach behind me and there it is, my tail, beautiful scales
and all.

This is not a concussion or a delayed acid trip or a dream.

I am a mermaid. Like, for real.

I peek above the surface, looking for anyone who can witness
this. I want proof. I want witnesses. But the rain has driven everyone inside. I'm completely alone.

Or am I? Vibrations pulse down my sides. They are different
than last time. Instead of a sharp prickle, it's more of a dull throb.
Still, I don't take any chances.

I go under, kick my tail, and fly. Water rushes over my skin,
my hair flutters behind me. It takes some practice to synchronize
the mechanics of my tail and torso, but when I do, I cut through
water like a dolphin. I am the fastest person alive. I am superhuman. I am a goddess of the sea.

I am shark bait.

Thoughts pass through me like electricity. I try to listen to what
my new senses are telling me. A faint vibration runs down my
side. It translates instantly into words: *small fish nearby.*

A knocking sound in the distance means *turtle.*

A steady electrical field up ahead tells me *something small and fast*. Immediately I know it's prey, not predator.

My vision is total crap. Dark, shapeless blobs loom in and out of my sight. Rocks. Slopes in the ocean floor. Inanimate objects. Everything is a blur. But living, moving creatures light up in pixels of bright light.

As I adapt to the language of my new body, with its inflections of scent, sound, taste, and touch, I realize I don't have to rely on my eyesight. My brain keeps telling me I should swim away and find shelter. There are sharks in this ocean, and they hunt mermaids. But my body isn't in any rush. I decide to listen to the wisdom of my body. Let go and give my body what it wants. And right now it just wants to swim, to explore.

I swim south into deeper water. Colors fade. Red becomes blue. Pink becomes blue. The blood in my veins becomes black in this light-starved world. I don't know where I'll end up or which route I'll take, but I don't care. When's the last time I went anywhere without knowing the destination? When's the last time I just explored? I must have been a kid, me and Kay roaming the foothills around Mount Wabanaki.

I test out my speed, kicking with my arms straight overhead, then by my sides, figuring out which is more efficient. On the sandy bottom I stop, then bolt straight up toward the surface and breach like a whale into the rainy sky. I feel the change in gravity between water and air and jump out of the water again, feeling the squeeze in pressure like a giant hug against my body.

I stop on the surface and look back toward Ne'Hwas. I am really a mermaid. I'm not dreaming this. This time I'm sure of it.

I tilt my head back and let the rain fall into my mouth, across my nose and forehead. I have to show Matthew what I can do. He has to know I'm not some silly girl with wild fantasies. I'll show Sheriff, too, and Sammy, and anyone who doubts me.

Suddenly something bumps me in the back. I jerk around to see what it is, but nothing is above the surface. I dive under. Through the haze, my eyes make out movement as thousands of neon dots. Whatever it was, it's swimming away. I should be afraid, but under water my senses are calm, the electroreceptors in my sides telling me to chill out.

The dots of lights come racing back toward me with alarming speed.

I freeze.

The thing rushes toward me. Then stops. A harbor seal is inches from my face. He cocks his head, twitches his whiskers. He tucks into a ball and somersaults backwards, his spine like rubber. He swims away and swims back. He makes another pass at me, blowing bubbles in my face, which tickle my nose. The bubbles make him look like he's laughing. I laugh, too.

I reach out a hand and brush his smooth coat.

His thoughts are like blips of Morse code. He wants to communicate. I let my body translate.

What are you? he asks.

It's as clear as if someone is whispering in my ear. I feel the words in a latent part of my brain. I pulse a message back to him: *Mermaid.*

He wants to know about me, his huge black eyes search me for clues. *Where is your kind?*

On land.

Air breathers?

Yes.

He swims away and then charges back toward me. *Me too. Let's play.*

Okay.

I pull my knees (or what used to be my knees) into my stomach, and roll. He mimics me. He blows more bubbles. I try to blow bubbles back, but I don't have air in my lungs and only water comes out.

He takes off like lightning and I take off after him.

To my amazement, I catch him easily. I must be swimming at least thirty knots, the top speed of the *Dauntless*, with its two-thousand-horsepower engine.

The seal stops. I stop. I put a hand out and he pushes his nose into the palm of it.

Concentrating on my words, I send him my message, through the nerve endings in my body: *I like you.*

I like you, too.

We are the same. Mammals. We breathe air. Our blood is warm. I can feel this deep inside of me. And I think he can, too.

Come with me, the seal says.

I swim like the seal, accelerating with my tail, steering with my hands. He jumps into the air and I follow. I explode out of the water into air, breaching like a giant tuna.

We're like little kids on the first day of school. I follow him for miles and miles out into the sea. I have no idea where we're going, but I'm all-in.

Thousands of new sensations come at me at once. My fish brain interprets them—lobsters caught in a trap, a pod of whales miles away, a kelp bed, a skate in the sand below, a fish pursuing another fish, the tide coming in, the currents sweeping south.

We pass schools of fish and solitary pelagics. Each species has its own language that I do not understand, like tribesmen from different clans.

As foreign and otherworldly as it is, it feels like I belong here.

When I was little, my mother would let me ditch school and we'd go on adventures in the wilderness, hiking Mount Wabanaki or wandering the vast dunes on the north shore. Nature's classroom, she called it. I remember those hikes, my legs trembling with fatigue, my lungs burning, making exquisite discoveries around every rock and every tree—bear scat or a fox's den or a thick slab of hardened pine sap for starting a fire. We'd pick berries, fiddleheads, and black trumpets, and catch fish in the little freshwater ponds to eat. My mother would teach me the Passamaquoddy words. *Kiyahq* is "bird." *Ktoton* is "mountain." *Nomeha,* "little fish," her nickname for me. And *koselomol,* "I love you." How my tongue would trip over the sounds. We would reach the top of the mountain, after those rigorous climbs, breathing in the cold air and feeling like being there was the greatest treasure on earth.

It's like that now. It feels like an exquisite treasure lies around every corner. It feels like I belong. And I feel completely free.

Cold and hot are no longer sensations for me. There is no comfort or discomfort. There is only a change against my skin, my scales.

Nomeha koselomol. I love you, little fish. My mother's voice sings every syllable.

I want to go everywhere and see everything, but suddenly my tail slows down and my muscles freeze. It's like my veins are filled with lead. I try to move forward, but I can't get my tail to cooperate. A dull, aching pain spreads across my stomach. Hunger, I realize. It's so much more intense than any sort of human hunger I've ever felt.

My body needs food. Energy. And it needs it now. For a moment, I think like a human—I can swim to shore, get my legs back, and walk down to the Lobster Corral. The thought of fried clams, onion rings drenched in ketchup, and coleslaw fills me with a kind of misery only someone who is hungry can understand. I know I won't make it to shore. Food is energy, and without it, my muscles stiffen, my movements slow to almost nothing.

Think. I'm in the ocean. I've worked on a fishing boat for many years. I should be able to catch a fish to feed myself. But the fish that light up in my line of sight are so fast, and I've become an underwater sloth. Can I eat kelp? There's plenty of that. Slowly I make my way to a strand of kelp and bite into it. I wait. It does nothing. I need protein.

With my tail lagging behind, weighing me down, I breast-stroke forward. When that becomes too difficult, I crawl hand over hand on the sandy floor. Will I be able to make it back to the island like this? I don't even know how far away I am. I was so focused on the seal, I've completely lost track of where I am. What if I can't make it home? Have I come through all this only to die of starvation?

I refuse to believe that.

I keep moving, feeling in the sand for crabs, scallops, bottom-feeders, anything I can get my hands on, the hunger hanging over me like a grenade. Minutes pass. Hours? Light is fading. I can't keep track of time because the hunger has crept into my brain now. No energy to think.

Bottom slopes up. Shallow water. A rocky mass in front of me. My hand fumbles around a hard edge. More hard, bumpy objects. The surface just above. Darkening sea. And then I realize where I am—an oyster bed. Protein pods by the thousands, all within my reach.

I'm so happy I feel like screaming, but first I need to eat. I yank an oyster loose from the thick carpet of shells. Is it even possible to shuck an oyster with bare hands? I slam the shell against hard rock until my palm is sore. It doesn't even crack. I'd give any-thing for a knife. I pluck another oyster and slip the narrow end into the hinge of the first oyster. I wiggle and twist, working it like a drill with a dull bit. It's slow going, but eventually the oys-ter gives. It opens a crack. I jimmy the other oyster into it until the top shell lifts away. My stomach grumbles with anticipation.

As I pull the meat from the shell, a little fish darts out of nowhere and snatches it right out of my fingers. Bits of oyster mucous drift around, and suddenly I'm swarmed by fish of all sizes looking for a free meal. *Thieves.*

I swat at them. Stupid fish. Stupid fish who are smarter than me.

I pry open another shell, twisting and pulling, until the top shell gives. This time I grab the meat in a fist to keep it safe, and pop it into my mouth. It slides down my throat. It's pure heaven, the finest thing I've ever tasted. Instantly my body responds. Energy comes back to me and I tear into the next oyster.

Now hundreds of fish school around me, pecking on the bits of membrane floating like snot in the water. They weave around me, jockeying for scraps, trying to steal my food.

As I crack apart another oyster, my friend the seal lunges toward me, teeth bared. Fish scatter.

I pull my hand away a split second before he can bite it.

He has no words for me now, only teeth and hunger. A fish-eat-fish world. He disappears into the dark distance, but the second I crack another shell apart, he comes flying back at me.

I hold up my fist. *Back off, seal.* But he doesn't know fists and he lurches at me, biting the oyster out of my hand.

I bonk him in the head. He backflips upside down and circles around. I try to communicate with him. *I will hurt you. I am deadlier than you.*

He doesn't speak back. We are no longer friends. There is food in the water and we both need to eat. He swims away into the darkness and I devour a dozen more oysters, letting the fish battle it out for the scraps of sinew.

I eat until I'm full, the scuffle of fish lighting up the water in neon light. As they swim away, they take all the light with them, leaving the water empty and dark. In fact, it's almost black. Are my eyes are playing tricks on me?

How long have I been down here? Has the sun already set?

I bolt through the darkness for the surface. My eyes take a few minutes to adjust. The sky is black and rain is pounding the ocean. I don't see Ne'Hwas. I spin around, looking for a bearing. Anything—land, a buoy, a lighthouse.

I search the horizon for Kotoki-Pun light, but the rain and darkness swallow everything. It dawns on me that oyster beds don't appear in the middle of the ocean. I must be at the tidal reefs near Wolf Rocks. We pass by here on the *Mack King* all the time. I try to envision the nautical chart of the gulf. If I'm right about being at Wolf Rocks, I'm probably fifteen miles from Ne'Hwas. How did I go that far?

My heart beats like a jackhammer. Rain stings my face. I dive down and swim faster and faster toward . . . what? I don't know if I'm heading toward the mainland or out to sea. I've completely lost my bearings.

Panic rises in my chest. It sounds like the clapping rain, like drums in my ears. Vibrations creep up my sides. Night. Feeding time. Predators closing in.

I reach the bottom and swim wildly through the darkness, bumping into sandy bottom, rocks, unseen things. The vibrations intensify.

I need to come to terms with my reality. I am a mermaid. I am lost. It's night and there's no way I can find my way home. Sharks will be coming out to feed soon; I can't stay on the surface. I have to spend the night under water.

I need to find shelter.

Staying close to the bottom to search for shallow caves, I swim with my hands ahead of me, feeling my way around the reefs of Wolf Rocks. But the reefs are low and jagged and don't have much in the way of hiding spots. Up ahead, I sense a change in the water. Not a predator or a prey, but a thing. Something dense. I swim toward it. Vibrations race up my spine.

An old cargo ship lies on the bottom, tipped on its side. It's in one piece, for the most part. There are lots of shipwrecks at Wolf Rocks. I've seen them at low tide. I've pointed them out to passengers as I served them cold beers and warm fish chowder from the security of my galley, never in a million years thinking that they might save my life.

Feeling my way, I find a hole in the ship's deck. I climb in, the darkness opaque and terrifying. How often is a person really in complete darkness? There's always a pinprick of a star in the sky, a crack of light beneath a door, the electric glow of a distant city on the horizon. Here, I curl up in a ball in pitch blackness, the world's deadliest hunters outside, metal below me, metal above me, an underwater coffin, and I try to sleep.

TEN

There are a dozen suns dangling on the horizon when I surface, their rays streaking the sky in orange and pink. I blink hard against the dry, harsh air. Slowly, the world comes into focus and the many suns converge into one.

It's a different ocean than it was yesterday. Today, it's a mirror. Not even a longboarder could scratch out a ride in this sort of calm. I've caught the ocean in her waking hour. A minute later the wind picks up and the mirror is broken into a million dark ripples. Somewhere, a foghorn blows.

Off in the distance, Kotoki-Pun light is a speck on shore. If I estimate in the way Matthew taught me—that at sea level, in open ocean, the horizon is thirteen miles away—I'm about ten miles off shore. Totally swimmable. But last night, in the dark, ten miles might as well have been to China.

I roll my neck and stretch my arms, unkinking the cramps. I'm sore from staying curled up all night. Tired, too. I was too scared to sleep. Afraid the sharks would get me. Afraid that I would stop breathing if I stopping moving water through my gills.

But I survived. What does that say about me? Humans adapt to the most rugged terrain on earth—the arctic circle, the Sahara, Mount Everest—but I've done what no one has. I overcame that human limitation, that breathless, desperate feeling of drowning, that hysterical fear that comes with being trapped in pitch blackness in an eternal ocean. I survived. Relief washes over me.

Maybe I'm not such a complete screwup after all.

Next time I'll be even more prepared. I'll bring a compass. An underwater light. A knife. Maybe a waterproof GPS.

Next time. Will there will be a next time? And a time after that, and a time after that? How does this work? Do I get to choose when to be human and when to be fish? Am I the only one? Are there other mermaids and mermen, having mer-parties and mer-jobs and mer-families? If there are, did we all get here the same way—surfing the barrel at Tutatquin—or are there other entries into this world? Can I bring someone else with me? Would anyone want to come?

My gut tells me that, whatever is happening to me, it has to be my secret. Maybe I'm being paranoid, but I need to figure out the rules before I share this. I don't want the Jay Delgados of the world out here with me.

As I swim home, I stay under water, out of sight.

By the time I make it back to Ne'Hwas, boats are buzzing around the harbor like flies. Under water, the roar of engines is magnified. At a lobster buoy, I peek my head above the surface. The passenger ferry is already motoring out for the morning trip, and the whale watch boat is close behind. I see the *Dauntless* cruise by. Matthew will be at the helm, wondering where I am. Jacqueline will be on board, filling in for me in the galley. Probably counting her lucky stars, along with her hefty tips, that I didn't show up for work. One of the guys will have to cover the galley aboard the *Mack King*. Cursing my name. Can't worry about that now.

I dive down and swim parallel to shore, following the slope of sand to North Beach. In the shallows, a tiny pair of legs is kicking on the surface, held close by a larger pair of legs that walks weightlessly in circles. Mothers and children are already out at this hour. This is not a place for reentry.

I keep swimming around the western edge of the island. Wabanaki State Park doesn't have any safe spots to land. Too many tree-hugging, bird-watching nature lovers rising out of their tents and lean-tos there. Once I make it around Tutatquin Point, I see the silhouettes of a dozen surfers and paddleboarders in the lineup at Nipon. Part of me wants to reach out and tickle some feet.

How am I going to make it ashore in broad daylight with eyes everywhere? If it weren't for the sharks, and the starvation, could I stay out here forever? Write Sheriff a note to explain everything? Send him a message in a bottle?

I keep swimming around the island, looking for a safe landing. I finally find it in the riprap seawall into Lobster Cove. Here, the docks are empty, the lobstermen long at work for the day. Only one boat's still docked—the *Jennie B*. It's been lobstering on Ne'Hwas for as long as I can remember. And it doesn't look like the owner is in any great hurry to make his numbers.

I swim to the stern, staying submerged from the nose down. No one's here besides an old fisherman with a white beard, sitting in the harbor house reading a newspaper. As silently as possible, I pull myself onto the transom of the *Jennie B*. My tail makes a loud thump against the hull. Nervously I look around, but the old fisherman doesn't flinch. With all my upper body strength, I heave myself over the stern.

The rig is rusty, the engine well coated in grease. A few lobster traps are tossed in a heap, along with the ship's ropes. Matthew would have a heart attack if he saw lines like that. He demands coiled lines, everything shipshape.

There are chains on deck, blackened with mildew and algae. Ladders, plastic buckets, and worn-down brushes are tossed around. The only clean part of the boat is the fish hold in the center. And here I am: a fish throwing herself into a fishing boat.

With a bit of trouble, I pull myself across the deck on my hands, my tail dragging behind me.

I half expect to find the captain of the *Jennie B* curled up drunk somewhere, but no one's on board. Inside, the cabin is caked in years of dirt and dust and cigarette ash. Empty beer bottles are strewn around, along with whiskey bottles, rusty tools, chewing tobacco canisters.

Once again, I'm starving. I'm so hungry, in fact, I lift the lid on an ancient, water-stained box of Wheat Thins crammed next to a cushion. It's empty, which is probably for the best. The lack of fuel sends a headache cracking through my skull. Food will come later, I tell myself.

First priority is to get my legs back. I look around for a towel and find, instead, an old canvas tucked into a forward compartment. I wrap myself in the moldy thing, suddenly aware of the temperature on my skin. The canvas is rough and scratchy, and a very poor replacement for a towel. I lie back, waiting to become human. Through the murky windows speckled with salt spray, I watch the sun rise higher and higher, and listen for intruders.

I fall asleep. When I wake up, my tail is gone, my legs are back, and I'm bare-ass naked. Where *do* my bikinis go?

The sun is high in the sky and the old fisherman is still asleep in his chair. In the forward cabin, underneath a pair of circa-1940 orange life vests, I find a work shirt and put it on. It's like a dress on me. A fish-and-diesel-stinking vagabond dress. But it beats walking home naked.

~~~

Lobster Cove is only a couple miles from town. I walk, barefoot and stinking like rotten fish, without drawing too much attention—except from Lady Victoria, who's out on her balcony, in drag.

"Walk of shame, hey girl?" Lady Victoria tosses her feather boa across her neck and regards me through eyelash extensions.

"No," I snap. "It's not like that."

"Ah, come on. I'm only playing with you."

Given my present situation, the catcalls of my drag queen neighbor should be the least of my worries, but her insinuation rubs me the wrong way. "It's not a walk of shame. I'm just going through some weird stuff."

"Kitty cat, whatever it is you're going through, take my advice—that which does not kill us, makes us utterly fabulous." She runs a hand down her sequined gown. "My word, what on earth are you wearing? You look like you've been run around wet and hung out to dry."

"Just an old shirt."

"Spin around for me, Minnie Mouse."

I don't have the energy that's required to argue with a diva, so I twirl.

"My, my, my," she says, pressing her hands onto her hips. "The ensemble is positively dreadful, but the girl beneath it has some potential. I never noticed those curves on you before. You take any supplements? I pop estrogen, but it only gets me so far."

"What do you mean?"

She snaps her finger. "Look in a mirror sometime, Betty Boop. And do yourself a favor. Buy something a little more formfitting."

Lady Victoria is obsessed with her wardrobe and is constantly giving style tips to me and Sammy, which I never take. "Have a good show tonight," I say. She blows me a kiss and I climb the stairs to the apartment. Luckily, the door's unlocked, since my keys are back at the beach, stuffed into my shoe—security system surfer-style. I head straight for the kitchen and find half a pepperoni pizza in the fridge. I don't even bother with a plate. I'm thrusting a piece into my mouth when the front door swings open.

"There you are!" Sammy says, running toward me. She throws her arms around my neck.

I swallow a hard lump of crust.

"Where have you been?"

"It happened again," I tell her. I can see the doubt in her eyes. "I know what you're thinking, but it wasn't a concussion. I shot the barrel and turned into a mermaid. I lost track of time and couldn't find my way back, so I slept in a shipwreck out at Wolf Rocks. Which was terrifying, by the way."

"Like, for real? Because if you feel like you're not getting enough attention, I understand. We can go out to the Schooner Wharf and let some boys buy us drinks. Always makes me feel better."

"I became a mermaid," I say, my voice sure and steady.

"As in fish tail, flowing hair, scallop-shell bra, the whole thing?"

I raise a Girl Scout salute—not that I was ever a Girl Scout, or that Sammy would even know what the Girl Scout salute is, but it gets the point across.

"Holy shit," Sammy says. She collapses into the papasan chair.

"I know. It's crazy. I don't understand it, but it's true." I take another bite of pizza. "Oh, and there's no scallop shells. I don't really know where my bikinis go. I might have to stock up on some cheap ones down at Kmart. I want you to see what it's like out there, Sammy. You have to come with me."

There's a knock at the door.

Sammy jumps. "I called Sheriff," she blurts out.

"What? Why?"

"I didn't hear from you. You came by the restaurant with that Count Dracula voice and that 'I need you to know where I'm going' business. I was worried. Like, *really* worried."

If Sammy was worried, Sheriff must be a basket case.

"Should I let him in?" Sammy asks.

"I don't think we have any choice."

Sammy opens the door and Sheriff walks in. Dark circles under his eyes. A slouch in his shoulders. I think about the morning they found Kay. The early call from the station. Sheriff on the phone. The color draining from his face. His eyes like saucers. Mom asking what happened. The phone propped against his shoulder as he holstered his gun.

Sheriff looks at me, and his face does a weird twitchy thing. I'm not sure whether he's going to laugh or cry.

"Thank God," he says, crossing the living room. He hugs me so hard I can't breathe. "Are you okay?" There's a crackle of anxiety I know all too well.

I nod, because I don't trust my voice.

He hugs me again, my head pressed into his chest. I can hear his heart fluttering. I can feel the tension in his muscles.

"Are you injured? Did anyone hurt you?"

"No one hurt me."

"What happened?" The fatherly tenderness in his voice is fading and the I-need-answers-right-now cop voice is taking its place.

As I think about the fresh hell I must have put him through these last few hours, the guilt rises up, catching in my throat. "Nothing happened. I'm fine." I want to tell him about the wave, and the swimming, and the seal, and the oysters, and sleeping in a forgotten shipwreck under the sea. The thrill, the fear, the magic of it.

"Where were you?" he demands.

"I . . ." I look to Sammy for help. She shrugs. Not going to touch this with a ten-foot pole. "I fell asleep on the beach after I went surfing."

"Which beach?"

"I don't know."

"You don't *know*?" His voice is full of daggers. He rubs his temples. "Do you want to know what's been running through my mind? Do you know what you've put me through? What you put Sammy through?"

"Just tell him," Sammy says, poking me.

He glares at her. "Tell me what?"

I look at my father, who is a shell of the man he once was.

When I was little, I thought my father was the strongest man on earth; everyone did. My friends were in awe and fear of him. Even his name—Sheriff—summed up his purpose in the world. The way he walked, the way he spoke, everything about him reflected the pride of a man who protects others.

Now, there's no one left to save. Except for me.

"Well?" he says.

I'm all he has left. *I* need to protect *him*. I need to lie.

"Nipon," I say. "It was at Nipon."

"You spent the night at Nipon Beach?" he yells.

I jump.

"Are you crazy? You slept in a place that you know is crawling with junkies and drug dealers and God knows what else? Do you have any idea how many arrests I've made at Nipon Beach?"

"I mean North Beach. It wasn't Nipon. It was North Beach. I had a beer and I didn't want to drive home, so I sat down for a few minutes. Next thing you know, I was asleep."

He blades his stance. A defensive posture. "You were drinking." It's a statement, not a question.

"No. I mean, yes. Just one beer, though. I was tired." I feel like I'm digging a hole for myself, a shovelful with each lie.

"So you're telling me you had one beer and then proceeded to fall asleep on the beach, all night, *in the rain?*"

And the hole gets deeper.

"Dad, can you just drop it?" The word *Dad* floats out there like a piece of driftwood.

He grabs my arms, turns them over, looking for needle marks. He has flipped the switch from Dad to cop. "Were you doing drugs?"

"No!" I pull my arms back and cross them over my chest.

"Who were you with?"

"I was alone."

"Baloney."

Nothing I say will help, so I just stand there in my ratty, borrowed shirt.

"Aren't you supposed to be at work right now?" Sheriff asks.

I shrug.

"Is that a yes? Is that a no?"

"I'm sure Harold found someone to cover for me."

"This is so disappointing." He shakes his head. "You're so disappointing."

"I know."

"You have responsibilities. You have a job to answer for. You have people who rely on you. When are you going to learn that?"

"I get it, okay?" I feel like I'm in fourth grade all over again, sitting outside the principal's office, waiting for my punishment.

"You don't get it. You never get it. You're an adult now, but you're acting like a child. You don't follow rules, Jess. You don't take responsibility for yourself."

"Neither do you," I snap.

He glares at me. "What's that supposed to mean?"

"It means you need to stop worrying about me and take a look at yourself." I choke back the dry lump in my throat. "You had responsibilities. Kay was your responsibility. Mom was, too. But you let both of them get away." I wish I could take it back, but my words have an unstoppable energy to them. They spin through the room like a blizzard.

A knobby vein on his temple throbs. His inhales sharply. The muscles in his neck quiver. His eyes gloss over and he looks like he's about to cry.

And then he slaps me across the face.

I'm so startled I can't speak. I put a hand to my cheek and feel the blood rising to my skin. Salty residue makes even the slightest touch feel like sandpaper.

He looks as shocked as I feel. "Jess, I'm . . ." He steps close.

He steps back. He steps close again. "I'm sorry," he mutters. "I'm . . . so sorry."

I can't look him in the eyes. My heart thrums in my ears. I feel a pain cross my chest.

The thing is, it's not the slap. I can get past that. I probably deserved that.

It's *him*. It's his sadness. It's the pity I feel for him. He's my father. He's the strongest man on earth. Not the weepy, broken man in front of me. I'm not supposed to pity him.

I look down at the floor. At the frayed edge of the Oriental rug. At my bare toes covered in dust from the gravel road at Lobster Cove. There's motion in the room, and I think Sheriff might be reaching for me, but I still can't bring myself to look up until I hear the door close.

"Dude," Sammy says. "That was intense. You okay?"

I nod. I think about my mother on her spirit journey, leaving Sheriff and me behind. I wonder if she worries about him? About me? I wonder how long she needs to wander to lose the sorrow inside of her? I wonder if I could get rid of my sorrows that way.

"Why didn't you just tell him that you're a mermaid?" Sammy strokes my hair, which has gotten so gnarled and kinky that I'll have to run through a whole bottle of conditioner to get it straight.

"Because he needs me to be his little girl," I say.

ELEVEN

I sleep for most of the day. I'm not usually one of those people who can crash on demand. Naps have never been my thing. The thwack of rolled newspapers hitting cobblestone on the morning paper delivery is enough to startle me out of bed. But today I'm a snoozing champion. I don't even get up when Lady Victoria starts belting out show tunes from her balcony.

I guess I've never been tired enough.

When I wake up and see that it's already four o'clock, I feel confused. A.M. or P.M.? My skin is tight with salt residue. The sting of the slap is gone, but my face is creased with pillow marks. I look out the window. The sun is shining. Must be P.M.

The fishing boats will just be getting in for the day. I think of Sheriff's words. I need to take responsibility. I need to grow up. I have a job. I have people who rely on me.

One of those people is Harold Stantos. As much as I hate to admit it, I need him. I need the tips, the reliable work. Time for me to do some damage control with Harold.

~~~~

The door to Slack Tide is propped wide, an afternoon breeze drifting in. Harold is at the counter, scrawling in his ledger. He keeps track of everything—fishing conditions, pounds of fish caught, tackle rented, tackle lost or damaged, numbers of hamburgers and sodas sold, debits, credits. He should have been an accountant rather than a fisherman.

Harold likes to tell about his rise from poor immigrant to

successful business owner as though it were a fairy tale. But the truth is, there's more to his story. He came to Ne'Hwas by accident. Back in Greece, he married his childhood sweetheart when they were both very young, and he promised her that he would strike it rich in America one day. His new wife had a cousin who owned a Greek restaurant in Hyannis Port, so the newlyweds bought their tickets to Boston and left everything they knew.

The restaurant turned out to be a simple little sausage cart, without a dolma or a cube of feta in sight. And the cousin had no need or desire to hire his cousin's husband for a job he was perfectly capable of doing by himself.

Harold, after trying his hand at a number of unsuccessful enterprises, decided it was time to put America behind him. With two young children in tow, he bought a sixteen-foot ketch he found through an ad in the paper. The seller even threw in a captain's hat for free, which, to hear Harold tell it, made him look like a full-bird admiral. Harold wasn't much of a sailor, but he was full of confidence. And he was Greek. Greeks know the water better than anyone, or so he believed. He packed up his wife and two young sons and all their belongings, sold their car, and shoved off.

Mykonos was his destination.

Thirty-two days later, he pulled into a mooring in Ne'Hwas. What's normally a day-and-a-half sail turned into a wretched disaster, in which Harold's wife began to seriously question his competence as both a sailor and a man. She stepped off the tiny boat, a child in each arm, and walked straight down Spinnaker Street to city hall to file divorce papers.

Harold stayed. Deep down, I think he has always regretted the path his life led him down.

Harold's eyes are cold when he sees me. "The galley girl is here at last. Only eight hours late for work."

I approach him cautiously, like you would a feral cat trapped in an alley. "I'm sorry, Harold. I really am. I should have been here. It's a long story."

He doesn't look up.

"Do you have any candy bars that need to be stocked? Any lures that need pricing?"

He looks down. Continues writing. Keeps up the silent treatment. I wish he would just yell at me and get it over with, but it's as though he takes some sick pleasure in making me beg.

"Look, I'm sorry I wasn't here this morning. It was out of my control."

"I don't need excuses. I need boys who can fish and girls I can count on to run the galley."

"And what's up with that? Why aren't girls allowed to fish and . . ." I stop myself. I breathe deeply and put on an appropriately contrite face. I need this job, I remind myself. "It won't happen again. I swear."

"I need workers I can count on, you understand this?"

"I'll do inventory to make up for today," I say.

He taps his pencil. "Summer is short. I have only two months to make my numbers for the year."

"I know."

Down the pier, I can see Matthew hosing down the deck of the *Dauntless*. Tony is at the fillet table, cutting up the last of the customers' catches.

"One day of summer costs me two weeks of winter." He taps his pen against the book. "You kids today. You don't appreciate the value of hard work. You know I came here with nothing but twenty dollars in my pocket."

"And a dream." I smile and force a laugh. Ugh, the story of Harold making good again. I want to tell him to stop being so melodramatic. I want to tell him I'm one of his best employees and he needs to cut me some slack. I want to tell him that I spent the night under the sea, in a place no other human has been, breathing water, swimming with the grace and speed of a goddess. What I actually say is, "I'll be here early tomorrow. I'll even clean the storage shed."

"Be here early. Be here late. It's no matter."

"Huh?"

He looks me in the eye. "You're fired."

I can't be hearing him correctly. I take a step back. "What?"

"Don't come back. I don't need you and your excuses."

My whole summer flashes in front of my eyes. No work. No tips. Season coming and going. Bank account dwindling to nothing. No way to pay rent by the fall. Me, moving in with Sheriff. Sheriff watching every move I make, getting on my back for every minuscule thing I do wrong, the constant concern over my well-being, my moral development. Losing the little bit of freedom I've managed to carve out for myself on Barefoot Lane.

My hands start shaking. I refuse to cry, but I have to choke back the tears.

"Harold, you can't do this. Not after all the years I have here."

"I can, and I have." *Tap, tap, tap* goes his pen. "Kids today. No ambition. You party all hours. You skip work when it suits you. At least it's early enough in season that I can train a new girl."

The next thought races through my mind like a movie. If I had a knife on me, I could pry him apart like an oyster, letting his juices flow into the street, for the stray cats and dogs to devour. I could crack his neck like a lobster claw. A surge of aggression and violence overwhelms me. I blade my stance. My hands form fists. That thing deep inside of me that lashed out at the seal to protect my food, my territory, comes out.

Calm down, a rational voice inside me says.

But my mind is turning black. Adrenaline surges through me. Someone other than me is in the driver's seat. I want to attack Harold, to rip him apart, strangle him. Give him a new story to tell. Instead, I back away from him, my legs carrying me from the terrible thoughts in my head.

I bolt out of the shop just as Matthew is turning the corner toward it. We collide. Matthew reaches for me and catches me, stops me from falling backwards.

"Sorry about that," he says.

"He fired me. Harold fired me."

"What?"

"Five years and he fires me just for missing one day of work. I want to kill him," I say. I turn and I start running, afraid of what I'll do. Afraid that the animal in me is in control.

I run down the gravel lot of Buster's Wharf, past the boat-yard and the marine salvage shop. I run down the last strip of road bordering the harbor, past the observation lot with its coin-operated viewers, and I keep going all the way down the jetty of Seal Point, jumping between rocks, escaping to the island's edge.

When there's nowhere else to run, I stop and catch my breath.

A strip of clouds hover low in the sky and the first star of the night shines like a lone pinprick. I can feel the pressure rising, like a barometer under my skin.

I can't believe I got fired from my crappy job. I'll have to find a waitressing gig, but anything good will be taken by now, which means I'll be doomed to the anemic shifts of breakfast and lunch. I could work as a chambermaid at a hotel, cleaning up after people and making beds. Or worse yet, I could ask Sheriff to get me a job at the park.

Hundreds of harbor seals crowd onto the rocks around me. I watch a big male hauled out on a rock just above the waves. A smaller male waddles up to him. The big seal barks and bares his teeth. You don't have to be a mythical sea creature to understand his language. *My rock,* he's saying. The smaller seal plunges back into the water.

Right near the ruckus, another pair of seals cuddles up together. One lies its head on the other's belly, and they close their eyes and sleep. I could be like these creatures. They play, they hunt, they stake out their rocks, they cuddle up to each other to rest.

I could inhabit that world. Go back to Tutatquin. Catch a wave. Never come back.

Forget about eking out a life by mopping up puke and forcing a smile for foreigners who may or may not leave a dollar in my tip jar.

As far as the sharks and the terrifying darkness—I could adapt, couldn't I? I have a human brain and a human heart. That has to count for something down there.

I try to picture it in my mind. How would I spend my days? Exploring and hunting? Could I learn to communicate with other animals? Could I observe life on Ne'Hwas from afar, maybe even check in with Sheriff and Sammy and Matthew right here at Seal Point?

All these thoughts are playing out in my mind, when I notice Matthew jogging up the jetty toward me.

"I got you your job back," he says. He's windblown and shiny with sunblock from a day on the water. "You'll be on the *Mack King* for the next week. It's the best I could do. And I think it's fair."

"How'd you manage that?"

Matthew shrugs, as if it was nothing at all.

"His heels were dug in. How did you convince him?"

"I told him I'd quit."

I laugh. "So you lied."

"I wasn't lying. I wouldn't work for Harold if you weren't there."

There's something in the way he's looking at me, like I'm the only person in the world, that tells me he's not joking. The last swell of anger inside me drifts away.

"You would leave if I wasn't there? Seriously?"

"I care about you, Creary."

A wave crashes into the rocks below us, and splits into a million particles, the fine mist soaking both me and Matthew on the side of our bodies facing the sea.

"I care about you, too." I want to spill my guts, because it's Matthew and he's like a big brother. And because it's Matthew with the biceps I've never noticed before and the smile that takes my breath away.

"Good. So you won't hate me when I tell you the other part of the bargain."

I groan. "What's the other part?"

"Come with me."

TWELVE

By the time Matthew and I get to the pier, the nightly circus is underway. Crowds of tourists amble up and down the pier, looking to be entertained, searching for a postcard ending to their summer-perfect day. And there to entertain them are Ne'Hwas's finest amateur artists. Community-theater types. Ordinary people who emerge from their winter jobs laying sheetrock or stitching canvas boat covers to become seasonal street performers. Musicians, jugglers, clowns, contortionists. Hustling for the summertime surplus of tax-free tip money.

Matthew and I plant ourselves between the bagpipe player and the flame-eater. A small crowd gathers close, (but not too close), as the flame-eater lights a wad of gauze on the end of a baton and twirls it over his head. He throws the fiery thing high into the air and tries to catch it midshaft, but it lands on the ground with a thump. The crowd gasps. He picks it up and keeps going. For the finale, he tilts his head back and extinguishes the flame in his mouth. People clap and throw cash into his jar.

I recognize him as one of the breakfast cooks at Kotoki-Pun Diner.

"This is stupid," I say, sounding more like a five-year-old forced into time-out than a twenty-three-year-old fighting to keep her job. I'm thumbing the stack of flyers Harold shoved into my hands back in the Slack Tide office.

"Come on, Creary," Matthew says. "A few flyers and you'll be back in Harold's good graces."

I hate the fact that I have to be in Harold's good graces in the first place. He was barely able to look me in the eye when Matthew coerced me back to the office to make peace. I had almost attacked Harold in his own shop, after all. He had seen the anger and wildness lurking below the surface, and it scared him.

It scared me, too.

So Matthew did the talking for both of us. "Jess will pass out flyers—off the clock. And she'll be at work on time from now on. And Harold, you'll let her keep her job. Okay? Okay." Matthew, the peacemaker. Matthew, the big brother who's always watching out for me.

Kay was the peacemaker in my family. It's the role of the oldest sibling. The firstborn is supposed to be reliable, conscientious, cautious. I wonder if my last-born traits—carefree, self-centered, irresponsible—get lost when you someone drops out of the birth order? Do I automatically lose my free spirit and become an overachiever like Kay?

I wonder if animals are affected by birth order like we are. Does the oldest seal in the herd take care of its younger siblings? Does the youngest slack off, exploring the kelp forests while his siblings hunt?

I hand a flyer to a father with the young girl on his shoulders. He looks at it briefly, then drops it onto the pier where it's trampled.

"Litterbug!" Matthew yells out.

I laugh and try to hand a flyer to a mom with three kids. She pretends not to see me. The next five people politely ignore me, too. One tells me to buzz off.

Trying to pass out advertisements to people who've been overcharged for every soda and taxi ride since they stepped on the island is pretty much a lost cause, I decide, so I sit on the concrete bench of the pier and read one of the flyers in my best Harold voice.

"*'Slack Tide fishing charters.* Voted *best, most excellent* party boat on Ne'Hwas. Experienced captains. Excellent service. *Deepsea* cod and haddock fishing. Mackerel. Voted *best* friendly crew on the island.'"

"That is the *best, most excellent* Harold impersonation I've ever heard," Matthew says, smiling.

"When were we voted best friendly crew?" I ask.

Matthew tilts his head and scrunches up his nose. "Probably when Harold asked Tony, Ian, and Stefan who they thought the best crew on the island was."

"And they voted for themselves."

He snort-laughs, which is completely adorable for a big, burly fisherman like him.

"You don't have to be here, you know. This is *my* punishment," I say, fanning my face.

He looks at his watch. "I've got ten more minutes to give you. Then you're on your own."

"Better get to work, then." All the anger disappears around Matthew, and a lightness takes over in me. The quiet rage lurking below the surface spills away.

"Don't you want to know where I'm going?" he asks.

"Okay. Where are you going?"

"Since you ask . . . I have hot date tonight." He smiles so wide I can't tell if he's joking.

"Oh," I say, and slip a flyer into the bottom of a baby stroller when the mother isn't looking.

"What's the matter, Creary? You jealous?"

The bagpipe player marches rigidly by. The silver mime is right behind him, crouching in a crab walk, covering his ears, like he can't stand the bagpipes. The mime stops in front of us. He places a hand over his heart, flutters his eyelashes, and points to both of us with puckered lips.

I can feel my face burning with embarrassment.

I shove a flyer in the mime's vest pocket. He takes it out, flattens it, starts folding it. When he's done, he hands me an origami heart. Then he points to me and Matthew again with puckered lips to let us know what he thinks we should be doing.

"Can't," I say to the mime. "He's got a hot date in a few minutes."

The mime wipes away an imaginary tear and moves on.

"Mimes freak me out," I say.

"Don't take it out on the mime. Admit you're jealous."

My heart is pounding. "I'm not jealous. I hope you have fun tonight," I say, trying really hard to sound sincere, but failing.

"You're practically green," Matthew says.

"No, I'm not," I say. Matthew is like a brother. We're coworkers. Colleagues. Friends. That's it. He probably flirts with everyone. Besides, I don't need a boyfriend. Especially not Matthew.

He's a fisherman; I'm a fish.

An attractive blonde woman in Lily Pulitzer and pearls walks by with her friends who look like they've just come from the spa. She flashes Matthew a smile which only seems to encourage him.

"Any of you ladies up for fishing? We were voted *best* party boat on the island," he says.

"Do we look like fishermen to you?" one of the ladies asks, placing a manicured hand on her slender hip.

"If the fishermen I knew looked like you three, then I'd never set foot on land again," he says, laying on the charm.

I roll my eyes.

They laugh and ask him if *he'd* be their fishing guide and whether or not there would be other young, handsome fishermen on the boat with them, and all I can think about is how high-maintenance these women would be if they actually did come out on the *Dauntless*, and how Tony would spend all his energy hitting on them, and fighting with Stefan and Ian over who had the best shot with them.

As the pearled Lily Pulitzer ladies walk away, Matthew turns his attention to me.

"Admit it, Creary. I want to hear you say it."

"What?"

"You're jealous."

What a flirt! What a terrible, gorgeous, sexy, charming flirt! "I'll admit I'm jealous if that will make you stop talking about it."

He puts his hands up. "All right, already. You don't need to throw yourself at me like that. Don't be so obvious."

I roll my eyes, loving and hating every minute of this.

"Since you ask, I'll tell you what Alice and I will do tonight. We'll probably hit the cafeteria right away to beat the rush, because she gets pissed when they run out of croutons and bacon bits at the salad bar. It's Tuesday, so they'll serve what I can only determine to be some version of beef Stroganoff. No salt, of course. Too many heart conditions. And it'll be weirdly soft beef because of all the dentures. Then we'll head to the TV lounge and watch *Jeopardy* and gossip about Mrs. Hansen's terrible grandchildren, and probably play a round of gin rummy with the ladies from the third floor. Afterwards, she'll give me a bag of Pepperidge Farm cookies, because I'm a growing boy, you know. We'll have a glass of Manischewitz and I will swear to her that I'll be back next Tuesday."

"So your hot date is at a nursing home?" I ask.

"Assisted care facility."

"Alice is your grandmother?"

Matthew smiles. "No. We're not related by blood. Alice and her husband, Roger, took me in after my mom died."

I start biting my nails, which I do when I'm nervous. I know the rough outline of Matthew's childhood. There are no secrets on an island as small as Ne'Hwas. People talk. They embellish. They lie.

The details of Matthew's mother's death are Ne'Hwas legend.

Overdosing on heroin after years of addiction. Sixteen-year-old Matthew finding her on the couch, dead. Matthew left alone in the world.

"You got a raw deal. I'm sorry," I say.

"I loved my mom. Despite everything she did. She had a good heart. She tried to do right for me," Matthew says. "But the drugs took away any chance she had. I always felt like she would have been okay if we lived somewhere other than Ne'Hwas. I think the island suffocated her."

Down the pier the tightrope walker blows a conch shell and announces that his show is starting. Matthew and I start walking that way. We stop at a jewelry vendor, who looks like she's about sixteen years old. Matthew picks up a sea-glass bracelet made of delicate green beads. "I wanted to help her," he says. "I did all the cooking and cleaning. I dreamed about making enough money to buy a place for us, away from Nipon. Away from Ne'Hwas. But by the time I was in middle school, things got out of control. Her dealers would come looking for her. She'd get hit. I stepped in more than once. Got pummeled, too, by guys a lot older and bigger than me. It was a rough time. Started fighting at school a lot, too."

I study the crescent scar under his eye, noticing the way the line is pearl white against his tan skin. I'm not so sure it came from a fishing hook anymore.

"Eventually I stopped going to school and started turning up at the fishing boats looking for work," Matthew says. "I was thirteen or fourteen at the time. Fishermen are a tough crowd, and they could have taken advantage of me. But there was one guy—Captain Roger Ballantine—who took pity on me. Taught me about fishing and driving boats. Gave me the sea hours I needed for my captain's license. His wife, Alice, took me in. She fed me, clothed me, cared for me. When I lost my mother, Roger and Alice let me live with them. I had no one else to go to. They saved my life. They knew all the history about my mom and they never made me feel like I was any less of a person for it."

"And now you look after them?"

"Roger passed away a few years ago. Alice was already in the home by then. I always check in on her. She never had kids of her own. I'm like the son she never had."

"Or the son she never wanted," I say, trying to lighten the mood.

"Smart-ass." He puts down the sea-glass bracelet and picks up a matching necklace.

"So all this time I had it wrong," I say.

"What do you mean?"

"All these years, I thought it was your loyalty to Harold that brings you back to Ne'Hwas every summer. When really, it's your love for Alice that draws you here."

Matthew smiles. He holds up the necklace and bracelet. "What do you think?" he asks.

"The necklace. She'll love it," I say.

He pays the jeweler and we step away from the crowd to the edge of the pier.

"So you see, Creary, when I tell you that you've got to move on, I know what I'm talking about."

I want to lean over and kiss him. And I'm terrified that I will.

He looks at his watch again. "Well, I got to run," he says.

Before he gets to the end of the pier he turns around once and looks at me. He smiles and I feel his smile move all the way through me. This is crazy, I think. Falling for Matthew Weatherby? I've got too much on my plate right now to entertain the thought of romance. I have to figure out what's going on with the wave at Tutatquin, and how far I'm going to let it take me.

Just as Matthew slips away, another familiar face comes through the crowd. Bree Hamilton. One of Kay's childhood friends.

She was in Kay's year at school. The two of them were insepa-
rable growing up. Girl Scouts. Princess softball. Sleepovers. I was
the annoying little sister constantly tagging along.

As they got older, they drifted apart. Kay was smart, ambitious,
innocent. Bree was a townie. She was one of those girls who ma-
tured early, ruled the lunch tables, always had a boyfriend, and
would have been a cheerleader if Ne'Hwas High School had a
cheerleading squad.

A month before Kay died, I saw Bree for the first time in years.
It was early in the season and the Rongo was hopping. I was in
the bathroom, rolling a joint. From behind the stall door, I heard
Bree and another girl talking, gossiping, while they fixed their
makeup. I heard Kay's name, which caught my attention. Bree
told her friend that Kay was a gold digger and a slut and that Trip
Sinclair better watch out or he'll end up with a baby mama on his
hands. She said Trip was too good for Kay. That Kay would end
up pregnant by the end of the summer just to seal the deal. That
Kay had stalked him and jumped into bed with him on their
first date. How else could a townie girl land such a catch?

I wanted to tell her she was jealous and bitter. I wanted to rush
to my sister's defense.

Instead, I hid. I waited in that stall, until the coast was clear.

How could I have let her get away with it? Why didn't I stand
up for Kay? What kind of sister cowers in the bathroom while
her sister's name is dragged through the mud? Did part of me
believe that Bree may have been right?

Quickly, I turn my back to Bree, praying she won't see me.

"Jess? Jess Creary, is that you?"

Too late.

I spin around and force a smile. "What's up, Bree?"

"Oh my God. So much. I'm getting married. Can you believe
it?" She sticks her bony ringed finger in my face, proof that
she's won.

"Congratulations." I look down at the water along the pier. The outgoing tide, dark and determined, rushes by, swirling around the wooden posts. I feel it tugging at me. At the thing in me that is not human. The things that belongs out there.

Bree pulls her hand back. "So what are *you* up to these days, Jess?"

Where to start? I'm treading between human and animal. I'm trying to figure out who I am and how to move forward. And right now, with Bree standing in front of me, I realize that I'm stuck in the past. Part of me is back in that bathroom at the Rongo, wishing for the courage to stand up for Kay, to protect her.

"You were wrong," I blurt out.

"What?"

"Kay wasn't a gold digger and she didn't want Trip Sinclair's money. She was going places. She didn't need a man to get her off this island."

"Uh . . . okay," Bree chuffs. Her face is hard, cold. "Look, I'm sorry for your loss, Jess."

I think about Kay riding on that yacht through the dark. Trip at the wheel. Kay on the rocks. Her body under the sea. Trip climbing to freedom, leaving Kay to die.

The storm is brewing inside of me. My ears start to ring. The thing in me that wanted to strangle Harold is beating hard in my chest.

I chuck the rest of Harold's flyers in the harbor. Watch them spin and twirl in the current.

I feel trapped by so many things—the pain that is always just below the surface. The memories of losing Kay. All the injustice.

Maybe Matthew is able to bury the past, to "move on." Not me. Drugs may be the villain in Matthew's story, but mine has a name: Trip Sinclair.

THIRTEEN

The funeral was on a Friday. A cop's daughter had died so every cruiser on the island joined the procession, blue lights flashing. Bree Hamilton gave one of the eulogies. Talked about what an inspiration Kay had been to her in school. Called her a role model. Remembered (fondly, of course) her smile and how she would light up a room, blah-blah-blah. What a phony.

At the cemetery, there were too many people to count. Childhood friends, neighborhood friends, school friends. The Ne'Hwas Police Department. The entire Passamaquoddy community. Everyone was there.

Except for Trip Sinclair, who was still under investigation at the time and advised by his attorney not to attend.

He sent a flower arrangement in his place—hundreds of red roses and white calla lilies. It dwarfed all the other bouquets, making them looking cheap and provincial.

As I walk down the pier, street performers pack up their props for the night. Tourists head toward the restaurants on Spinnaker Street.

All the sadness I feel for Kay sours. It becomes something primal and powerful. Rage. Disgust. Shame.

Whatever it is, it propels me through the crowd. I bump into a woman walking too slowly for my maddening pace. "Watch it," the woman says and shoots me a dirty look. But I don't care. I surge forward, knocking into people, pushing, plowing, forcing myself forward.

As I cross the pier and march down the harbor road that curves along the edge of the island, I feel the heat in my body rising. My legs carry me ahead, to where, I don't know. My mind is filled only with the three syllables of his name: Trip Sinclair. My pace quickens. Before I'm even aware of where I'm going, I arrive at my destination.

The Ne'Hwas Yacht Club. The spot where Kay took her final steps on solid ground.

I ignore the PRIVATE PROPERTY sign and scurry past the trimmed boxwood hedges to the side of the building.

I've never been here before, but if you've lived on Ne'Hwas as long as I have, the image of the clubhouse is seared into your brain. It has appeared in page one pictures in the *Daily News* dozens of times: when the Sinclair yacht won both the Ne'Hwas Regatta and the Saint Barth's Bucket Race in the same season; the year the Sinclairs hosted a charity ball for the Ne'Hwas Hospital, when it was in danger of default.

The year that reporters were stationed out front, trying to get a quote from a member of the Sinclair tribe about Kay's death.

At the head of that tribe is Bennett Sinclair, Trip's grandfather, a ferret-faced man whose charitable donations have landed his name on park benches, a reading room at the library, a Little League field, and even the sea otter exhibit at the Ne'Hwas Cultural center.

Despite his reputation as a philanthropist, he's known on the island as a tightwad tipper, and a real jackass. He once sued a local teenager for trespassing after the boy's lure got stuck on the Sinclair's yacht. The kid boarded the yacht to retrieve the lure. Bennett sued. The kid's six-dollar lure ended up costing him thousands in legal fees.

It was no different with my sister. She was a local. A townie. A nuisance.

As the president of the club's board and a big player in the yachting world, Bennett Sinclair had a lot to lose by having his name dragged into a scandal like a manslaughter investigation.

He stood by his grandson's side during the entire investigation, the two of them smug and silent while the lawyer, Grant le Carre, did all the talking: "We have no comment on this" and "We aren't permitted to speak about that."

Le Carre is one of those high-profile defense attorneys who wins the unwinnable cases. Got some Wall Street bigwig off on assault charges by blaming a doctor for overmedicating him.

One night that summer, a reporter from the *Daily News* caught Bennett Sinclair coming out of a restaurant and asked him, in an unguarded moment, a few questions about the nature of the relationship between Trip and Kay. Got him on record saying his grandson "wouldn't have had anything to do with the dead girl."

Not that he *didn't* have anything to do with her. "*Wouldn't* have had anything to do with the dead girl." Like the whole thing was hypothetical. Or else, that Trip was too good for my sister.

He had it backwards.

I walk around back to the patio that overlooks the sculpture garden. A wide green lawn sweeps down to the edge of the water, and mega yachts sparkle in the apricot glow of the setting sun.

Trip brought Kay to this exact spot. They boarded his boat right here. Was he already drunk when he got behind the wheel, or did he booze it up out on the water?

Does he have any remorse for what he did?

I make a wide arc around the patio, circling like a mako, searching for Trip Sinclair's face. Women in dresses and men in blue blazers with shiny buttons move around in groups like bait fish. Champagne is popping, glasses are clinking, but there's no sign of Trip.

I spot Bennett Sinclair standing at the bow of a sleek, black sailboat at the docks. *Sea Nymphe,* the boat says in gold lettering across the transom.

Grant le Carre is on the deck, too, holding court with a gathering of beautiful people. I look up and down the gorgeous, shimmering yacht. And then I see him. Trip is standing at the stern, hand wrapped around a scotch, smiling. The smug smile. Plastered across his face during the investigation. It was always there. He smiled through the testimony. Smiled through the arraignment. Smiled during the hearing.

Smiled in all those pictures over the years on the pages of the *Daily News* that tracked his sailing victories.

Bennett Sinclair cracks a bottle of champagne across the bow of the *Sea Nymphe*. A christening. He pats his grandson on the back and gives a long toast. I'm too far away to hear what he says, but it's clear that he's proud of his new boat, *Sea Nymphe,* and even prouder that Trip is captaining her.

This must be why he's back on island. His much-anticipated return to the racing circuit. The Sinclair family is finally emerging from the dark cloud of a manslaughter investigation, stepping into their day in the sun.

The beautiful people mill around in their own solar systems. They cheer for the Sinclairs, and for their charmed lives. They are far removed from the working-class natives who live off their tips during the season. A thousand light-years away from mothers who overdose and leave their teenage sons to fend for themselves.

I don't even realize how angry I am until I look down and see that my hands are shaking. I feel adrenaline coursing through me. I think about Trip Sinclair and the apologies that will never come. If I stay here any longer, there's no telling what I will do—or rather more accurately, what the animal in me will attack. A breeze blows in and I catch the briny scent of the sea, the wild, green stench of seaweed and sea life decomposing on the shore. I need to get out of here.

But first I swear to myself that I will make Trip pay for what he did. I'm not like Matthew; I can't leave the past behind.

FOURTEEN

My penance to Harold continues the rest of the week aboard the *Mack King*, with its piddly tips and buckets of oily mackerels. To make matters worse, two back-to-back hurricane systems have kicked up in the Caribbean this week, sending high seas all the way up the East Coast, which means we're averaging about five chunk blowers on every trip. Only a handful of them make it to the rail in time. I spend more time mopping up puke than flipping burgers.

Being kept away from Matthew is the worst part of my punishment. I want to ask him about his visit with Alice and hear every detail of his life story. I want to talk about the past and the future, and figure out what a relationship with Matthew could be like. When I close my eyes at night, I think about his biceps and his smile, and the way his eyes sparkle when he calls me Creary.

I find myself thinking about him all the time, anticipating when I'll see him next. Each morning I search the docks for him before my boat heads west and his heads east. And I wonder if he does the same for me.

The one good thing about working on the *Mack King* is that the day ends at two o'clock, and I can go surfing.

~~~~

All this obsessing over a boy has me feeling a bit out of my skill set. I need an expert. Luckily Sammy is lying on the couch watching a cheesy romance when I get to the apartment.

"What do you think of Matthew Weatherby?" I ask, lifting her feet onto my lap to steal a spot on the couch.

"Gorgeous," she responds immediately. She sits up. "Deep, too. Like there's more to him than just beer and fishing."

"He visits the nursing home every week," I say.

She sits up. "I think I just had an orgasm."

"You're demented."

"Seriously, I'd do him in a second. If I weren't dating Spencer, of course. Youngest commercial captain on Ne'Hwas. Island legend. And he's got that quiet, smoldering, captain thing going on. Like he's about to rip his shirt off any minute and reveal a perfectly ripped six-pack." A smile breaks across her face.

"Yeah, something like that."

"So what do *you* think of Matthew Weatherby?"

"I've always thought of him as a big brother," I say.

"Erase that image from your mind."

"He's only here for the summer. What's the point of getting into a relationship if he's just going to leave and head back down south?"

"The point is . . . he's hot. He's here now. And you need to get laid."

I can always count on Sammy to say it like it is.

"Thanks for your insights," I say.

"Are you going to do him?"

"Not today," I say, although I am kind of wondering the same thing about the future.

~~~~

Once Sammy leaves for work, I decide to go surfing, but this time I don't tell her where I'm going. She doesn't need to worry about me. Besides, who's to say that I'll be able to go back to mermaid-ville again? Maybe the magic is gone. Maybe I'll chicken out. Why would anyone want to go into a world where so many things want to eat you?

Just in case the portal is there, and just in case I decide to go through it again, I dig through my old scuba gear and grab a dive knife. If I decide to go, I'll be prepared.

It's a beautiful day and there are a few people climbing the rocks at Tutatquin Point as I paddle out through the boneyard. They're tourists, so they won't think anything of a surfer going into unsurfable waters. They won't question why I have a dive knife strapped around my arm. They won't even blink when they see me paddling through a maze of jagged rocks and eddies even though there's a perfectly good surfing beach just a mile away.

To be safe, I wait it out once I'm past the break. They'll lose interest. Surfing is an exciting spectator sport. But watching surfers miss wave after wave after wave gets boring pretty fast. As an hour goes by, the tourists leave, the tide comes in, and the waves build.

When the last group leaves the rocks and heads back into the pines, I paddle for a wave.

I'm not afraid anymore. I've never had such an easy time catching and taking the drop on an overhead wave. My confidence is back. I'm stronger, more agile. I suspect it's a lingering side effect of the first two times I've gone through the barrel. Like one of those fitness regimens they advertise on TV that promise a "new you" in thirty days. That, but on speed.

Paddling is easy, and right away I feel the rush of the wave beneath me. In one swift move I pop to my feet and take the drop. The sheer face of the wave spreads out in front of me. I carve a bottom turn and get into the pocket. I hope the wave will transform me again. I hope I'll get another chance to enter that magical realm. Despite the dangers—the crippling hunger, the pitch blackness of night, the shark—I need to be out there again. Something in me feels like "out there" is where I belong. "Out there" is better, more real, more like home to me than my life on land.

The wave curls around me, and I'm inside the barrel.

I ride it all the way over the sandbar and past the boneyard to shore, every bit as impossibly as the last two times it happened. It's a good thing no one is on the shore when I feel that first gasping breath, that sensation of drowning on land. No one sees me stash my board behind a thick stand of pines, run into the ocean, and disappear beneath the waves.

~~~~

My tail seems even longer this time, my movements more graceful. I stop and listen for the vibrations, subtle shifts in electrical fields, infinitesimal sounds and smells that drift on the current, letting me know if predators are nearby.

My eyesight is a little better, too. Things are only blurry in the distance. Up close, I can see the ridges of sand swept north to south by the long reach of the Atlantic currents. I can make out the fine detail in my scales, right down to the spectrum of colors they capture. Greens and blues deep underneath, reds and purples on the shimmery surface. My other senses are more finely tuned, as well. A fluttering down my sides tells me a school of mackerel is nearby. I can taste the distress of an injured lobster in a trap. I can hear the difference between a diving bird like a cormorant and a jumping fish like a salmon.

And sharks, well, they're the loudest silence in the ocean. I can feel their absence. *She's* not near.

I swim by Smith's Point and peek above the soft waves at the mansions situated regally above the ridge. Somewhere up there, Trip Sinclair is playing tennis is his white whites, drinking expensive wine, wooing women, and getting away with murder. A guy like that wouldn't last five minutes in the wild sea. Money buys you nothing out here.

I decide to find food right away. Swimming through miles of open ocean burns through more calories than anything in my human life, and I don't want to run out of energy again.

I swim east, toward open Atlantic, then parallel to land. There are lobsters in traps all along the coastline, marked with bright buoys on the surface. I follow the vibrations to a trap with two lobsters in the interior compartment. Lobster traps haven't changed much in the last hundred years. All that keeps them in the trap is a funnel-shaped net that's easy to enter and hard to exit. Carefully, I reach in and pull one out. It's as easy as robbing a candy store. God knows I had my share of shoplifting experiences growing up. Small things. Gum. Rocky candy from the counter at the grocery store. A CD from the used-record store. But this doesn't feel like stealing. This is survival, and these traps are in my world, not the world of men.

Since it's molting season, the lobsters have soft shells, which makes them easy to slit apart with my knife. The meat is tender and delicious and I wonder why they never serve lobster raw like they do tuna or salmon.

I eat both lobsters and head to the next trap. I plunder a few more traps until I'm stuffed.

I'm about to head home, when, in the distance, I hear singing. It gets louder and closer, until a pod of dolphins emerges out of the blue.

At first it's their sound that mesmerizes me. Each dolphin has a distinct voice with a range of noises. There are high-pitched squeals, clicks, whistles, calls, grunts. Some of the voices are sweet and childlike, some are relaxing, some insist on being heard. Some sound like words, others like emotions.

The dolphins swirl around me and nudge me with their fins. I don't know what aggressive behavior in dolphins looks like, but these guys seem like they just want to play. They blow bubbles at me. They bob their heads. One of them lets me pet her smooth skin and presses her snout into my hand. They are the friendliest, most fantastic creatures I've ever seen in my life.

Nothing Professor Sherwood ever taught me could prepare me for what happens next. They each introduce themselves to me, their individual names specific and unique.

I try to tell them my name. "Jess." But it comes out sounding muffled and ugly, and this makes the dolphins laugh. They try to repeat my sound. It almost sounds human, but coming from them, it's more musical than any noise I could make.

They swim around me, watching me, chatting. Frolicking.

Another pair of dolphins joins us, and when they get closer, I can't believe what I see.

They each have a bikini top in their mouth. One yellow, one red, just like the ones that have disappeared during my transformations from human to mermaid. Something tells me these dolphins are frequent visitors to Tutatquin Point.

When the dolphin holding my yellow top swims up to me, I try to grab it, but the dolphin darts away. The dolphin with my red top takes his place. He swims inches from me, then dives away before I can grab my bikini. The little rascals come back again, teasing me with my missing bikini tops, getting close to me but never close enough.

Since they enjoy the game of keep-away so much, I play along, grabbing for my bikinis as they pass from dolphin to dolphin.

The other dolphins find this funny and laugh hysterically. They take turns doing corkscrews through the air and zipping past me. They dance pirouettes around me, wave their pectoral fins, swim upside down.

I get the feeling that I'm being tested. They wanted to see what kind of swimmer I am, so we dive down and I swim in the middle of their group. They speed up; I speed up. They slow down; I slow down. They swim fast and close together, clicking and squeaking, but never colliding. We resurface and I do my best to match their jumps and dives and twirls, although I'm not nearly as graceful as them.

I marvel at their physical skill, their complexities, their total synchronicity with one another. I follow them for a while, until the dolphins finally slow down. All at once, they swim away, a school of sardines off in the distance calling them to hunt.

They are gone as suddenly as they appeared, and I'm all alone.

As I swim east, back toward Ne'Hwas, the bottom suddenly plummets over a deepwater canyon and I realize I must actually be heading west. I hang on to the edge of the underwater cliff, my hair fluttering behind. Below me, hundreds of pollock congregate in a huge school. They look like birds gliding on drafts of wind. I think about how stoked Matthew would be to discover a hot spot like this.

I decide I'll find a way to lead him here. My gift to him. I just need a land bearing.

As I swim to the surface to find triangulation points on land, a terrible cry stops me. It sends a wave of grief through me. Immediately, I know it's a humpback. I don't know how I know. It's that primal animal brain in my primal fish body. But it's unmistakable. The sound of the humpback is sharper than the sound of pilot whales, or sperm whales, or right whales. It's got more depth than any human language. It's filled with emotion.

And it's heartrending.

I stay under and follow the sound to a shallow ledge. The massive gray shape of the whale looms in the hazy water. Its head is pointed downward, its white fins stark against the blue water. It rolls in slow circles as it groans a melancholy song. As I get closer, I see what all the fuss is about.

A baby humpback is pinned to the sand, trapped underneath an enormous fishing net. The animal is leaning on its side. It thrashes its tail, but the net is heavy and thick and unmoving. I understand instantly that the moaning whale is the mother. Her baby is in danger.

But it's not just something I see with my eyes.

I can feel her despair like a deep pain in my chest, in my heart. The pain immobilizes me. I understand something else about this creature: She makes no distinction between her baby and herself. There is no "I." There is only "we."

The smell in the water is acrid. It smells like despair.

I look around. Larger whales circle nearby. They're males. From the distinctive stench of hunger in the water, I can tell they want to feed. They aren't as connected to the baby as the mother is. They want to feed and mate. Typical men.

But the mother is singular in her purpose. I feel her desperation, and without even thinking, I swim toward her. As I get close, her massive eyes land on me. With a wild grunt, she charges at me. Thirty-five tons of mama bear heading my way.

I try to communicate with her. *I can help.*

But she is too distraught to communicate.

I keep swimming. She keeps charging.

And then she stops. Her eyes look into mine.

I don't want to sound corny or melodramatic, but we have a moment, she and I.

I am here to help you, I try to say.

She lifts her head and moans. I hear it all through my body.

The mama whale turns around and we swim side by side toward her baby.

The poor pup is twisted in the massive net, which is weighted down with anchors. It's an old gill net—the kind outlawed years ago. It's slimy with seaweed and sharp with barnacles. I tug at the section in front of the baby's face, but it doesn't budge.

Up close, the thing is a graveyard. Fish bones poke out of the rope fibers. A dead turtle is stuck inside, its body decomposed, the shell coated in algae. As I start pulling the rope, more gruesome things emerge—a dolphin skull, beaks, feathers, soda cans, mangled lobster traps, plastic bags decayed in the salt water.

I unsheathe my knife and slice at the rope, but it's so thick my blade doesn't make a dent. Slicing with my knife, working away layers of net with my hands, I look for weak spots. It's like untangling a gigantic wad of Mardi Gras beads tossed in the street from the Lobster Parade floats. Every time you think you've got it, a new knot appears.

The mother whale cries out, and the baby responds by bucking his giant body up and down. He's so ensnared that he slices himself on barnacles with every movement.

Professor Sherwood's biology class comes back to me all at once. Humpbacks are baleen whales. Filter feeders. They don't have sharp teeth. Whales aren't fish. They can't breathe under water. I try to remember how long a humpback can hold its breath. Fifteen minutes? Thirty minutes? Two hours?

Mothers nurse their young for up to a year, and they form tight family units. But nothing in a book can make you feel the connection between a mother and baby humpback. Or a mother whale's anguish.

The mama whale moans.

I'm going as fast as I can, I try to tell her. I pick up on some dangerous vibrations nearby. A predator in the area. The urge to run is powerful, but I stay with the whale, slicing and pulling, stress building with every passing minute.

Suddenly, helping this family becomes the most important thing in the world to me.

I finally manage to free a pectoral fin, but the baby gets so excited he thrashes it around, which just gets him more tangled.

The mother swims to the surface, breathes. When she returns, she blows a stream of bubbles, encircling us in a protective wall of air.

Minutes tick by. I keep slicing at the net. I can feel my energy fading. And darkness is setting in.

If I leave, the baby will die. If I don't leave, *I* might die. I need food and shelter as much as this whale needs air. I look back at the mother. She swims in circles, one gigantic, humanlike eye trained on me and the baby.

It's not my fault, I try to tell her. *I didn't put the net here. I didn't make him swim into it. Nature is a cruel teacher.*

I flutter my tail. It feels heavy, my energy slipping. If I leave now, I'll be able to find more lobsters. *There's no hope for this whale,* I think. But as I look at him, so vulnerable and so majestic, something comes over me.

Sheriff's words move through me: *You have responsibilities. You have people who rely on you.*

People and animals. I won't quit. I'm going to stay and rescue this whale if it kills me. I'm going to do the right thing. The honorable thing.

So I keep at it, and darkness creeps in around me. As I pull off a large section of net, I feel someone behind me. Not a fish, or a whale, or a shark, but a some*one*. I turn around. There's a shadow of movement. I widen my eyes, try to see. A large tail flashes by. Purple. Not like any fish I've ever seen. But the eyes play tricks on you under water. And hunger jumbles your thoughts.

Time is ticking. The baby whale isn't moving anymore. Is he still alive? I go after the rope with more vigor, shredding strands, pulling it apart, my hands raw and bleeding.

Finally, I pull off the last piece of netting. The baby doesn't move. His body drifts motionless. With amazing dexterity, the mother wedges her head beneath him, pushing him off the bottom. He starts to float. Using her head and fins, she pushes his body to the surface and holds him there.

I sit back and watch. And pray.

A minute goes by. Nothing. Another minute. The baby wiggles his tail. His pectoral fins move. With a sudden burst of energy, he gulps air and swims downward, his mother right beside him. He rubs his entire body up and down her belly.

And the mother's song is different now. Still lonesome. Still haunting. But beautiful and soulful. I feel an overwhelming sense of pride. Proud to have saved a life. Proud to be what I am. A mermaid.

The scent in the water has changed from fear to relief. As they sing back and forth to each other, I can hear the whale word for "we."

The whales swim off into the darkness. Suddenly, I'm alone, the sunlight slipping away. I'm too far from shore to make it home. I'm going to have to survive another night alone out here. No shipwreck to hide out in this time. No way to get to land at this hour. Sharks will find me. As the reality sets in, so does the fear. I curl up in a ball.

Then I hear a voice in the dark. Well, not a voice exactly. A sense.

Land creature, it says.

The mother humpback is calling me. She swims to me, her baby by her side. It's her turn to rescue me.

Follow, she says. I hold on to her pectoral fin, and she swims me all the way to Ne'Hwas Harbor.

~~~~

Inside the harbor, boats buzz overhead. The water here tastes foul. Compared to the sea, it's a wasteland, devoid of life. Trash litters the muddy bottom. Cinder blocks, old tires, bottles, and cans sink into the mud. Food wrappers drift midwater. Even the smell in the harbor is ugly. A haze of silt makes visibility poor. Noise is amplified. At the ferry pier, I overhear bits of conversation from the tourists. Their voices are loud and clear under water. They talk about human things. Insignificant things. The weather. Which restaurant has the best lobster roll. Where to find a pharmacy.

Cautiously, I pop my head above water. A fog has rolled in fast, covering the harbor in a gray calm. I watch tourists milling around, kids running down the boardwalk. I watch ducks and plovers digging in the seaweed-covered rocks for mussels, and seagulls

swarming overhead looking for handouts. I see kayakers paddling in from one of the ecotour companies.

I dive under the water, through mucky water, looking for a spot
to make landfall, when out of nowhere I feel a shiver down my
spine. Not like a shiver from being cold, or a vibration when a
white shark is near. It's the feeling you get when you know someone's watching you.

I turn around.

Through the muck, I see a face. A nose. Eyes. Dark hair drifting like seaweed.

Another mermaid?

It turns and races off, disappearing into the gloom.

I go after it.

FIFTEEN

I race toward the other mermaid, but the harbor is pea soup.

I'm barely ten yards in when I slam headfirst into something hard. I squint and try to make out the shape. A pickup truck is stuck in the mud in front of me. I rise toward the surface, rubbing my head. I listen for vibrations, sounds, smells, anything that will lead me to her. Or him. Or *it*.

But the harbor is an earsplitting mess of grinding engines in all directions. I swim toward the surface, toward the hazy light of the streetlamps on the boardwalk. A boat zips by, the prop missing my head by a foot. I dive back down.

Who am I chasing? How many others like me are out there? Where did they come from? How do they survive like this? How can I even be sure it won't try to eat me, like so many other things out here?

If it is another mermaid, I need to talk to her. I need to find out why this is happening to me, and what will happen if I keep shooting that barrel.

Staying close to the mucky bottom, out of range of propellers, I swim blindly through the harbor. I nearly collide with a refrigerator, a mast that's stuck straight up in the mud, fishing line, sunken wreckage from old boats, slabs of concrete. An underwater junkyard.

Where are you, other mermaid? Maybe it was just my eyes playing tricks on me. Sight is the least reliable of all my senses down here. Maybe I saw a seal. Maybe it was my own reflection in a piece of broken glass.

I try to communicate through the lateral lines, like I did with the humpback. *Who are you? Show yourself.*

I try again, with a different set of muscles:

I come in peace.

And, nothing.

I scour the harbor, chasing a ghost. Whatever I saw, it's long gone, and I need to get out of the clanking noise, the dirty water. In the gunmetal dark, I swim to White's Wharf, directly behind my apartment, and climb aboard a little fishing trawler that's so derelict it doesn't even have a name.

I'm still amped on adrenaline from the whale encounter as I pull myself hand over hand into the wheelhouse. How many people can say they've rescued a baby humpback with his mother right beside them? How many people can say they've done any of this?

Inside the cabin of the trawler, I make my way into the berth. Tightly rolled towels are tucked into storage hammocks in the ceiling, along with sheets and pillows. I wipe myself down.

The transition back to human is tedious. My eyes have a harder time adjusting to air. My tail looks bigger to me than the last two times I transitioned. My scales thicker. It's as though the animal part of me is evolving. Even my brain is slower to transition. It still listens for signs of danger. Predators. Hunger.

When I finally have my legs back, I wrap a sheet around myself, tie it over my shoulder, and head out.

Barefoot Lane is quiet, except for a few stragglers window-shopping for seashells and driftwood wind chimes. Someone whistles, but my eyes aren't working worth a damn. All I can make out are feathers and sequins. Lady Victoria.

"Where's the toga party, sunshine? And why aren't I invited?"

"Um. Well . . ." I stall for a reasonable response. "You wouldn't like it. Bunch of townies. All beer, no champagne."

"Sounds deliciously pedestrian," she says in her sultry voice. "I do like the toga. It works for you, kitty cat."

"Thanks." I smooth down the sheet, hoping she can't smell the fish and diesel on me.

"Girlfriend, you have *got* to give me some of what you're taking. Is it estradiol? Progestin? Don't tell me you're on antiandrogens?"

"What are you talking about?"

"Honey, curves like that don't just pop up after puberty. You must be getting a little *supplemental* help. No judgment from me, baby. I'd positively *kill* for a body like yours."

I smile and head up the stairs to the apartment. "Good night, Lady Victoria."

"Good night, darling. And remember: be good. Or be good at it."

In the apartment, I check my phone. There's a message from Sammy. Her voice is slurred and barely audible through music in the background. She and Spencer are at the Schooner Wharf Bar and I should join them. It's locals' night. Three-dollar-a-plate spaghetti and meatballs. Full-price drinks. Take your perks where you can get them.

The message goes on and on and on. Tony, Stefan, and Ian are there. Jacqueline and West, too. Spencer's being a total ass. I need to come and rescue her. There's a bunch of hot guys from the catamaran charter there, and a bunch of those wankers from the Half Shell Restaurant.

"And Matthew's here." Incoherent babble and giggles. "Thought you'd be interested." Her voice rises into a question mark at the end.

Matthew never goes to locals' night. Too many sloppy drunks, too many reminders of what he's escaped. But he's there tonight, and he's made a point of telling Sammy. I'm sure I'm the cause of his sudden interest in three-dollar-a-plate spaghetti.

I'm exhausted from my swim and consider blowing Sammy off. But I would love to see Matthew. My hands feel jittery just thinking about him. I wish I could tell him about the baby humpback. The thrill of saving a creature as magnificent as that. The gratitude I felt from the mother. The beautiful language of "we" that they sing.

It was the best day of my life, I realize. Better than winning the regional surf championship. I want so badly to share it with someone. I want to sing a song of "us" in my heart, like the humpbacks. I don't want to just be a "me."

In my bedroom, I slip on a pair of cutoff shorts, fringed, with the pockets hanging below the hem. They feel a little tighter than usual, but when I look down I can't make out the details. White thread and blue denim are indistinguishable. I find a clean tank top and pull it on, look in the mirror. Everything's a bit hazy. I blink hard, but it's as though I'm still under water. Maybe I need glasses. I wonder, briefly, if poor eyesight is an irreversible side effect of being a mermaid.

I use my hands to see what Lady Victoria was talking about.

My shoulders feel broader, my arms chiseled. The ribbed cotton of my tank hugs my body, stretching tight across the chest, narrowing to a taper at my waist. My thighs and butt round out into a grand sphere. As I press my hands down my body, I'm astonished. There is no fat anywhere. I am all muscle and curves.

Every which way I turn, sumptuous lines appear through the hazy film of my reflection. My waist is tiny; my hips and rib cage flare out so much like an hourglass that I understand for the first time what that term means.

I can't stop looking at myself, moving my hands down my body, admiring my new figure. All from swimming like a fish. I've always been in good shape. A tomboy. An athlete. But these new curves, these aqueous lines . . . these can't belong to me. Kay was always the pretty one, the one with the womanly figure. I was like the smelly little brother.

I'll have to cover up. People will notice. Matthew will notice.

Hell, I *want* him to.

I reach into a drawer and pull out a faded flannel, roll up the sleeves, button the bottom two buttons. It's going to be hard to hide these curves. Hopefully plaid will do the trick. I throw on some flips-flops and I'm tomboy-ready.

My hair is coarse with the salt water, and I twist it into a loose bun. I add some shimmery lip gloss and head out.

The Schooner Wharf Bar is at the far end of the Galleon Marina, and I still don't have my vision back when I leave the apartment and head down to the harbor. My legs are a little wobbly. I put my head down and focus on the sidewalk, trying not to trip. As I cross Spinnaker Street in the middle of the late dinner rush, I can feel eyes on me. I'm hyperaware of the new curves of my body swaying as I walk, even though, inside, I still feel like the skinny tomboy I've always been.

When I get to the Schooner Wharf, I slouch my shoulders to hide what's underneath and walk in.

The place is packed. A Jimmy Buffett cover band plays on the tiny stage outside on the deck, where the masts of tall ships stand as tall as giant pine trees. Laughter rings out from the tables of people. The smell of warm bodies and spaghetti sauce fills the air. I don't see Sammy anywhere. I don't see much of anything right now, other than vague shapes and shimmering bottles of alcohol behind the bar.

I walk around, squinting at everyone, looking for familiar faces, feeling lost and self-conscious. A fish out of water.

I fumble my way around the perimeter of the deck, hoping Sammy or Matthew, or even Tony, will find me, but no one calls after me. It's too crowded. People are packed in as tight as the pollock at the edge of the cliff. As I head back into the main bar, I feel a pulsing down my sides, like the vibrations of a shark.

I bump into someone, or rather, someone bumps into me. Strong hands clasp both my arms in a way that's too familiar. At first I think it must be one of the Slack Tide guys—Ian, Stefan, Tony. The hands linger. Hands like bear claws.

"Sorry about that," says the man who belongs to the hands. It's a voice I don't know.

His face is blurry. I can tell that he's tall and built like a lumberjack. Older. In his forties, at least. He's got a beard and a red ball cap, and his breath reeks of cigarettes.

"Don't worry about it," I say, and step to the side so he can pass, but his hands stay. They slide down my arms to my wrists.

I give him the best back-off-motherfucker expression I can manage, although I don't know how effective it is, since I can't even be sure that I'm looking him in the eye.

"Why in such a rush?" the man says.

I shake his hands away.

"Let me buy you a drink," he says.

"Buzz off."

He laughs. "Aren't you a little spitfire?"

I turn my back to the lumberjack and step away from him into the anonymous crowd. My eyes slowly adjust. *Where are you, Sammy?* Through all the chatter and music, I find my answer. That laugh—an explosion of gasps and whoops that ends in a snorting fit—that only Sammy can get away with. I follow it to the bar.

Sammy hugs me. "How come I've never noticed how cute Matthew is before?" she whispers, and I can tell she's been drinking. "And he's sweet, too. Did you know he was so sweet?"

I look around the bar, but I don't spot him. Maybe he already left. "He is sweet," I say.

"Why doesn't *he* have a girlfriend?" she says. "You should get all over that. I mean, he's *hot*. And he's actually *nice*. What are you *waiting* for?"

"Well, he's a fisherman and I'm a fish, for starters," I whisper.

"So?"

Spencer walks up to us before I have a chance to explain any more of my hang-ups.

"You been working out, Jess?" Spencer asks.

Ugh. I knew I should have covered up.

"Your legs are . . . really . . ."

"What?" Sammy says, getting in his face. "Why are you noticing my best friend's legs?"

"They're really strong," Spencer says, eyes glued to my cutoffs. "I mean big. Bigger than normal. Like a dude's."

"Nice save, Spencer," I pat him on the back.

He plants a kiss on Sammy. She kisses back aggressively. Then they start making out, right in the middle of the bar, and I'm just standing next to them like a big dope.

"I guess that means more spaghetti for us," Matthew says brightly, sneaking up beside me.

"I think I lost my appetite," I say.

"Not into public displays of affection?"

"Public display of disgustingness is more like it."

He smiles and leans his back against the bar so our arms touch. Standing next to me, broad-shouldered and sun-kissed, he looks like a sea god. Rugged. Tough. Like someone who could survive in the ocean. How *have* I ignored his hotness all these years?

"How was your penance aboard the *Mack King*?" Matthew nudges me.

Fisherman by morning, fish by afternoon.

"Mackerel fishing isn't exactly glamorous," I say.

"Neither is watching Tony and Sal fight over who's on chum duty."

I can feel the heat of his skin against mine. "Ben drives to the same spot every day."

"Wolf Rocks?"

"Yup."

"Mackerel are pretty consistent out there."

"You're a better captain," I say. "You understand the fish."

He laughs. In the dim light of the bar, my eyes adjust. I catch a glimpse of myself in the mirror behind the bar and do a double take. My hair is wild, my eyes seem lit from within. The light overhead accentuates my cheekbones and the strong lines of my jaw. Even my skin sparkles, with remnants of salt.

I look like my mother in pictures I've seen of her when she was young.

"At least I'll have you back on my boat in a couple days," Matthew says. He's so close I can smell soap on his skin. I sweep a hand down my thigh.

"How about a drink?" he says. "Dark 'n Stormy, right?"

"Yes. Thanks."

The bartender is an older woman, tattoos up her arms, wispy bangs around her face.

My scalp itches and I scratch it, only to find, tousled within the gnarled dreadlocks of hair, a hermit crab. I steal a quick look at Matthew, but he's trying to get the bartender's attention and doesn't notice. I close my hand around the crab and stick it in my pocket. Poor little thing. I'll release it later, where it can find its way back to the sea.

While Matthew hails the bartender, a burst of tremors travels down my spine. I look up. The lumberjack in the red ball cap is staring at me from a high-top table across the bar. *Predator*, the vibrations are telling me.

Leave me alone. The words vibrate out of me.

But he's only human and can't hear them. He continues to stare at me.

"To the end of your exile," Matthew says.

"I'll drink to that."

We clink glasses.

He asks about the spaghetti, since he's never been to spaghetti night at the Schooner Wharf.

I have to lean in close to hear him, so close I can smell beyond the soap on his skin, deep down to his chemical makeup. I can smell his desire.

"It's food and it's cheap. And if you don't get here by eight, it's gone."

"Sounds impossible to resist," he says.

He says something about the fishing this season. It's good; it's bad. I can't pay attention because now the vibrations from the lumberjack are jolting me to attention. I look at him, my vision sharp now. He smiles crookedly and tips his grungy hat my way, as if he might stand a chance. There's a buzzing in my ears. And the Jimmy Buffett music, and the laughter of strangers all around.

"Jess?"

"Yeah?"

Matthew looks at me expectantly.

"Did you say something?" My senses are too fired up. The sounds are overwhelming—shoes shuffling sand on the floor, the fizz of a beer tap, the drainage pipe dripping into the marina, the clanging of rigging on sailboats.

"I was wondering if you have plans this weekend?" Matthew asks.

I try to focus on his words, on his delicious smell, on the notes of desire in the air. But too many other smells creep in. Rancid trash in the street, mosquitoes burning into lightbulbs, spaghetti sauce, seaweed, and seawater, and lust.

I feel my heart beating and the bass thumping and the air growing thick and humid.

Suddenly Spencer appears. "Jay Delgado says he saw you surfing Tutatquin Point today. I told him he must have been high."

Sammy's right behind him. "Jess can surf wherever she damn well pleases. She's better in the water than all you guys." A drunk finger points indiscriminately around. "You have no idea what she can do."

"Sammy, please," I whisper.

"Jay swears you caught a barrel there," Spencer says.

Sammy, emboldened with Corona, keeps going. "Jess is part fish. She lives in the water. Bet ya didn't know that." She jabs a finger into Matthew's chest with each word.

"No one can surf Tutatquin," I say. "That would be suicide."

"Yeah," Spencer says. "That's what I told him. 'No way, bro,' I said. I mean, *I* wouldn't even be able to surf there."

Sammy's about to do battle with Spencer and his ego, but her attention is snatched away by Spencer's wandering eye when a pretty blonde from the catamaran crews walks by. Sammy, on the verge of spilling my secret along with her drink, grabs her boyfriend by the arm.

"Whoa," Spencer says. "I think it's time to get you home."

"In a minute. I want to dance," Sammy says, shimmying her way to the dance floor.

I turn back to Matthew. I feel the heat of his skin. I feel desire.

And I smell the blood of the haddock from the fillet table on the dock, and a diesel engine, zinc and steel. I smell fudge from the shop down the road, garlic frying at a nearby restaurant, beer on the floor.

There's too much stimulation. I'm like a caged animal. I need to get out of here.

But first . . . I put my drink down and look Matthew in the eyes. "Will you go out to dinner with me?" I ask. It just comes out fully formed. I can't take it back.

Matthew laughs. "Well, if you insist."

"Good." My heart is beating like a jackhammer.

"A real date," he says. "Just the two of us. Someplace a little quieter than this. How about Saturday?"

"Yes." I smile, but my ears are thumping and my senses are on overdrive and I need air.

"I'll pick you up at seven o'clock."

I smile and nod. "I need to go."

"Now?"

"Right now."

"Let me take you home."

I press a hand against his chest. "No. I live right down the street. I'm really, really tired. Lots of surfing this week. I'll see you tomorrow at work."

~~~~

I step outside and let the fresh air fill my lungs. It's a welcome relief. I start walking home, thinking of Matthew, our date, taking it to the next level. Maybe, in a quiet moment, I can tell him about the humpbacks and he'll believe me. I'm daydreaming about it, when I hear that voice again.

"Hey, baby, where ya going? Why in such a rush?" The lumberjack with the red ball cap is smoking a cigarette in the alley.

I smell his aggression and testosterone. There is no fear in his smell. The vibrations pulsing in my body are screaming *predator*.

"Leave me alone."

"Come on, I won't bite."

He reaches for me.

All I can hear is my heart pounding. And all I can taste is the surge of adrenaline like metal on my tongue.

SIXTEEN

It all happened so fast.

His hands on me, the weight of his body pushing me into the wall, the crack of bone. Cigarettes on his breath. The raw, rancid smell of aggression.

Did I scream? I don't think I did. I don't think I felt fear.

Instinct took over.

This I know: I struck his neck first, the way a shark, bear, or cat stuns its prey before it goes in for the kill. He froze, stunned, shocked by what was happening. I swept his legs out from under him. He fell to the ground. The rest is a blur.

There were punches, mine mostly. Kicks. Also mine. A small voice deep inside me pulling me back, telling me to stop. I overpowered him so easily it was like the time Sheriff took me spearfishing at night for black crappies in the creek behind our house. We shone a light into the dark water and the crappies raced toward it, rubbing themselves onto the tip my spear. There was no sport in it.

The lumberjack had that stunned look in his eyes. Like he couldn't believe what was happening. And then he was flat on the dirt, a rivulet of blood beside him.

Had I killed him? Did I want to?

I checked for a pulse, but the carotid artery was hidden in the depths of his thick neck. Was he breathing? I leaned toward his face to listen, but all I could hear was the thrumming of my heart. There were people nearby, people spilling out of the bar. I could hear voices coming toward the alley.

I fled, a small voice inside of me tearing me away. I ran and only when I started running was I afraid.

<center>~~~~</center>

I check the *Daily News* the next morning, and the morning after that, for anything about an assault at the Schooner Wharf. The police blotter has a wide assortment of freaky crimes: a teenager hiding a potato gun in his pants, a woman who was reported by neighbors for keeping a five-hundred-pound pig in her living room, a guy who stopped traffic by riding his bicycle naked down the middle of Ocean Road. Island living can screw with your mind. It can send you over the edge. There are also plenty of run-of-the-mill crimes: drunk-and-disorderly arrests, traffic violations, petit larceny, fire, a breaking and entering at Nipon Beach.

But no dead lumberjacks at the Schooner Wharf.

It's a huge relief.

Lumberjack man didn't report the assault. It makes sense. A guy like that would want it swept under the carpet. Wouldn't admit to being beaten by a girl.

Sheriff used to warn me and Kay about scumbags like that. He taught us a thing or two about self-defense, showed us how to strike with an open hand. He explained which parts of the body to aim for. The red areas—the head, the neck, the spine—that's how to take someone down. As a cop, you have to aim for the green areas first—the big muscle masses. Yellow areas second—the elbows, knees, and ribs. Red areas are only when you're sure.

I went straight for the red areas.

<center>~~~~</center>

On Thursday, there aren't enough customers to take the *Mack King* out, so Harold tells me I can leave, after I sweep out the shop and clean the windows.

Sammy has the day off, too.

"You going surfing? Doing your mermaid thing?" she asks as we eat leftover scallop mac and cheese out of Lobster Corral boxes.

"No."

"No waves?"

"There are waves." I plop a scallop in mouth, appreciating for a moment how easy it is to survive on land. "I need to know what's happening to me, Sammy. I feel like I'm changing. I feel like I'm losing control." I don't tell her about lumberjack man.

She sips a Diet Coke. "So, how can you find out? I mean it's not like there's a mermaid expert on Yelp, right? Actually, maybe there is. I once Googled 'How to know if your man's cheating on you' and I got, like, fifty thousand results. All experts. Can you believe it? You can probably Google 'What do mermaids eat?' and get, like, a million opinions. Isn't Google amazing! I'm always telling people 'If your name ain't Google, don't act like you know everything.'"

"I have an idea of where to get some answers."

"Not on Google?"

"No. Right down the street."

~~~~

The sign out front of the little shop says "Truth Within"—not "Psychic Readings," like Madame Irene's palmistry shop in the strip mall near the Stop & Shop, or "Fortune Teller," like the woman who comes down from Nova Scotia every summer, dresses like a Gypsy, and reads tarot cards on the ferry pier for fifty bucks a pop.

Truth within. Like you're already supposed to know the answers.

When I was little, my mother and I walked past this shop together. I stood outside, watching the new tenant move in, while my mom crossed the cobblestones to Bob's Fishmonger to buy dinner. An old woman hung dreamcatchers and animal skulls, sharks' teeth, turtle shells, and strange-looking talismans in the wavy display window. *What on earth kind of store sells such things?* my little mind wondered. I was drawn to it the way honeybees descended on the crab apples in our yard every fall. The woman in the window was just as fascinating as the treasures she was laying out. I could tell by the contour of her jaw, the slant of her nose, and the hazel circle in the dark brown irises that she was like us.

I waved at her. She waved back.

I said hello. She mouthed the word back.

There was something about her that was so familiar.

She had a friendly face, and there was something in her eyes that made me think she wanted to talk to me. Then her mouth turned down and she got very serious looking. Her gaze fell behind me. When I turned to look, my mother was there, a brown bag from the fishmonger in her hand. My mother and the old woman were in a stare-off. Even as a little twerp, I understood that there was something between these women. The air around us was electrified. The hair on my arms stood up straight. I remember looking at it, thinking how strange that I'd never noticed hair on my arms until then.

Before I knew it, we were scrambling down Barefoot Lane, my mother's hand tight around mine, pulling me away.

"Stay away from that place," she said, in a scary-mom tone I'd never heard her use before. It startled me. My mom never yelled or threatened.

Of course, it just made me want to know everything. What kind of shop was it? Who was the old lady? How did she get all the animal skulls? Where did she find the turtle shells, and how could I get my hands on one?

Most importantly, why wasn't I allowed to go in?

"No one can tell you your destiny, nomeha. You must decide for yourself. That's the only chance you have at finding happiness."

"What's a destiny?"

My mother said, "Destiny is who you are meant to be. It's the story that's written about you before you are born."

"Who writes it?"

My mother sighed. "Jess Creary, promise me you will *not* go in that shop."

"But the woman in the window was Passamaquoddy, wasn't she? She looked like one of us."

"Not our kind."

After that, I never went back. So powerful were my mother's words over me. And I never saw the old woman again, even though her shop has been here the whole time, and only a couple blocks down from my apartment.

❧❧❧

"So, knock already," Sammy says, gum snapping.

I pause, waiting for lightning to strike, or the garden gnomes out front to rise up and stage an intervention, or some other supernatural force to stop me.

The old woman answers right away, her eyes rimmed in hazel, her face unchanged.

She smiles. "Follow me."

Not "Hello." Not "Hi. Can I help you?" It's like she's expecting me.

She leads me and Sammy to the back room, which smells like animal hide, but not in an unpleasant way. A large turtle shell hangs from the ceiling. There are fish skeletons mounted on stands. Dozen of maps, tinged yellow with age, line the walls. The Maine and New Brunswick coasts. Nova Scotia. Cape Cod. Islands I cannot place. They're creased and smeared with handwritten notes. Dozens of Xs appear on them like marks on a treasure map.

There are also dreamcatchers, fossils, dowsing sticks, soapstone carvings of animals—a mishmash of artifacts. What did my mother know about this place? About this woman? Is she a witch? A shaman? A treasure hunter?

"I'm a seer," the woman says.

I spin around. She's seated at a small table, staring at me. Was I thinking out loud?

I take the seat facing the woman, and Sammy sits on a bent-hickory chair near the window.

"You are from the Upriver People," the woman says.

I shrug. "I don't know. My mother's Passamaquoddy. She's from the mainland."

"You are Passamaquoddy, too."

"Yeah. I guess so."

"There is no guessing. You are what you are."

"My mother didn't talk about her family much. I'm a Ne'Hwas islander, born and raised." Miles of ocean separate me from my Native American heritage.

Out the plate glass window a fleet of small skiffs and fishing trawlers is docked at White's Wharf, and I spot the little derelict boat I boarded the other night. The night I saw the other mermaid.

"What do you want to know?" the woman asks. Spikes of sunlight illuminate her face, revealing the tight, shiny skin of her high cheeks.

Sammy speaks up. "If you're a seer, shouldn't you, like, already know what she's going to ask, before she asks it?" She crosses her arms and gives me a conspiratorial wink. Holmes and Watson, the two of us.

"I don't see the future and I can't read minds," the old lady snaps. "All I can do is help you see the present."

"Well, okay then." Sammy rocks back on her chair. Mystery solved. Case closed.

The woman folds her hands on the table. They are ancient hands, brown and lined in wrinkles. "Your mother was with you when you saw me before. Does she still forbid you to see me?"

"She doesn't live on Ne'Hwas anymore."

Her eyes are piercing. "Are you sure?"

"Of course I'm sure. She was devastated when my sister . . ." I stop myself. "She's on a spirit journey."

"What do you want to know?"

I take a deep breath and look out at White's Wharf, at the skiffs listing sideways on the hard-packed sand of low tide, thinking how, in a few hours, they'll be floating.

"Something has happened to me," I start. I pause. It all seems too foolish. She'll laugh at me. Who wouldn't?

Across the table, she takes my hands in hers. It's an intimate gesture. I close my eyes, and suddenly I can feel the sway of the current, the weightlessness of being in water. A school of herring swims by, flashing silver as it parts like a curtain for me. Images come at me like a movie—the shipwreck, the seal, the inside of the barrel.

The old woman squeezes my hand, snapping me back into the room.

"I can breathe under water," I blurt out. I look from our entwined hands to the woman's face.

Her eyes light up. She smiles so completely, with such radiance, it looks like she might spontaneously combust. She doesn't laugh. She nods as though she's heard this sort of thing a thousand times. "Tell me what happened."

"I surfed a big wave and something happened and I can swim like a fish. I'm like a fish. I *am* a fish. It was scary at first, but then I liked it. It felt right. It feels . . . natural. And it's so beautiful down there, and I'm beautiful when I'm down there.

"I got scared a few times. It's a dangerous place. And then, last time, I thought I saw another mermaid, but I can't be sure."

I look up at the fish skeleton, at the precision of bones lining its spine, and wonder what my skeleton looks like when I'm under the water.

"I'm a mermaid," I continue. "And I want to know why. And

I want to know if there are others out there. And I want to know if I should keep going back."

"Do you believe her?" Sammy asks, practically leaping out of her chair.

The woman puts up a hand to silence Sammy.

"Well," I say, "do you believe me?"

She closes her eyes, then opens them. "There is a legend that the Upriver People tell. It's where your story begins."

"*My* story?"

"You are in a story. We all are. The story was written long ago, from beginning to end. All there is for you to do is decide which character you are."

"Dude, it's like one of those old Indian legends," Sammy says. "Like, where some animal talks to a little kid in the woods and the kid's supposed to figure out the riddle and save the village. They used to tell us these legends on class field trips to the lobster cannery."

"Not another word out of you," the woman says.

Sammy sulks.

"Long ago, in the land of the pollock spearers, there were two girls, twin sisters, who lived with their parents by a river. They were very close and shared all their secrets. One of the girls was very good and obedient and did all she could to please her parents. She was thought of very highly by others and was often rewarded for her efforts. Her name was Sipayik."

The woman clears her throat. "The other had a wild streak in her. She was known to wander off alone and lose herself in her thoughts. She was often in trouble with her parents for failing to finish her chores. Her name was Ne'Hwas."

"As in Ne'Hwas Island?" Sammy says.

"Hush," the woman says. "You talk too much. You have much to learn and you need to listen."

"Jeesh, all right."

"One day, the girls went to the river at the edge of a waterfall to collect water for their household. It was a hot day and Ne'Hwas wanted to swim. Sipayik told her they did not have permission from their parents to swim. She said that they needed to get their work done and go home.

"But Ne'Hwas looked down at the sparkling blue water and couldn't resist. She got undressed and stood up on the high rock at the edge of the falls. It was a very tall cliff and very dangerous. She summoned her courage and jumped into the pool below.

"The water was cool and refreshing. She called for Sipayik to join her. Sipayik was afraid to make such a jump, but Ne'Hwas kept calling to her until she agreed. Now they were both swimming in the clear, blue water, and they felt a fine sensation wash over them. After a time, they swam to shore to return to their duties. But when they got to shore, they could not stand. The weight of their bodies dragged them down. They had grown long tails in place of their legs. This made them very afraid.

"When it grew dark and they still had not arrived at home, their parents came to look for them, fearing they had run into trouble. Seeing their parents on the shore, the girls called out.

"The parents were stunned when they saw what had happened to their beautiful girls. They believed it was the spirit of the river, cursing the girls for disobeying their parents' orders. The parents wept for their girls, for they could not bring them onto shore.

"Each day, the parents came to check on Sipayik and Ne'Hwas, to see if the river spirit had cut them loose from the spell. For a month, from new moon to new moon, the girls lived in the river, eating mussels and raw fish. Every day, Sipayik would wait on the shore, hoping for her legs to return, missing her parents and her life on land. But Ne'Hwas found great pleasure in the world under the surface. She became a great hunter, and enjoyed the freedom of the river.

"One day, the parents were paddling their canoe and capsized in strong wind and waves. The girls came to their parents' rescue and carried them to shore safely. Now, after performing such a good deed, the girls could get their legs back and return to land. Sipayik walked up the sandy shore and joined her parents.

"Ne'Hwas stayed back. She decided to remain a creature of the river. The family wept and pleaded for her to return, but Ne'Hwas needed to stay. She had found the place for her wildness to live. She slunk back into the water and was never seen again.

"Some people believe that she lived the rest of her days as a goddess, roaming the rivers and ocean freely. Some people believe she's out there still."

The old woman sits back and lights a clove cigarette. Sweet smoke drifts through the room.

"I'm supposed to be the wild sister in this story, right? I'm Ne'Hwas?" I ask. "And Kay was Sipayik."

"That's for you to decide. You will need to choose which world you belong to."

"You mean I have to give one up?"

"That's correct."

"Dude," Sammy interjects. "Bummer."

"There's always a catch," I say. There is no such thing as getting everything you want. Things slip away from you. People slip away. Life is unfair.

"You have been given a very special gift, little fish."

Little fish. *Nomeha.* That's what my mother calls me. Is it a coincidence, or does she know that? Is it a common Passamaquoddy nickname? "How do you know my mother?"

"I knew her a long time ago."

"How?" I ask. I feel tears building inside of me. I swallow hard.

"Remember, I don't tell the past or the future. I can only help you see the present."

"Can you tell me where she presently *is*?" I ask, sounding more sarcastic than I intend to. "Or, at least, can you tell me if she's still on her spirit journey?"

"That's not important right now. Now, you need to focus on the choice before you."

"Between human and mermaid."

"Yes."

I sigh, wishing she could be a little more helpful. "Can you at least tell me more about Ne'Hwas? Why did she choose the river? Didn't she miss her parents? What about her sister? Weren't they devastated to lose her? Wasn't Ne'Hwas lonely out there? Wasn't she scared?" I ask.

"Ne'Hwas was following her nature."

I pull down my hoodie and scratch my salty scalp. "I don't know what my nature is."

She blows a long trail of smoke into the air. "Jumping off that waterfall took a great act of courage, and it led Ne'Hwas to her destiny, just like surfing the wave led you to yours. The question before you is whether or not you have the courage to stay. Like Ne'Hwas and Sipayik, you will have one full cycle of the moon to make up your mind. By the next full moon, the world you choose becomes permanent."

"What if I don't want to be alone."

"You won't be alone."

"So there is another mermaid down there?" I ask.

She takes another drag of her cigarette. "A goddess cannot die. Ne'Hwas is out there."

"What about the sharks? How am I supposed to survive in a world where they're constantly trying to eat me?"

"You have something the sharks don't have. A human brain. And a human heart. Use them."

The woman stands and walks toward the door. "We're finished now," she says.

"Finished? But wait a minute." I stand up, too. There's so much more I need to know. "Tell me what to do. Can I ever come back? Will I ever see my parents and friends if I become a mermaid?"

She laughs deeply. "You are much like your mother. The animal in you is strong." She leads me and Sammy out of the room, and then out the front door. I walk out of there in a daze.

～～～

"What a drag," Sammy says. We stop at Scoops Ice Cream Shop on the way home. "You only get to be a mermaid 'til the next full moon. Enjoy it while it lasts, right?"

"Yeah," I say, licking my cherries jubilee with sprinkles on top.

"I mean, you can't really be thinking that you'll be a mermaid forever, can you? It's not like going to Albuquerque. You'd be a fish. Like, forever."

I lick my cone and ponder this. Why wouldn't I leave once and for all? My sister's dead, my mom's gone, and my dad and I aren't exactly on good terms. I'm in a dead-end job with no sort of future ahead of me. I scrape by, season to season, on handouts from tourists. Why shouldn't I be a mermaid and live my life as a goddess?

"How do mermaids even have sex?" Sammy says. "Doesn't your tail cover everything up? Oh my God, do you think there are some hot mermen out there? That would be so-o-o kinky!"

"Did you think there was something off about the old woman?" I ask.

"Ye-ah! What was up with all the bones? Totally creepy. And she told me I talk too much, which is kind of rude, considering we were there to talk, but I'm used to that."

"What I mean is, I feel like she knows more than she's letting on."

A couple of teenagers walk up to the ice cream line. They flirt and goof around in that awkward, self-conscious way that teenagers do.

"She's a seer, dude. She's supposed to know more than she lets on."

"Sammy, promise me you'll keep it a secret. If anyone knew, they'd try to get there themselves. They could die in the surf at Tutatquin Point, and I'd be responsible. Or worse, they could make it. What if someone else discovered the legend of Ne'Hwas? What would they do? Flag down the six o'clock news? Try to land their own reality TV show?"

"Wicked. You could totally have your own show." She licks her ice cream and flips back her hair. "Until the next full moon anyway. It'd be kind of short-lived."

"You can't even tell Spencer," I say.

"Okay, okay."

"Pinkie swear."

Sammy huffs. "What are we? Seven?"

I lick the last of my cherries jubilee and toss the napkin in the trash.

"Do it."

We do the pinkie swear. Kay was the only other person who knew it. She used to make me give her a pinkie swear whenever she wanted to keep a secret from Mom and Sheriff. Not that there were that many secrets. Kay was the good one; I was the one sneaking out of the house to meet my friends, go night surfing, or skip school.

I was the sister with the wild streak in me. I was like Ne'Hwas.

Sammy has it backwards. I only get to be *human* until the next full moon.

SEVENTEEN

Am I really considering ditching my legs for a tail? Swimming with whales, killing fish with my bare hands, running from great white attacks every day?

Living like a goddess?

Do I follow the path of Sipayik or Ne'Hwas?

According to the tide chart, the next full moon is the same day as Regatta, the big midsummer yacht race. I have ten days to figure out my destiny.

No pressure there.

On Saturday, I'm back on the *Dauntless* and life is back to normal (minus the whole choosing-which-species-I-belong-to dilemma).

Saturdays are my favorite aboard the *Dauntless*. That's when my buddies Nick, Joey, and Mario join us. Harold loses money on these guys because they bring their own sandwiches and don't buy anything in the galley, but I've come to think of them as family.

They're always overdressed in goose down vests and wool caps, as if they're crossing the North Sea in February. They're all over sixty-five, retired, and they've been fishing on Harold's boats for as long as I've worked here.

There's Nick. He spent his life as an electrician and constantly recites his philosophy of life: "Work was invented by people who don't know how to fish." Nick brings a cooler on board to store his catch, even though coolers are technically prohibited. The years are marked on the lid in Sharpie ink, with a Jesus fish under each year to record the number of times he's won the fishing derby. Nick never takes a break. He jigs all day in the pulpit. Happiness, to him, corresponds directly to the number of fish he's caught.

Then there's Joey, the builder of houses. He spent thirty-five years building homes, from the Shenandoah Valley to New Brunswick. He likes to tell people that his beard is twenty-one years old.

Mario is the leader of the group. He wears dark, wraparound glasses, "Not because I'm mafia, you know, but because of the cataracts." He has a bulbous nose, a broad white smile. My first conversation with Mario went something like this:

"Hey galley girl, what kind of deodorant do you use?"

"Excuse me?"

"Do you wear Ban or Speed Stick?"

"Isn't Speed Stick a man's deodorant?"

"Ban then?"

"Actually, I wear Secret," I said, feeling like the conversation was getting a little too intimate.

He reached into his gigantic duffle bag and pulled out a half dozen sticks of deodorant. "Sorry, don't have your brand."

"That's . . . okay."

"Here," he said, and offered me a bottle of French's mustard instead. He was proud of his gift. Mario's a coupon clipper. Goes on about how much he saved on two-liter bottles of orange soda, or how he got a free oven mitt during a promotion the Stop & Shop was running on baked hams. He offers to take me shopping, to show me "how it's done."

They play poker on the trip out and always give me a five-dollar tip from the group. It's what they can afford, and I accept it with a smile.

They're always concerned about my love life. They give me

advice, even though I really don't need to know the inner workings of an electrical circuit or the best days to pick up the *Penny Saver*.

When Matthew keeps popping down to the galley for drinks and snacks, they want to know what's going on with the captain. Even Nick, who's never aware of anything other than the end of his fishing line, thinks that Captain Matthew might have a crush on me.

"You should play hard to get," Nick advises. "Girls who put out too easy end up with their phone numbers on the walls of the men's urinal."

"Will do," I tell him.

"And boys who ride motorcycles are usually trouble. Watch out for them. Find yourself a boy that respects his mother and obeys his father. You know, a good, wholesome boy."

I think the sum of Nick's relationship advice was gleaned from *Happy Days*.

Nevertheless, I find myself watching the cabin door, waiting for Matthew, excited to see him, to have a quick little exchange before he steals away to check the fish finder.

Finally, when he comes down for his third bag of potato chips, he smiles and asks if we're still on for tonight.

"Where are we going?" I ask. Even though *I* was the one who asked him out, *he's* the one taking me out.

"It's a surprise."

When I'm all alone, chopping onions for the chowder, Mario comes up to the galley and puts a five-pack of flavored ChapStick on the counter for me.

"What's this?" I ask.

"Little something extra for you today, Jess." He flashes me a big, white smile. "Maybe you can share with the captain later on." Wink, wink.

〰〰〰

That evening, all the anticipation has worked its way through me and I'm a basket case. I think about faking food poisoning, which wouldn't be such a huge stretch, since my stomach is in knots and I feel like hurling any minute.

Sammy can read me like an issue of *People* in the checkout line.

"Don't even think about flaking." She is attempting to unspaz my hair, which has taken on epic dreadlocks over the course of my mermaid summer.

"It's too weird. Matthew and me on a date. He's like a brother."

"He *likes* you. What's weird about that? And he's hot. And he's not a drug addict."

"Maybe you should set the bar a little higher."

"Are you going to tell him about the whole mermaid thing?"

"Not yet," I say. It's not the kind of thing you throw out there casually. *Hey, so I'm a fish and I saved a humpback whale and fought off a great white. Could you pass the ketchup?*

"Right. Good. Increase your chances for a second date."

"I'm going to call him. I can't go."

She grabs my phone out of my hand and stuffs it in her back pocket, then spritzes me with detangler. "When's the last time you went on a date? It's been, like, three years, right? Girl, you must be wound up like a bottle of champagne, ready to pop. You *need* this."

Granted, I don't have a fraction of the sexual expertise of Sammy, but I don't feel the need to hook up in order to validate my existence. My needs are much more complicated than that.

"Great advice. Where did you hear that . . . Spencer?"

"I'm serious. You can't keep pushing people away."

I give her a push.

"It's time," she says.

I hate it when people say that. But Sammy was like Kay's sister, too. She's got more skin in the game than the rest of the free-advice-giving public.

"Okay, so I can't use Kay as an excuse. What about the fact that I'm a mermaid? Huh? What about that?"

"Minor bump in the road."

I think about the beating I gave to the lumberjack. *The animal in you is strong,* the seer said. What if I've already lost a part of my human self? I feel different than I did before I caught that barrel. I'm not as in control as I used to be. And I don't know if I can stop what I'm becoming.

"Are you sure this dress isn't too much?" I ask for the millionth time. After much debate, Sammy helped me settle on a hip-hugging crochet dress with a cool surfer girl vibe to it.

She shakes her finger at me. "I don't know how you ended up with a bodacious bod like that from turning into a fish, but you have *got* to flaunt it. Look at you! You are banging!"

"Shut up!"

"You are a bootylicious mama with some junk in the trunk," she says, and slaps my bootylicious bottom. "Where's he taking you, anyway?"

"Wouldn't say. And what's up with that convention anyway? Why should *he* take *me* out? Why does the man get to be in charge?"

"Poor Matthew."

~~~~

Everything is wrong from the start.

Instead of sitting outside and honking his horn like every other guy I've been out with, Matthew actually walks up the stairs to the apartment and knocks.

He's standing there with a look on his face that I can't quite place, except to say it's a look I haven't seen before, and I don't even notice the bouquet of flowers in his hand until he sticks them out in front of me. "You look beautiful. These are for you."

"Oh. Flowers," I say, trying to act totally cool and casual. So this is like a real Date, with Flowers and Everything.

He smiles.

Then there's a really long, awkward pause where I'm standing on one side of the threshold and he's on the other and I just want him to turn around and start walking so we can get this date out of the way, but he obviously wants to drag it out. So I take the flowers and invite him into the apartment.

I poke around the kitchen looking for a vase while Matthew talks to Sammy, but I don't have a vase, since no one ever brings me flowers. I settle on a Big Gulp cup from the 7-Eleven. When I put the flowers in, it tips over, and I have to rummage around for something taller and heavier. I find a glass pitcher that we use for margaritas sometimes.

At least the pitcher doesn't fall over like the Big Gulp cup, but the mouth is too wide and the stems splay out so that the flowers look spindly. I decide that giving flowers to someone kind of sucks and lead Matthew out the door.

Sammy does an obnoxious pelvic thrust dance for me when Matthew has his back turned.

⌇⌇⌇

The big surprise he has planned is a reservation at Au Pied de Cochon—which is literally French for "the Pig's Foot." It's the fanciest restaurant in all Ne'Hwas. Booked all summer long. He must have pulled some strings to get us in.

The inside is elegant, with starched linen tablecloths and place settings that include more silverware than a person can possibly use for one meal. The tables all have floral arrangements that are not jammed into Big Gulp cups or margarita pitchers.

The hostess seats us at a special table on the porch with a fantastic view of the ocean. Matthew pulls my chair out for me, which throws me for a loop. There's a whole bunch of very polite and extravagant offers by the hostess, who assures us that our waiter will be over to serve us shortly, and that she wishes us a pleasant evening, and she insists that we let her know if there's *anything* she can do to make us more comfortable. (I resist telling her that leaving us alone would make me more comfortable.) She isn't gone two seconds before our waiter comes over and goes through the whole rigmarole again.

Then another server comes over and fills our water glasses, and by the time Matthew and I are left alone, we are both so out of place and disoriented we can't find anything to break the nervous silence.

"So . . ." he says, after a dramatically long pause.

"So . . ." I repeat.

I rack my brain for anything to say, but nothing pops up.

"Who do you think's going to win the fishing derby this year?" Matthew finally says.

"Probably Nick." I ponder this thoughtfully. "Yeah, Nick."

He nods like he's considering the depth of my answer. "Yeah, probably right."

"Nick usually wins."

Silence.

"Unless Joey wins. Then I think Nick would come in second." Thank God for Nick, Joey, and Mario. At least we have *something* to talk about.

There's more excruciating silence. The minutes tick away. Matthew smiles and looks away. I look away, too.

The first waiter brings our drinks. I slam my Dark 'n Stormy and Matthew orders me another one. It's obvious we're going to need a little liquid courage on this date. But why? We've had a million conversations about a million different things over the years. There's never been any of this awkward smiling and looking out the window and reaching for things to say to each other. Is it because we're both so focused of how the date will end—i.e., with a kiss, like dates are supposed to end, or without a kiss, which is how really bad dates end?

The fact that I'm in the middle of a fairly big existential

conundrum also looms large. In ten days I'm either going to stay human and continue life as I know it or I'm going to surf through that barrel and never return. And if that's the case, then what am I doing here? Leading on a man I really, really care about?

And that, I realize, is what's truly eating at me. I really, really care about Matthew. I care about him in more than just a guy-I-work-with kind of way. No matter what happens ten days from now, today, I don't want to blow it.

Finally, Matthew comes up with something: "You look really beautiful tonight."

I fake a smile. Not exactly the conversation starter we need.

The waiter comes back with menus and this, at least, gives both of us a distraction. However, it's in French. All I can read are the prices, which are so outrageous that at first I think it must be a joke. This meal will cost a week's worth of tips.

"What are you going to get?" I ask.

Matthew frowns at the menu. "Maybe we should ask the waiter for a suggestion."

"Yeah, they didn't exactly teach French at Ne'Hwas High, did they?"

Matthew forces a smile. "I don't know."

School. Another conversational dead end. He dropped out to help support his mom and started working for Roger. His youth cut short.

At the table next to us, a group of yacht club types orders their food, speaking in fluent French. Even their laughter sounds French.

"Maybe we can ask them to order for us," Matthew says.

I smile, and this forced, fake laugh comes out of me, which is more embarrassing than the silence.

Things don't get any better after that. I finish my drink and order a third. The waiter, who agrees to order for us, brings us an appetizer of escargot, which neither of us knows how to eat and which tastes like snot dipped in butter.

The group next to us only makes things worse, with their booming, confident voices telling stories of their wonderful, worldly lives. One has a son who just graduated from Stanford. Another just closed on a house in Aspen. Someone else is fired up about the trip to India they're taking in the fall. They all have lives elsewhere, but Matthew and I are stuck right here. I've never felt like such a townie as I do while eavesdropping at Au Pied de Cochon.

At least the drinks are softening the hard edges and making me care less about how I might look to the yacht club types.

I get up to go to the bathroom. There's a massive fish tank in the foyer, which faces the dining room on the other side. I stop and look at it. Orange roughies, bonitos, and black bass are packed together so tightly that they bump into one another. Powerful pumps at the top of the tank stir the water into a mini current. A whirlpool spins on the surface. All the fish are on the menu; fresh seafood taken to the extreme.

It might be the three drinks, but I imagine myself jumping in and swimming with them. I crave the weightlessness of it. I want to breathe the dense salt water and hunt for my dinner. A bit of drool gathers at the corner of my mouth.

"Are you all right, dear?" a woman asks as she passes me on her way from the restrooms to the dining room. I must be quite a sight in my hip-hugging dress, drooling at the fish.

"I'm fine, thanks," I say, wiping my lips. I go to the bathroom, splash my face with cold water and return to my seat.

We manage to get through the meal by talking mostly about Harold and the *Dauntless* and the ever-revolving hookups and breakups of the Slack Tide crew.

When the waiter asks us if we'd like to look at the dessert menu, we both give an enthusiastic no.

~~~~

The awkwardness carries over into the truck, but at least now there's a light at the end of the tunnel—an end to the evening.

Matthew and I like each other. We tried to be more than friends. We failed. Simple as that.

Probably for the best. I'm probably leaving to be a fish for the rest of my life. Even if I stay human, he might leave at the end of the summer, head south, and never come back. We're doomed either way.

Thank God for radio. I reach over and turn up the volume.

When we get to Barefoot Lane, Matthew keeps driving.

"Where are you going?"

"One more drink?" he says.

~~~~

Once we're perched on bar stools in the musty air of Dick's Bar, where people still smoke cigarettes inside, I start to relax.

"Do you remember the first time we met?" Matthew asks.

"Nipon Beach. My first time paddling out past the break."

"You were, what, twelve years old?"

"That's right. You took pity on me and gave me pointers," I say.

"It wasn't pity. Not even close." Matthew swivels his stool toward me. "I mean, here's this little grommet paddling out all by herself in these peaky, six-foot swells, getting knocked around, falling off her board every time a wave rolls in, attempting the worst duck dives I've ever seen in my life. I thought, oh man, this girl is going to get slammed and one of us is gonna have to rescue her. All the guys were thinking the same thing. They were already making bets on who would tow you in."

I remember it well. I was young. I had no business attempting the break at Nipon. I swallowed more seawater than a right whale feeding on krill. "Are you hoping to get lucky tonight with all this flattery?"

"Is it working?"

I smile. "Dredging up memories of what a cocky little misfit I was is not going to get you laid."

"I'm not finished," he says.

"Please. Let the humiliation continue."

Matthew smiles. "You made it past the break. Then you caught this wave, right on the shoulder, perfect drop, down the line. There was no hesitation in you. No backing down. You were all-in. Absolutely fearless. You carved a perfect bottom turn, and spun right off the lip. I couldn't believe it. Then, you turn around, paddle back out, and do it again and again and again. I didn't even bother riding any waves that day. All I could do was watch you go. I thought, Wow, this kid knows the secret to life."

I smile. "I remember being scared shitless when I got out the back that day."

"That's not what I saw," he says. "Back then, surfing was my escape. When things got really bad at home, I'd disappear all day in the waves. I'd skip school and surf so I didn't have to explain to the teachers why none of my paperwork was signed by my mom."

"That blows."

"It did. I surfed to get away. The other guys surfed to prove themselves. But you were different. You weren't running away. And you didn't care who you impressed. You were running *toward* something. I was in complete awe of you."

I nearly lose my breath. No one's ever spoken to me like that before. "So you were checking me out when I was twelve years old?" I punch him in the arm. "That's really pervy of you. Sheriff would arrest you."

Matthew's cheeks get red. "It wasn't like that. Not 'til much later."

"What's it like now?" I'm feeling warmed by all the drinks.

"I like you, Jess. I always have." He clears his throat. "I look at you and I see this wildness in you. You never think about the next wave, or the one after that. You go for whatever wave you're on. I love that about you. I loved it about you then, and I love it about you now." Matthew's eyes sparkle this time when he looks at me.

"All-in," I say.

"Exactly."

God he's sexy. I lean toward him until we're touching, and I can feel the warmth of his breath.

"Why did you wait so long to tell me?" I ask.

"I've been waiting for you to be ready. When I saw you at Kay's funeral, I saw how you were. How sad. I was sad for you. I was sad for myself. The world can't afford to lose something as rare as a badass surfer chick."

The knots in my stomach have turned to butterflies and have flown off. I lean in and kiss him. Right in the middle of the bar. And he kisses me back, a kiss as deep as the ocean.

Eighteen

The kiss keeps running through my mind all day. The tenderness in his lips, his strong hands, the taste of cherry-flavored ChapStick. The way he stood at my door and we kissed again before saying good night. I play it over and over as I'm frying up burgers and cleaning gum from underneath tables. I think about it while I'm emptying the grease traps and as we pull into Buster's Wharf in the lazy afternoon, where seals sun themselves on slick black rocks. Captain Ben is at the wheel because Matthew has to do repairs on the *Mack King*.

Is he thinking about me right now like I'm thinking about him?

I keep wondering about Ne'Hwas, too. What kind of life did she carve out for herself? Did she make it to the ocean, or did she stay in the river forever, safe from sharks?

Was she lonely?

After work, I start walking home down the pier, the air thick with ocean, my head full of things I have to do before I leave this human world. I'll have to tell Sheriff where I'm going. Write my mom a letter. Let Sammy know.

And Matthew. I will tell him good-bye.

Instead, I find myself window-shopping along Spinnaker Street, stealing glimpses of the harbor between buildings. I notice the beauty in everything. The wisteria-covered trellises, the antique onion lights, the cobblestone paths built before the first car ever came to the island. A pot filled with marigolds fills me with a sense of wonder.

Even the kitsch shops that sell driftwood lamps and river rock tables seem charming. I peek in the windows of the haberdashery, the silversmith, the marine salvage shop. I study the selection of bleached corals, starfish, and conch shells in Capt. Steve's Shell Shop, none of which come from local waters.

At a shop called Chez Eloise, headless mannequins show off delicate lingerie. Lace bras, teddies, camisoles.

Things other women wear.

I walk in.

The salesclerk, a well-dressed woman in her fifties whose bright red nail polish matches her lipstick, is immediately at my side. I'm vaguely aware that I smell like fish and Lysol.

"Can I help you?"

"No thanks."

She presses her chin into her neck and her eyes are hard and I can feel her watching me as I walk around the racks of expensive, small-enough-to-slip-in-your-pocket merchandise. I have townie written all over me.

A group of girls walks in, all dressed in pretty summer colors. They're talking about the wedding banquet, the wedding night, the wedding dress, the wedding flowers, and it becomes clear that they're here to buy the wedding lingerie, which sends them into bursts of hysterics.

At least they get the salesclerk off my back.

The mother of the bride picks out a white silk bustier and holds it up, but the daughter has something less traditional in mind.

I think about the first time I went bra shopping with my mom. I was thirteen. Mom announced to the saleslady that I was a late bloomer and needed a bra with modest coverage. But the way she said it, dragging out the end, like "bra-a-ah," made it so much more embarrassing than it already was to be shopping with your mom for your first bra at the ripe age of thirteen.

It was pale pink. A-cup. When I got home, I modeled in front of the full-length mirror. Kay walked in. "You got boobs. Congratulations." Kay had already had boobs for quite some time and didn't quite understand the pride I took in producing a tiny patch of cleavage between the pale pink mounds.

I wish my mom was here now. She would know what to do. Choose human or mermaid. But she's on her spirit journey. Shedding her sorrow.

My phone pings with a text from Matthew: *Dinner tonight? I'm cooking.*

I start composing my message: *I'd love to!!!*

Three exclamation points *and* the L word. I delete it and try again: *Didn't know you could cook. Depends on what you're making.*

Delete. Delete. Delete.

Finally I settle on *OK*.

I walk over to the rack of panties on the hangers, with individual price tags—a different class of underwear than the three-for-fifteen-dollars bin at the Kmart. Flipping through the price tags, I choke on my saliva. A day's tips for a pair of panties.

I think about that kiss. Matthew's lips.

I buy the lace panties and head home.

〰〰〰

I keep both hands on the wheel as I head out of the crammed downtown streets, past yacht club row, and out to Kotoki-Pun Point. What am I doing? I'm a fish. I'm leaving this world for the deep, dark, exquisite places of the sea. Where, I remind myself, I won't ever have human suffering, ever again. I'm going to where life is simple and beautiful and free.

Only a coldhearted bitch would lead on a guy as sweet (and hot) as Matthew and then disappear from his life.

So I won't lead him on. I will let him cook me dinner. Then I will tell him I just want to be friends. I'll tell him I'm heading out on a spirit journey to find myself, or some lame excuse like that.

Matthew opens the door, his hair still wet from the shower, his blue eyes brilliant against his sun-kissed tan, and I immediately start to rethink my plan. He's dressed in a button-down oxford shirt and jeans without holes in the knees. His smile peeks out beneath his beard, and I want to lean in and kiss him right there.

Instead, I jam my hands into my pockets and stand miserably at the door, wishing I had never found that barrel. Wishing I didn't have to choose.

I'm also feeling really underdressed. I could have put more effort into my old flannel shirt and running shorts, which together don't add up to the price of the underwear beneath them.

"Uh. I should have brought some wine, or a six-pack, or something."

"I've got everything here, Creary. Come in."

Alice and Roger's house used to be the lighthouse keeper's cottage at Kotoki-Pun Point, back when the lighthouse required a keeper to climb the stairs each evening and light the mantles by hand. But electricity came to the island, then computers, and the job became obsolete.

Inside, the walls are papered in faded floral print. Peonies. Alice's favorite, Matthew tells me.

"I bet you've got some needlepoint pillows shoved in a closet somewhere."

"Only bring those out for special occasions."

I pick up a glass candy bowl. "Do you by any chance have a grandma fetish?"

"You can read me like a book, Creary." I follow him down a hall. "I'm just taking care of the house until Alice decides to sell it. It's a great place. And wait until you see this."

The hallway opens up to the bedroom, which takes my breath away. The room is sparsely furnished. Only a bed, mirror, and bureau. It has a high ceiling and is flooded with light. An entire wall of windows faces east, revealing a panoramic view of the ocean. It feels like we're standing on the edge of the world.

I can feel my heart skip. His house is perfect. And he's perfect—this beautiful, sensitive man who braves the roughest seas and saves time to do good deeds for old ladies in nursing homes.

"So is this how you lure women into bed? Show them the kick-ass bedroom and tell them how beautiful the sunrise will be in the morning?"

"No. It's not . . . I'm not . . ." He looks deflated. "That's not really what you think I'm doing, is it?"

There's an agonizing silence, and I wish I could take the words back. But snarky and apathetic is my go-to defense mechanism, honed over years in principals' offices and in front of Sheriff.

"I'm going on a spirit journey," I blurt out.

It's totally abrupt and it makes him laugh. "Okay. Would you like some cod before you go? Because I've got some in the fridge that needs to be grilled."

~~~~

Dinner is perfect and torturous. He's grilled the cod with lemon and fresh ginger. He's made a salad and picked wild daisies and black-eyed Susans from the fields that surround the house. He tells me about the long, hard trips out in the Gulf of Mexico, where the seas get so rough that sometimes you don't know if your boat will hold. He tells me how incredibly boring it is, until all of a sudden you've got a full catch and it's the opposite of boring. When the work is good, the adrenaline drives you through, from night all the way into the next day.

"I think you'd love it down south," he says. "The work is hard, but there's a lot of opportunity for someone like you."

"Someone like me?"

"You know, a true waterman. Not many people can handle being out there. The waves get to them. The sun. Fishing all day."

"Do you think you'll ever stay down there? Leave Ne'Hwas after season and not come back?" I ask.

He grimaces. "That depends." I feel my heart pounding.

This is my opportunity to tell him. This is when I let him down easy. Tell him I just want to be friends. But when I look into his eyes, I feel like the cowardly lion.

"What about you? What's in your future?" he asks.

"In the future . . . I would like one of those warm chocolate chip cookies I saw on the stove."

"Jess Creary, I've held eels less slippery than you," he says.

He gets the cookies and I clear the plates. We meet in the middle of the floral kitchen. He puts a hand on the small of my back, where my tail meets skin, and kisses me.

My heart is beating so hard it's pounding in my ears. It might even be shaking the whole house.

We move from the kitchen to the living room and can't keep our hands off each other. He tastes like warm cookie. Once we're on the floral couch, I let my hands explore his chest, his arms, feeling the solid mass of muscle underneath. He caresses my shoulders. Then he pulls away. "I want to take it slow. Is that okay?"

I don't have time for slow, I want to say. But I tell him yes, it's okay.

We decide to watch a movie.

Matthew opens a closet stocked with VHS tapes. I find *Splash*, that movie from the early eighties with Tom Hanks and Daryl Hannah. He sticks the old relic into the VHS machine and the picture comes on.

The movie is hysterical, just like I remember when I watched it as a kid. A mermaid wanders naked into New York City, looking for her long-lost love. Hilarity ensues as she navigates the human world, and her commitment-phobic man friend finds the true meaning of love. It's a light-hearted romantic comedy with a mermaid twist. There's nothing about how mermaids are the apex predator of the sea, or the great act of courage required to cross into that world.

And then the last scene plays. With the help of the quirky scientist who exposed her, and the nutty brother, Tom Hanks breaks Daryl Hannah out of captivity to release her back into the wild. There's a car chase scene, which is pretty ridiculous. And then they get to the pier. Daryl Hannah kisses him good-bye and jumps into the Hudson River to return to her world. Tom Hanks is left standing alone and morose. Then he has one of those Hollywood moments when he realizes that love conquers all, and he throws himself into the water. Daryl Hannah comes back for him and they swim hand in hand to happily ever after.

As I burrow my head into the crook of Matthew's arm and he kisses my forehead, an idea forms in my head. Maybe he can surf that barrel, too. Maybe giving up his life for his girlfriend can be his act of courage that transports him to the mermaid world. Maybe he can come with me.

The question is, will he?

NINETEEN

Aboard the *Dauntless,* Matthew and I try to keep our relationship hush-hush, but I'm drawn to him like hydrogen to oxygen. Sal notices first. "I'm feeling the vibe between you two," he says, nodding his head, blond locks tumbling over his face. Stefan catches Matthew kissing my shoulder and wants to know if we're mutually exclusive or if he still has a chance with me. Finally, Tony catches us touching hands in the galley, and once Tony knows, it takes about three seconds for the rest of the Slack Tide crew to find out, including Harold, who gives us both a stern warning about the pitfalls of love and marriage, as well as about the sin of putting pleasure before business.

For the first time all summer, my mind isn't on waves. I don't worry about sharks. I don't see swirling schools of fish when I close my eyes. All I can focus on is the fisherman.

After work, Matthew asks if he can take me to Lobsterfest.

"It's so touristy," I say.

"I love Lobsterfest. Those claw hats just kill me. Come with me," Matthew says.

His enthusiasm is irresistible. Besides, we only have eight days left before I leave him for good, or convince him to come with me. I'll take all the time I can get.

Lobsterfest started out small and authentic. A vacant meadow near the airfield in mid-July, when the lobsters are molting and lobstermen have a glut of soft shell lobsters on their hands they can't ship any great distance. They'd throw a huge party with all-you-can-eat lobsters and unlimited butter.

Over time, it's grown up. The venue was moved. T-shirts were made. Someone hands out funny hats with lobster claws sticking out the sides. Musicians were brought in. A writer from *Travel + Leisure* stumbled on it. Now it's in every tourist brochure. "The hidden gem of Ne'Hwas," they proclaim.

~~~~

As soon as we step out of Matthew's pickup, my ears start ringing. Pressure is building in the atmosphere.

"There's a storm coming," I say.

Matthew looks at me curiously. "A system's rolling in from the south, but it'll hold off until early morning."

"Rain. Tonight," I whisper. I know it the same way that horses predict hurricanes or service dogs warn their humans of epileptic seizures before they happen.

"Do you know something the radar doesn't?" Matthew asks. "Is divining the weather one of your many talents?"

Black birds circle low in the blue sky and then dart off to the tree line on the far end of the field.

"What other talents do I have?"

"Too many to count, Creary."

Matthew grins and holds my hand as we walk through the crowd. Smells of fried dough and boiling lobster fill the air. The small festival I remember has morphed into a bona fide fair, with food trucks, vendors, beer gardens, and street performers. Even the mime from the pier at Galleon Marina is here. He sees us, points to me and Matthew, brings his fingers together, and makes a kissy face. This time, we oblige.

Little kids run around in lobster claw hats, and everywhere we go, fishermen stop to talk to Matthew. They want to know how the cod are running out in the basin, or if he has any leads on pollock runs. They slap him on the back and throw their arms around his shoulders, and make sure he's placed his bet on the live lobster race.

A boy of about ten or eleven runs up to us. "Hey, buddy. What's happening?" Matthew says, and fist-bumps the kid.

"Will you take me out on the boat this week?" the kid asks.

"You bet. I'll let you drive," Matthew says.

The boy rubs his hands together and runs back to the other fishermen-family kids to share his good fortune.

"Roger and Alice's niece's kid. I've known him since he was a baby," Matthew tells me.

"He worships you," I say. "It's obvious." Everyone worships Matthew. Kids, old men with raccoon eyes from sunglasses and hours spent at sea, women.

And, I realize, these are his people. His family.

"Everyone loves you," I say, awed myself.

Matthew blushes. "These are good people. Hardworking. They looked out for me when my mom died, along with Roger and Alice. They're all the family I've got."

Everyone here knows what he went through. They helped him out, showed him love, and like the golden son, he rose above his crappy circumstances to become the pride and joy of Nipon Beach.

Why would he ever give this up to spend his life in the sea with me? Would I do that for him?

Could we ever have a family of our own in the sea? Or is the way of Ne'Hwas a genetic dead end? I've never thought about having kids. I've never given much thought to the future. But suddenly these questions seem important.

We wander over to the lobster tent, where the line is about a mile long. There's a separate station entirely for butter. It occurs to me that I haven't eaten a cooked lobster all summer.

"Welcome to the hidden gem of Ne'Hwas." I say.

"Let me see what I can do."

As we head over to giant steel pots billowing steam, there's a commotion near the row of vendors. A girl screams. In between the Holy Cannoli truck and the head shop guy who sells glass pipes shaped like skulls, a man is peeing in the grass. He teeters back and forth, and flashes a toothless smile to bystanders.

Some people are laughing, some look horrified, and then there's the girl who keeps screaming like she's witnessing a murder.

The sideshow turns into an even bigger spectacle when Sheriff pushes through the crowd. In his uniform, he looks very official. He tells the drunk to zip up his pants, then cuffs him. With authority, Sheriff settles down the crowd and restores order.

It always feels strange to see Sheriff in action. To see him the way the world sees him, protecting and serving.

"Jess. What a surprise," he says. Then he notices Matthew standing beside me and makes a funny face like he's concerned and happy all at once. "What are you doing here?"

"Trying not to get urinated on, apparently."

"Sorry 'bout that," the drunk says, quite sincerely.

"Stay there, Teddy. I need to talk to my daughter."

"You got it, Sheriff," the man says, and stays put while Sheriff steps out of pee-puddle range, toward me and Matthew.

"Aren't you worried he's going to run?" I ask, nodding toward the drunk.

"Nah. Teddy Abbott's a frequent flier in lockup. I think he enjoys it. Rap sheet like *War and Peace,* that guy. Totally harmless, though."

Teddy Abbott interrupts to ask if cell number four is free this evening. "That's my favorite," he says, a dumb smile plastered on his face.

Sheriff ignores him. Sticks a firm hand out to Matthew. "Good to see you, Matthew."

Matthew shakes his hand. "You too, sir."

Sir? I get the feeling that my father and Matthew have met before under different circumstances. It adds up. Sheriff worked the Nipon Beach beat for years. And Matthew lived in Nipon

Beach, with a rap sheet—though more like a haiku than *War and Peace*.

I'm sure Sheriff has a less flattering image of Matthew than his admirers at Lobsterfest. I wonder if Sheriff noticed that Matthew was at Kay's funeral. There were so many people in attendance. True friends who shed real tears. Fake friends like Bree Hamilton. All those peers shimmering with potential, paying tribute, making promises. They will call you every week. They will change their lives for the better to honor the dead. They will live every day like it's their last. They will keep her memory alive. They will never forget.

But they forget.

"Are you two dating?" Sheriff asks.

Oh my God. Why must fathers be so socially inept? "Kind of," I snap.

"I see," Sheriff says. He peers at Matthew. "Are you still living out at Nipon Beach, then?"

"No, sir. I'm staying at Kotoki-Pun Point, in the old lighthouse."

Sheriff smiles crookedly. "Very good. Nice place out there."

"Can I get you lobster, Officer Creary?" Matthew asks.

"That's mighty nice of you, son, but I need to get this character into booking."

It's pretty adorable how Matthew is trying to impress my father. "Would you grab lobsters for us? I'll find a spot on the grass," I say.

When Matthew is out of earshot, Sheriff says, "Matthew Weatherby, hey?"

"Yeah."

"Is it pretty serious? I mean, are you looking at a future together?"

The million-dollar question, I think. "Honestly, I don't know yet."

"He's kind of a drifter, isn't he? Spends summers on Ne'Hwas. Takes off the rest of the year."

This makes me a little defensive of Matthew. "He works the commercial fishing boats down south. That doesn't make him a drifter. It makes him seasonal. Like a lot of people here."

"I don't want you to get hurt, Jess."

"Dad," I say. That word again. So generic, and yet so incredibly specific. "I need to talk to you about something."

"I need to talk to you, too." He rubs the bridge of his nose. "I've been feeling just awful about what I did to you. I'm ashamed of myself."

I bite my nails. "What are you talking about?"

He tilts his head. "The morning after you didn't come home and I was out looking for you. It was wrong of me to raise my hand against you. I wish I could take it back."

"Oh. That. Don't worry about it."

"I've spent my entire career chasing after scumbags who hit women."

"I can be difficult. Believe me, I know that. I probably deserved it."

"No you didn't." He looks like he might cry. "It was a terrible thing for me to do. I am truly sorry."

"I forgive you."

"Well, I can't forgive myself."

I hug him. I'm the one who should be sorry. I'm the one who's going to swim away, out of his life forever. "There's something I need to tell you, Sheriff."

Suddenly, the speakers on the bandstand crackle to life. There's a sound like someone tapping the microphone, and an earsplitting squeal of feedback from the loudspeakers.

"Uh. Oh. Hi. Is this thing on?" a voice echoes out.

I look up. Trip Sinclair is on stage.

"Hi, folks. This will only take a moment of your time." That smile. Plastered across his face. "I'm here on behalf of the Sinclair Foundation, a nonprofit organization run by my family."

I look at Sheriff. His lips disappear into a tight line. His hands are in fists.

Trip's voice penetrates the air. "As you might or might not know, the Sinclair Foundation runs charities throughout the Northeast. With the strong ties to Ne'Hwas that my family shares, we wanted to bring our philanthropy a little closer to home. Today, we're happy to announce that the Sinclair Foundation has set up a college scholarship fund for one student from Ne'Hwas." Trip clears his throat. "The Kay Creary Scholarship will help ensure that Ne'Hwas residents will have opportunities for generations for come. We hope that honoring the memory of this intelligent, dynamic young woman . . ." He pauses and puts a fist to his mouth like he's going to cry. "A woman I was lucky enough to call my friend . . . We hope that by remembering her, we can help bring hope for the future."

The muscles in my body become rigid. There's a ringing in my ears. The pressure is closing in around me.

I am headed straight for the stage. This is not right. Trip got away with murdering my sister and now he's trying spin it into good press for his family.

When I get to the stage, a photographer from the *Daily News* is taking Trip's photo. A reporter is asking questions and Trip is answering with his usual arrogance. "My family is here to help those less fortunate," I hear him say. I'm near the stage. The reporter walks away. Trip pulls out a cigarette and lights it.

I'm in front of him. "You have no right to use Kay's name."

He chuffs out a line of smoke. "First of all, you're welcome," he says. "This is a big honor for your family. Kay's memory will be preserved forever."

"You don't care about Kay's memory. You're just trying to make yourself look good."

There are people all around us, staring at us, waiting for the train to wreck.

"Kay was a friend. I'm trying doing the right thing."

"The right thing would be not killing her."

"It was an accident."

"It was your fault!"

I'm right next to him now and I can smell whiskey on him. He leans toward me, his hot breath on my ear. His eyes are raw and red. "You want to know the truth. I wish I'd never met Kay. It ruined my life."

"Your life? You have a life. Kay doesn't."

I can't move. My head is spinning. The animal takes over. I push Trip Sinclair hard in the chest. I'm stronger than he expects and he falls down, coughing. Grant le Carre, scumbag lawyer, steps between me and Trip. "This is assault," le Carre announces.

Trip pulls the cigarette from his mouth.

Sheriff is beside me now. "That's enough," he says.

"He can't get away with this!" All I can see is red. The sky is red. The trees are red. Trip's eyes are devil red.

"Don't make it worse," Sheriff says, and his voice sounds so small and broken that I want to die right here.

"Control your daughter or we will press charges," le Carre is saying, somewhere in the ether around me.

"Get her out of here, please." It's Sheriff voice. I realize that he's talking to Matthew, who's holding two lobster plates in his hands. Matthew drops the lobsters in the grass and takes me gently by the hand.

The first drops of rain splatter on the field.

Trip is absorbed into a group of people, *his* people, congratulating him. They flash me looks that say *I'm* the psycho. I'm the criminal. I'm the ungrateful townie who has just snubbed a gift of charity by a great and generous family.

Then the deluge comes. All around, people run for cover. Trip and his people are whisked away in town cars parked behind the stage. Children splash in puddles and are pulled away by parents. A sudden exodus for the parking lot.

I let go of Matthew's hand and run.

I run and run and run, the rain beating at the earth.

I run because I'm angry and afraid and sick. I run because people like Trip Sinclair get to go on living golden lives while my sister stays twenty-three forever. I run until I slip and fall to ground. And then I start crying.

I close my eyes and turn my face up to the sky. The temperature drops, but I don't care. Mentally, I send myself back to ocean, where everything is simple, uncomplicated. Where no one feels betrayal or hatred or cheated. I try to put myself in that world, flying weightlessly through the water.

When I open my eyes, Matthew is kneeling in front of me, blinking rain from his eyes, letting it run down his hair.

"Are you okay?" he asks.

"I need to get away from all this."

"You don't mean that."

"I can't stand it anymore, Matthew. I need to leave here and never come back."

"Then I'll come with you."

"You don't even know where I'm going."

"Don't need to. Wherever you are, that's where I want to be." He wipes the water out of his eyes, and it's instantly replenished. "I love you, Creary. Don't you know that?"

I thrust myself into his arms and kiss him. The rain washes over us, drenching us in its magnificent splendor.

TWENTY

The great white is near. Vibrations pulse down my sides. Her heart beats in my veins. There's a slight rise in temperature against my skin.

I smell the sour note of fear and realize the fear is coming from me.

The water is gray and murky. My eyesight fails me. There are no animals lit up in neon pixels of light. Not a living thing is near. It's getting darker with every moment; the edges of my vision are closing in. Soon it will be pitch black. I need to get home.

Little by little, I inch my way out from my ledge, exposing my forehead, my neck, my shoulders. Maybe I can outswim her. The electromagnetic impulses intensify, throbbing down my spine now. I slide backwards into my ledge.

I watch and wait. And worry.

She grabs me from behind and pulls me violently into the cave. I reach for rock, seaweed, sand, anything to grasp onto. I'm being pulled backwards, farther and farther into the dark recesses. Blood darkens the water black. But I don't feel pain.

I turn around. A thousand gleaming white teeth are clamped onto my tail. Scales sail through the water.

I struggle to break free, but I can't get away. She thrashes her head, shaking me like a chew toy, bumping my head against the cave.

There's a noise outside the cave. A pounding, then a clanging. Laughter. The sound of someone trying not to make noise. My heart races.

≈≈≈≈

I bolt upright in bed.

The noises are outside my bedroom. Matthew is lying beside me, breathing heavily, lost in his own dreams.

Glass crashes on the floor. A thump.

In one move, I fling off the quilt, fly across my room, and open the door. Darkness blankets the apartment. I detect movement near the window. My senses tell me it's bigger than me. My brain screams *attack*.

I am a predator.

I leap on top of the intruder. He is a big man. Strong. But I am stronger. I push him to the floor, grinding a knee into his abdomen. I lay punches into the side of his face. Across his nose. I'm vaguely aware that he is saying something. Screaming something. He gets a hand free from my legs and pulls on my arm, so I force the hand back under my knee.

The lights go on.

But my eyes don't see.

Sammy is screaming at me to stop.

Matthew is yelling at me to stop.

There are hands on me. My brain is telling me *three against one—fight!*

Slowly, the details of the room come into focus—the papasan chair with the patched cushion. The lobster trap coffee table. The Oriental rug worn thin on the edges. The tapestry on the wall. The smell of incense and candle wax. The dead geranium on the windowsill.

Spencer lying on the floor, crouched in pain, and Sammy tending to him. I am in Matthew's arms. He's holding me, but not in a gentle embrace. He's restraining me.

Sammy is crying. "What the fuck, Jess?"

"Dude, I think she cracked a rib," Spencer says, and there's pain in his voice.

"What happened?" I ask.

"You went totally ballistic on me."

"You must have thought he was breaking in," Matthew says. I search Matthew's face for a clue. His eyebrows are furrowed and I can't read his expression. Is it disgust? Horror?

"I lost my key." Spencer says, rocking on the floor. "Sammy wasn't answering her phone, so I came in through the window. I've done it a million times."

"I'm sorry," I say, wrapping my arms across my chest.

Matthew helps Spencer sit up.

"Thanks, bro."

Together, Sammy and Matthew get Spencer to the couch. Sammy finds a pack of frozen peas in the freezer and covers Spencer's eye with it.

"Dude. Jess," Spencer says. "You been taking steroids or something?" He looks at Matthew. "She's really strong. Like freaky strong, bro. I felt like I had a linebacker holding me down."

"I'm sorry, Spencer. I'm so sorry. I was asleep. I heard noises."

"You're like the female version of the Hulk, man. You're like a jacked pro wrestler." Blood seeps from Spencer's nose.

Sammy comes back from the bathroom with a first aid kit and rifles through it. "There's no fucking Band-Aids in this stupid thing." She dumps the contents on the floor and starts patching Spencer back together with gauze pads and Neosporin.

Matthew is helping Sammy with the first aid kit, and all I can do is keep apologizing to Spencer.

Sammy's face is twisted in a knot when she looks up at me. She's angry at me, but it's more than anger. She's worried.

"You have to stop it, Jess," Sammy says. Her cheeks are wet with tears.

"I felt threatened. I reacted," I say. "It's natural."

"You're not an animal! You've got to stop going out there. It's turning you into something you're not."

"Sammy, please. Don't say any more," I plead.

Spencer chimes in. "Don't worry about it. I was about to turn it around on her. She was getting tired. It's the whole cop's daughter thing, right? Yeah. That's it. You've got that killer attack instinct cops have. Ow, my ribs."

"You're turning into a monster," Sammy says.

Matthew looks at me, waiting for me to say something to set this straight, but I don't. He speaks for me. "I think she heard noises and thought someone was breaking in."

"Spencer wasn't breaking in. He's here all the time!" Sammy yells.

Spencer's lying on the couch half moaning, half laughing. "She's got some power behind those punches."

"Lie still." Sammy dabs his lip with peroxide.

"Oo-w-www." Spencer brushes her hand away. "Dudes, listen. No one can know that I was tossed by a girl. They'll never let me live it down. The story is I fell down the stairs. Got it?"

"She almost killed you," Sammy says.

"Give me a break. She was getting tired." Spencer starts laughing hysterically.

"At least he might be drunk enough to kill some of the pain," Matthew says.

Sammy won't look at me. I've never seen her so pissed off. I have to hand it to her, though—as angry as she is, she's not giving up my mermaid secret. She mumbles about how I've crossed the line, how I have to give it up, how I'm out of control. But nothing about my magical double life.

Matthew, ever the gentleman, offers to run to the pharmacy to pick up some Advil and bandages.

"Why don't you come with me?" he says.

~~~~

It's still pouring out and we're in the parking lot of the pharmacy. Matthew's fingers rest on the key in the ignition, but it doesn't move. The windows of the truck fog over from the inside as we sit there, waiting for the words that need to be said. An employee in a red vest smokes a cigarette under the eaves of the pharmacy, blowing rings at the LET'S QUIT TOGETHER and OPEN 24 HOURS neon signs.

"I ruined everything, didn't I?" I say.

Matthew stares straight ahead, every exhale audible through the patter of rain. He looks at the truck parked next to us, with a dreamcatcher dangling from the rearview mirror.

"I'm worried about you," he says.

The night comes back to me in delicious flashes. Lobsterfest. The way Matthew's eyes looked even bluer in the mottled sky. Trip Sinclair on the microphone. The rage inside of me. The sky turning gray. The downpour. Matthew and I kissing in the rain, the water washing over us. More kissing in the truck. Inviting him back to my place. The tender way he stood outside my door as I fumbled with the keys, telling me he didn't want to rush anything. Me, pulling him inside.

Tossing off our wet, muddy clothes in a corner and taking a hot shower together. Surrounded by steam. Matthew telling me I'm beautiful, telling me that he loves me. Going back into my bedroom.

Making love.

Hearing the words "I love you."

Realizing that I'm in love with him, too. Ever since I can remember, I've always wondered how people know they're in love. What mysterious force compels two people to utter those words to each other? Is it something you just say to make the other person feel good about themselves? Does it just happen casually over time? I've wondered, and now I know.

It's like how a baby discovers gravity. It's something that's been there right along, but finally they trust it. It's ten years of friendship condensed into a single moment. I knew it in my heart, my mind, and my body, all at once.

Now the distance between us is like the Mariana Trench. Matthew twists his beard. Rain thrums on the roof of the truck, filling the silence.

"It was an accident. I heard a noise. I reacted. I didn't mean to hurt him."

"That was a big reaction."

Rain coats the windshield, blurring the world outside.

I choke back a tear. "It must have been the adrenaline. Please don't make a big deal out of it." His truck smells like WD-40 and metal tools. Maps of Texas and Florida are stuffed in the side pocket of the door. I think about him leaving at the end of the season, heading south. I think about me leaving through that barrel, never coming back. And wondering how in the world I can convince him to come with me.

"You know how you asked me why I keep coming back to Ne'Hwas?" he says.

"Why *do* you keep coming back?"

"Because of you."

I inhale so deeply that I might suffocate all the living things around me.

He continues, "I don't want to be stuck on this island forever. I don't want to depend on ferries from the mainland. I want a life as deep as the ocean. Fathomless. And every time I'm down south, thinking of what I want my life to be, you're always in it." He looks into my eyes. "You're the reason I keep coming back, Creary."

I lean toward him, but he doesn't move toward me. He turns away.

"But what I saw back there was not the girl I know. First you attack Trip Sinclair. Then you almost kill Spencer. What's going on with you?"

I hiccup. "It's hard to explain."

"Try me."

"I just . . . I'm going through some changes."

"I've seen behavior like that before." He puts both hands on the wheel, the tension in his shoulders visible.

"What do you mean?"

"Are you using?"

"Using what?"

"Drugs."

"No," I say indignantly. "Of course not."

"No meth? Heroin? Crack?"

"No!"

"Because I've seen how aggressive meth heads can get. How unpredictable they are. My mother was pretty . . . unstable at the end. There were users who came around the house, looking for a score." His voice is strained. His eyes are watery. "I had to step in a few times. With guys much bigger than me. They had that same sort of look in their eye that you had. Disconnected from reality. My mother had that look, too. Do you have any idea what it feels like to have someone you love with all your heart disconnect from the world around her?"

"I swear I'm not using." I cry.

He cries, too. "I wish I could believe you."

"Matthew, I'm sorry that you had to go through that with your mother, but it's not like that with me."

"I can't be around that again. Not ever."

"I swear to you, it's not drugs," I whimper. I look at my legs, at the chiseled lines of muscle that have formed over the past few weeks.

"What, then?"

I take a deep breath of air, wishing it were water. Wishing I could be swimming through the ocean with Matthew beside me, where the past can't hurt us anymore.

"I need to show you," I say. "Will you come surfing with me?"

TWENTY-ONE

The next day, Matthew and I load our boards into the back of his pickup. His is black from years of dust and neglect. Once upon a time it was a hot fish board that ripped; now it looks like it's held together with spit and wax. I hope he's not as rusty as his board.

As we head across from the lee to the windward side of the island, the wind whips the road, flattening the dune grass and bouncing our boards around. It's a strong onshore wind, which means waves will be steep and will close out fast.

I can feel his anxiety in small pulses down my spine.

"It'll be fine," I say, trying to sound confident, but when we pull into the main lot at Nipon Beach, I'm not so sure. Waves break in random peaks in every direction. Wind shears off the tops of the big rollers, sending spray into the sky. Crashing waves echo like a drum across the beach. I can sense his apprehension.

"Can't you just show me what you have to show me?" Matthew asks.

"It's out there," I say, pointing to the water.

"I don't know, Creary. Looks a little too rough."

"You can do it. You can surf this."

He shakes his head. "I know my limits."

The wind drowns out our voices. I look out at the surf. Waves like this are tough even for someone who's in fantastic surfing shape, not to mention for a guy who sits behind the wheel of a boat all day.

"You'll have to show me another time," he says.

"I can't," I yell over the wind. "We're running out of time. You need to see it today so you can decide for yourself."

"Decide what? What is with all the mystery? Just tell me what it is."

"I promise, you'll understand everything once we're out there." If only I can get Matthew inside that barrel and transport him to the other side, let him feel what it's like to swim like a dolphin, to experience the majesty of it, he'll have to come with me.

He twists his beard. "I'm not the surfer I used to be, and I'm not half the surfer you are. Those are big waves."

"I'll help you."

"I don't think so," his voice rises over the wind.

Fine. If he won't come with me, he's going to have to watch me. "Then just wait for me on the beach at Tutatquin Point."

"You're really going to surf? And you say you're not on crack."

That makes me smile. "I can handle this."

"Now you're just getting cocky."

We look out at the surf. There's only one brave soul hitting the waves today. Freddie Collins catches an ugly wave that breaks in both directions. He does a hard bottom turn, cuts up to the lip, and jumps the whitewash. It's a subtle move but it buys him an extra few seconds of standing time. The next wave breaks behind him and he gets raked over. His rides the whitewash on his belly all the way in.

He un-Velcros his leash, tucks his board under his arm, and runs over to us. "I'm glad you're here." There's a look in his eye you don't often see in a waterman like him. Fear.

"What is it?" I ask.

"I tried to stop him," Freddie says, out of breath, the wind blowing droplets of water off his hair. "It's heavy out there, man. Not a day to try something stupid."

"You tried to stop who?"

"Jay."

My eyes search the waves, but no other surfers are out.

Freddie points. "There."

"Tutatquin Point?" Matthew asks.

"He says he saw you catch a barrel there, Jess. Swears you disappeared in the wave. He saw you go under and didn't see you surface. Thought you were dead. Then you showed up the next day without a scratch on you. I told him he must have seen a seal or a cormorant."

"Oh, no." My heart races.

"I tried to stop him," Freddie says. "He was half crazed. Couldn't stand the fact that you discovered virgin territory. He knows every break on the island."

"He can't surf there!" I can feel the blood rush to my head. I feel protective of my secret portal. And Jay Delgado! Ugh. Of all the people to share that magical world with.

"That's what I told him. Even on a good day, he'd never make it past the boneyard," Freddie says.

I squint over at Tutatquin Point, searching the unrelenting crash of waves for Jay.

Matthew pulls out his phone. "I'm going to call the harbor police. At least they can pick him up if he got swept out in a rip."

"No. I'll get him," I say.

Freddie and Matthew both look at me as though I just threatened to bomb the president.

"You won't make it," Freddie says.

"I will."

"No one's questioning your abilities, Jess, but you can't risk your own safety," Freddie says. "We don't want to pull two bodies out of the water today."

I put my hand over Matthew's phone. "Harbor police are on the other side of the island. Sheriff works patrol boat shifts all the time, so I know. They won't get a boat out here for at least thirty minutes. I can get him."

"I'm coming with you, then," Matthew says, his voice deep.

"I'll be okay." There's a flash of understanding between us. What I'm really saying is I'll be better off on my own.

"Fine," he says.

That's a pretty emasculating thing for a guy to admit. But Matthew isn't like any other guy I know. He's not afraid to show his vulnerable side. If anyone is going to go through that barrel and join me on the other side, I want it to be Matthew. Not Jay Delgado.

I run back to the truck, strip down to my bikini, and grab my board. I run down the beach and into the breaking waves.

"Be careful," Matthew screams.

But I don't need to be careful. I am of the sea.

I paddle like a rocket. I paddle like my life depends on it. I paddle like someone who doesn't want her secrets exposed. Even when I duck dive, I keep my momentum forward, kicking under the water, throttling ahead. By the time I make it past the break, I'm not even breathing hard. I am a shark in a human suit.

Past the break, I turn so I'm parallel to shore and paddle toward the face of Tutatquin Point, my arms pulling a steady rhythm through the water. Wind whips in my ears and the spray stings my eyes, but nothing slows me down. My board slices through water like a powerboat. In no time, I'm all the way at Tutatquin, past the sandbar. I stop to get a land bearing: tallest spruce and parallel to the last outcrop. This is the sweet spot; this where Jay should be. But he's nowhere in sight.

I scan the water for him. *Jay! Where are you? Jay Delgado!* My view of shore is swallowed up every time I dip into a trough. As I rise up onto the peaks I look west to east, east to west. At the edge of the boneyard, a smear of yellow against the blue-black waves catches my eye. Jay's board. A frothing mass of white water tosses the board into the rocks. But no Jay.

For a second, I panic. He must have caught a barrel. He

grabbed one of these heavy waves, locked in, and rode into mer-
maidville. Ditched his board in the wash as his body went through
the terrific transformation to cold-blooded.

Then I notice a speck in the field of whitewash. A head. Jay
is in the boneyard. His head goes under and resurfaces, his arms
clawing at the surface. He goes under again with the next wave.
A minute later, his head breaks the surface and his struggles to
keep it up.

He's not transforming into a merman.

He's drowning.

And a different type of panic sets in.

I lie flat and start paddling toward him. If Jay dies out here,
it's on me. Maybe no one else would see it that way. They'd blame
it on his own arrogance. But I would know better.

As much as I despise the guy, I'm not a monster.

"Hold on. I'm coming."

I race toward him. A wave crashes behind me, sending an ava-
lanche of white water my way. I need to bail out or I'm going to
get a facial against the rocks below.

I sit up and pull hard on the rails of my board, against the force
of water behind me, putting on the brakes. It works. The churning mass of white passes without dragging me into its trail. I lie
back down and paddle straight for Jay.

His head goes under one last time and doesn't come up. I
unleash, roll off my board, and dive. Under water, I can see his
body as a dark shadow against the blue water. I swim to him, grab
him by the arm, and pull him up to the surface. My board is ten
feet away. I can't tell if Jay's unconscious, dead, or alive. I loop
an arm across his chest and swim with him to my board.

"Jay. Jay!"

He doesn't respond. I shimmy my board beneath him and lay
on top of him to paddle us in. But with an extra hundred and
eighty pounds on my board, there's not enough lift for both of

us. I have to slide off and push the board from behind while holding his weight on the center of the board. A wave topples Jay off. He starts to go under. I grab him again and lift him back on the board.

Kicking through the boneyard is a struggle. I slash my knees on a rock. We get swept sideways in a swirling eddy. Finally, I get us in to waist-deep water, where I can stand and push Jay to shore.

Freddie and Matthew run toward us and spring into action.

Together, we lift the board, with Jay on top of it, over the rocks to the stand of knotty pines on shore. Out of the howling wind, in the quiet of trees, I can hear how hard the three of us are breathing; Matthew and Freddie from running all the way down from Nipon Beach, me from swimming. How Jay isn't.

"Lay him down," Matthew says.

Blood runs from gashes on Jay's shoulder, above his eye, and other places I can't see. Freddie checks for a pulse.

"Ambulance is on the way," Matthew says.

"He's not breathing," Freddie says. He kneels in the sand and starts mouth-to-mouth.

Matthew and I stand back and watch. Adrenaline is coursing through my body, and I can smell it in the air.

I feel Matthew's gaze turn from Jay to me.

Gently, he takes my hand. "Are you okay?"

I nod. "I'm fine."

Matthew's eyes are like saucers. "How did you do that?"

I shrug. Freddie presses the butt of his palms into Jay's chest, coaxing it to beat. "One and two and three and four and five and six . . ." Versed, like every Ne'Hwas native, in the language of drowning victims.

"What, exactly, did you want to show me today?" Matthew whispers.

"Matthew, I . . ." I want to tell him, but not like this. I need him to *see*.

Water spurts out of Jay's mouth.

"Help me roll him on his side," Freddie says.

We drop to our knees and roll Jay onto his side. He coughs out seawater and blood. The relief I feel is as solid as the carpet of pine needles below us.

"What happened?" Jay asks, as Freddie helps him sit up.

"Jess saved you," Matthew says. "You would have drowned."

Jay looks at me. "But how did you . . ." His words drift off.

"You could have died, Jay. And worse, someone else could have died trying to rescue you. You're lucky to be alive right now," Matthew says.

"But I saw Jess do it the other day. She nailed a barrel right out there. She disappeared."

"No," Freddie says. "Your eyes were playing tricks on you. It happens out on the water. Tutatquin is unsurfable."

Jay leans forward, cradling his head in his hands. Matthew takes off his shirt and wraps it around the gash on Jay's shoulder. "But how did you make it out? Those are twenty-foot sets. I couldn't even get out the back . . ."

"Just say 'Thank you,' man." Freddie says. "And maybe next time Jess is in the lineup, you should show her some respect."

"Yeah. Well." A pained look crosses Jay's face. "Thanks."

~~~

"You saved his life," Matthew says, for the millionth time since we left the beach.

We're at Binky's Wicked Chowda, a local hole-in-the-wall with great chowder and cheap beer. Matthew insisted on getting me a big meal after my "ordeal." He's told me over and over how brave I am, what a badass. "I've never seen anyone move through waves like that."

Our waitress comes over and asks if we need extra oyster crackers for our chowder.

"No thanks," I say.

"She's a hero," Matthew tells the waitress.

"Please don't." I look at him, a frown tugging at my face.

"She's the bravest person I've ever seen," he says, and the waitress giggles and tells us what an adorable couple we are, before walking away.

"You are a badass, Creary."

"Just stop. Please."

"What's the matter?"

"I didn't jump in to save Jay, all right? It wasn't supposed to happen like this. I just wanted to take you surfing. I wanted you to see for yourself."

"I saw for myself," he says, a little injured. "I get it. You're incredibly strong. More than any athlete I've ever seen. Maybe you're some kind of physical anomaly. Whatever it is, it looks good on you. It's what made you go after Spencer. And Trip Sinclair. Some people have to talk their shit out; you let your strength do the talking. You're amazing." He leans toward me and whispers, "It's kind of a turn-on."

"No. That's not it at all." I poke at my soggy chowder bread bowl. "I went in after Jay to protect my barrel."

"Your barrel?" He laughs.

"If Jay had managed to make it out past the break, and surf that barrel at Tutatquin, he'd be . . . he'd be . . ."

"He'd be what?" Matthew is losing his patience.

I bury my face in my hands and rub my forehead, my skin tight with salt. I can't tell him the truth. I can't. Even if he believes me (which is seriously, seriously doubtful, as in there's no way in hell that he's going to believe me), he'll think I'm a freak. A mutant. An animal. Who can love a freak? I'll lose him. Just like I've lost everyone else. Kay's gone. My mom's gone. Yes, gone.

I said it. The spirit journey is just one of those things people say to postpone the truth. She's gone. Her heart got broken so she left. Sheriff's gone, too, in his own way. I have no one.

"I'm not a freak," I blurt out.

Matthew sighs. "I didn't say you were. You did a good thing today. I'm proud of you. You should be proud of yourself."

"*No!* I didn't do a good thing. I thought Jay would find my wave."

"Why can't you take credit for this? If you didn't risk your life saving Jay Delgado, he would be dead."

I stand up. "You don't understand! If Jay had caught that wave, he'd be flagging down the six o'clock news right now. Or trying to sell his story to some tabloid. Or getting his own reality TV show. Because right now he would be a merman, or whatever the dude equivalent of a mermaid is called."

I move over to Matthew's chair and kneel in front of him. "I'm a mermaid, Matthew. That's what I wanted to show you today. I found a barrel, and it turned me into a mermaid. All summer long I've been going through the barrel and becoming a fish. I swear to you. I'm not on drugs. And I'm not a hero."

I lean into him. "I'm a mermaid, Matthew. A mermaid."

I look into his eyes, but they are vacant.

I keep talking. "You can come with me. All you have to do is ride that barrel at Tutatquin."

"I don't know what to say."

I reach for his hand. "Say you'll come with me. Please." Tears are sliding down my cheeks and my face is hot and I can't control my breathing. I hiccup. "I want you to be part of it. I want you to come with me. In six days I'm leaving to be in that world forever. And I want you to come with me. Please. Please. Please." People are staring at us, and this is all wrong, wrong, wrong.

"Why would you say all this?" Matthew looks around, aware of the scene I'm making.

I feel so exhausted, I might collapse. "Come with me. You'll see. We can make it work."

"This is getting weird. You're being weird."

I look him in the eye. "Tell me you believe me."

He pauses. "You know what I believe? I believe that every time you do something irrational, like the night you practically assaulted Trip Sinclair at the Rongo, or the day you jumped off my boat in the middle of the ocean, you have this little story that excuses you from your actions. Every time you do something wild, you say it's because you're a mermaid. But it's a fantasy. It's not real.

"Even now, when you do something incredible like risking your life to save Jay Delgado, who you hate, you use this fantasy to make it seem like you're tougher than you really are. It lets you off the hook. It lets you keep your hard exterior. You don't want people to think that you're soft.

"I believe what this is"—he circles his finger—"is you pushing away anyone who tries to get close to you. I believe this is your way of delaying your life from happening. You don't want to move on. That's what I believe."

I reach for his hand. "No. That's not it."

He pulls it away. My hand dangles in the air, grasping for nothing.

He stands up. "I love you, Creary. But I'm not going to let you off the hook like this. When you're ready to commit to something, or someone, give me a call."

He walks out, paying the bill on the way.

TWENTY-TWO

My bed feels empty without Matthew in it. It's still dark out, and I roll over and pull the blanket over my head. I thought I could make Matthew understand what I am. In my pea brain, I thought he would actually want to go there with me. What was I thinking? He doesn't even believe me. He thinks I'm just inventing another excuse to run away from my life. In a way, maybe he's right.

I wake up a few hours later and decide to blow off work today. Matthew doesn't want to see me, and I refuse to spend my precious few human days cleaning grease traps and mopping up after seasick frat boys. I will lie in bed and wallow in self-pity instead.

All the wallowing makes me hungry. I tiptoe down to the kitchen, careful not to wake Sammy and Spencer. I don't want another confrontation. I don't want to apologize. I want to be what I am.

A mermaid.

A hunter.

Someone who attacks when she hears threatening noises in the middle of the night. Someone who protects her turf. Someone who cannot control the animal forces inside of her.

I rifle through the fridge, then the freezer. It's slim pickings—milk, frozen waffles, a Styrofoam container of cold french fries from the Lobster Corral. A box of Cap'n Crunch in the cabinet. I need real food.

I crave meat.

And not just a waterman's steak from Kotoki-Pun Diner. I need something raw and writhing in my hands. I need to hunt.

〰〰〰

First, I make a quick pit stop at Lobster Cove. The marina is bustling. Fishing is done for the day and lobstermen are loading their catches onto trucks. Housewives gather on the docks to buy lobsters and scallops from the fishermen. Selling directly to customers is against the trade laws in Maine, but everyone turns a blind eye.

While they exchange dollars for dinner, I slip down the dock to the *Jennie B* and toss my bag onto the deck. I've packed a towel and dry clothes for my transition to human.

I wait until dinnertime, when the tourists thin out, before I head out to Tutatquin Point.

The sun is low on the horizon and the moon is a waning crescent. I have a sick, scared feeling in my belly: scared that someone will see me and try to copy me and I'll have another Jay Delgado situation on my hands; scared about sharks and the darkness and the infinite loneliness of the ocean; scared that Matthew won't talk to me and I won't get a chance to say good-bye; scared that losing me will be the final nail in Sheriff's coffin.

Scared that I'm making the wrong choice.

The beach is empty. An offshore wind shapes the waves into perfect lines. It sheers off the tops of the waves, spraying sheets of white water high into the air. Against the dark blue expanse of ocean, the waves look like the jaws of a shark.

There is still time to decide my destiny. Today I'm just going hunting, I tell myself, as I run into the water with my board. The straps of my knife rub against my arm as I paddle through the boneyard, avoiding rocks. I pause for a minute on my board, gazing back at the rugged shore of Wabanaki, wondering what it would be like to see that view from the water and not be able to set foot on it again. How lonely would it feel? How liberating?

Then a set comes in. I spot a massive, right-handed peeler.

I paddle for it, pop up to my feet, and ride the barrel down the rabbit hole.

~~~

Under water, the world is calm compared to the churning surface above. I lie still on the sandy bottom, close my eyes, and let my body sway in the current.

When I open my eyes, my vision is perfect. Better than perfect. I can see the minutiae of life in the rocks. I can see tiny organisms so small they're almost invisible. Shells no bigger than grains of sand appear in splendid detail.

My body is changing, adapting, evolving.

I pluck a tiny crab the size of my thumbnail off a rock and let it crawl up my arm to my shoulder. Then I pop it in my mouth while it's still alive. I chew, swallowing shell and meat in one gulp.

My body craves more.

There's a flicker in the sand. My senses fire up. Smell, sound, taste, touch. Electrical currents in the water. Pulses down my side. They all lead me to a small skate camouflaged against the sand.

Swiftly I unsheathe my knife and thrust the blade into the soft, flat wing. It's as easy as spearing crappies in the creek with Sheriff. The skate wriggles wildly, twisting itself on my knife.

I cut off the wing and stare at the raw hunk of meat. The smell of blood sends a shiver down my body. Something inside of me takes over. Hunger. Desire. It's not like the hunger I feel late at night, when I'm standing at the open fridge, scanning for munchies. This is a thousand times stronger.

I bite into the skate. It slides down my throat. It doesn't taste good or bad. It's food. Fuel. Life-sustaining energy. My teeth tear apart the tough cartilage, the thick skin. I swallow half a wing before I'm swarmed by smaller fish looking for a free meal. They rush at the drifting carcass, ignoring the threat of bigger fish nearby. They gnaw off bits of flesh and retreat into the dark.

This is nature as my mother taught it. She despised Disney movies with cute cartoon characters. Couldn't stand how they showed animals singing happy songs and species intermingling with reckless abandon. She thought kids needed to see what nature was really like. Bloodier than the movies. And more beautiful.

I sit in the ruins of the skate, bits of bone and pointed ray tail drifting around me.

As I sheathe my knife, I feel a prickling sensation on the back of my neck.

When I look up, there she is, hovering in the water like an angel. I gasp a lungful of water and rub my eyes.

Her tail, like mine, shimmers with color, oscillating from purples to reds to greens. Her hair flows around her in luscious black waves. She smiles. It's her best smile. Exactly the way I remember her smile in happier times. It's the smile she reserved for me whenever I showed her one of my treasures, unearthed in the creek behind our house—tadpoles, salamanders, tree frogs. "What beauty you've found, little fish," she would say, and we'd make a temporary home for the creature in one of the fishbowls we stored next to the pots and pans. It's the smile that only a mother can give.

I swim to her and she hugs me with all her might.

She opens her mouth and a glorious voice comes out—not human, not like anything I've ever heard. "Jess."

I open my mouth and try to respond, "Mom," but it comes out sounding more like grumbling belly.

She laughs and her eyes light up. I try to speak again, I need to ask her how long she's been here. Is she permanently a mermaid now? Is she happy with her choice? Does she think I should stay? Does she know the legend of Ne'Hwas? (Which is a stupid question, because of course she does, and she's probably known it her whole life.) Where does she live? Do the sharks bother her? Is it scary to be out all night? What does she eat? Are there other mermaids out here? Did she know I would find my way here? Is it in our blood? Does she ever watch me and Sheriff from the water?

And then I start to think of all the other questions I want answered, and I start to get angry. Does she know how sad and lonely Sheriff is? How could she just leave him without saying good-bye? How could she leave *me*? Why didn't she tell me where she was really going? Does she understand how selfish it is to leave one daughter because you're devastated by the loss of the other?

Has she at least gotten rid of her sorrow? And if I stay a mermaid, will I get rid of all *my* sorrow?

She holds my face in her hands, which feel soft and familiar. She strokes my hair. The whole time, the smile spreads across her face, the joy in her heart impossible to hide.

I try to talk, but my vocal cords don't work under the water. As much as I want my answers, I also don't want to ruin this moment by stewing on the past.

Neither does she. She takes my hand and we start swimming in silence.

A massive school of sardines appears like a silver cloud in front of us. Sunlight shimmers off their metallic bodies. They explode through the water like fireworks, lit up by the sun and the crazy neon light of energy surrounding them. They move in perfect synchronization, mimicking each other's moves so quickly and precisely they appear like one organism. We swim through them and the silver cloud splits in two. Their little eyes dart at us as they speed ahead.

I want to talk to her, but I can't make my voice work, so I point up with my thumb to the surface, where we can have a conversation. She cocks her head. I point to the surface again with my thumb, the universal symbol for "Go up."

She stares at me blankly.

Suddenly, I feel a cold tremor up my sides. The vibrations are so strong I can feel them in my bones. I feel the rise in temperature. The sound of the great white's beating heart. She is near. She is getting closer, fast.

Move, my body screams.

In the murky distance, the silver sardines scatter like dandelion seeds in the wind and the great white shark appears.

I look at my mom, searching for the fear that I feel. But she's cool. Calm. Serene, even.

"Swim," she says, in her melodic voice.

I try to screech out the words "Let's go, let's go," but my voice won't cooperate.

The shark circles.

"Swim," she sings, and then, "fast."

I pull on her hand and try to swim, but she drags behind like deadweight.

She lets go of my hand. "Swim."

I shake my head. *I'm not leaving you.*

The shark makes another circle, this one tighter. It's the same full-grown female who tried to eat me for dinner before. Circling is aggressive behavior. She's going to strike.

I grab my mom's hand and try to pull her, but she doesn't budge.

What is she doing? Why is she giving up so easily? Doesn't she know that sharks hunt mermaids? Why won't she talk to me?

She looks me in the eyes and the smile disappears. "Go." She points west, toward Ne'Hwas. I shake my head again, violently. *I'm not going to leave without you,* I try to say with my eyes.

"Go," she says again, and there's something in her voice that I can't ignore. It's like I'm eight years old again, standing in front of the seer's storefront, my mom coming across the cobblestones from the fishmonger's, warning me not to enter that place.

I make prayer hands, hoping she'll understand what I want.

But she points west and I know I have to go. I start to swim away, feeling more scared than ever.

I turn around one last time. My mother is kicking toward the great white. She's sacrificing herself for me. I stop. Terrified to look. More terrified to look away.

The great white swims slowly toward my mom. They're going to cross paths any second. She's going to end up as dinner.

But they don't touch.

The shark swims right past my mother. I'm the one the shark wants.

My body sense is telling me she won't pass me up the way she did my mom. A stream of logical questions run through my mind, but right now I need to listen to instinct instead of logic.

I swim with everything I have. We're at the far edge of the shelf. There are no caves or rocks to hide in. I will have to outrun her.

I speed ahead, riding a burst of energy fueled by fear. The vibrations thump through my veins. Without slowing down, I look behind me. She's there. Her teeth shimmer white and the lines of her mouth curve downward in a menacing frown.

She is only a few feet away. Her heart beats in my throat.

Change course!

I skim along the bottom, using every last bit of speed I have. I zig left, then right.

She copies my zigzag pattern.

This is it. I'm done for. Forget about choices. Human or mermaid. Matthew or no Matthew. Nature is making my decision for me, right here, right now.

Faster!

I swim as fast as my body will allow. The chase takes us way out into the basin, past throngs of fish.

Any energy I gained from eating the skate is starting to fade. I won't be able to outrun this shark forever. Professor Sherwood's lectures run through my mind. Great white sharks cross thousands of miles every year to breed. They can reach speeds of thirty-five miles per hour. They can swim without food for up to two weeks.

I can only last a few miles. Tops.

I'm not going to last.

Faster!

Professor Sherwood's class comes to mind. White sharks have highly complex brains. They are older than the dinosaurs. Humans are their only natural predator.

I am human. I have a human brain and a human heart.

And a knife. I have a knife.

Despite the weakness I feel working into my body, I swim up from the bottom. The shark follows immediately behind me. Then, with all the speed I can muster, I bend at the waist and do a flip turn, just like I did a million times in the pool at Ne'Hwas High, racing the hundred meters. Coach Flanagan telling me to tighten my form.

The shark passes right over me, so close that our white bellies touch.

Her eyes are black pools. She is a fish, nothing more. I am fish and human. I have the courage of the Passamaquoddy.

And I have hands. Ten digits with powers not found in the fish world.

I reach up and grab her tail fin as she whizzes past. I hold on for my life.

The drag of my body slows her down. She knows I'm behind her, but the great mass of muscle and cartilage can't bend. I'm out of the reach of her jaws.

She thrashes her tail to shake me off. I tighten my grip. The rough skin is like sandpaper against my palms.

We swim along the seafloor like this for a while. I can feel her heart beating. The vibrations course through my body.

When we get out of the bay and into open ocean, she dives down into the cold darkness. And I hang on.

We travel far, the sun disappearing into a wash of aquamarine, then dark blue. Then black. I don't know how far we swim like this. My energy is low. I'm not sure I could swim all the way to the surface from this depth. My hands are the only thing keeping me alive.

Eventually, she slows down. Darkness closes in around us. There is only enough light to make out the broad shape of her body. She keeps moving, to flush water through her gills, but her power and speed are gone. If she makes a sudden move, I'm not sure I'll have the strength to hold on. It's now or never.

Kill. The word is coming from a place I can't name. An instinct deep in my bones.

I reach for my knife and unsnap the buckle of the sheath. The animal in me knows what it wants.

I pull my knife.

Find its weakness.

I could slice through the narrow section of her body just before the tail. The "caudal fin" as Professor Sherwood would say. The only fin that connects to the spine. Paralyze her. Bleed her out. Save myself. I move my blade to that skinny part of her tail.

I stop and tune in to my senses. The vibrations running through my body and spine are gone. Her predatory signal is turned off. Is she trying to make peace with me?

Professor Sherwood's words play out in my mind, my human brain. Sharks are essential to the ecosystem. Populations have been decimated. Humans are their only threat. They face extinction.

I move my hand along her sides. Even in the darkness, I can feel the complex structure of muscle beneath her skin. I'm suddenly awed by her power and beauty.

I try to communicate with her like I did with the seal and whales. I pulse out a thought: *Truce?*

But there's no response.

Leave me and I will leave you, I say.

Again, there are no words. She's a fish. I'm a mammal and a fish. We're wired differently.

But I do feel something from her. Not with my senses. Not a taste or a tremor or smell. I feel a connection—my heart to hers. One apex predator to another. Can she feel it, too?

I sheathe my knife and let go of her tail. Still, she doesn't move.

Slowly, I pull myself along the great expanse of her back to her dorsal fin, and I hold on.

Slowly we begin to ascend.

As I ride the great white shark into shallower water, the ocean brightens, everything taking on a pink hue, my eyes adjusting to the spectrum of light. Soon, dappled rays of sun shine through waves.

Her dorsal fin breaks the surface and I ride along, half in air, half in water. There are no vibrations. No electrical current warning me of an attack. Is she done with the chase?

I let go and the shark keeps swimming.

When she realizes I'm not riding her back, she makes a wide, slow circle and swings back to face me.

I am a hunter.

She is a hunter.

One apex predator to another, we shall do no harm. At least, that's what I try to communicate.

She doesn't understand.

She moves toward me.

I swim as fast as I can. The island must be close. In a burst of power I leap out of the water, looking for landmarks. We are right near the rock jetty of White's Wharf. I race toward it, the shark close behind me.

TWENTY-THREE

It's low tide and Lobster Cove is too shallow for a three-thousand-pound great white shark to safely swim. It's almost too shallow for me. But I stay submerged and wedge myself between two boats, listening for people, waiting for the coast to clear.

And hoping. Hoping my mom will have followed me here so I can ask her all the questions that are burning inside of me. Why didn't the shark attack *her*? How extraordinary is life as a mermaid, and should I join her? How can she just leave us like that, without saying good-bye?

I wait and wait and she doesn't come. The sky darkens and the water darkens around me. Something tickles my tail. I look, hoping it's her. An eel. I shoo it away and watch it slither over the bottom, leaving an S trail in the mud.

It's just after sunset when I thrust myself onto the transom of the *Jennie B.* Unlike the last time, the end of my tail dangles in the water. My dimensions are changing. My fish parts are getting bigger, stronger, more powerful.

I'm evolving.

I'm becoming the apex predator of the ocean. I've faced off with the fiercest animal on earth. And I've won.

I am invincible.

I am also flopping around naked on the back of a crappy old fishing boat like a total klutz.

My tail is too unwieldy to maneuver. I have to grab the back gunwale and pull myself over the rail. I land on the deck with a terrific thump.

I'm about halfway across the boat, at the fish hold, when footsteps rattle the dock. Boards creak. I freeze, scared to breathe. A man's voice yells something in the distance. My heart beats so hard I feel it in my ears. Footsteps are getting closer and closer. I'm a sitting duck.

I pull my knife.

Adrenaline surging, I drag myself toward the wheelhouse. I get to the threshold, only to see a wide-eyed little girl in pigtails staring at me from the dock. I blink, my eyes still adjusting to air. Her dress is the color of carnations and she wears a tutu that sticks out on the sides. She holds a glittery wand over her head and a pair of wings on her back. Our eyes meet.

I sit up and put a hand over my tail, as if that's going to hide my massive appendage. This is it. This is where I'm caught, my fate sealed by a four-year-old. I'm as much prey here as I am at the mouth of the great white.

I try to stay calm as the girl and I face off, but the panic rises to my chest. I wait for her to scream.

But instead, she waves.

I wave back.

She swings her tutu from side to side.

"Whatcha doin'?"

"Uh . . ." I put the knife down. "Going for a swim."

"I'm a fairy," she says. "Like Tinker Bell."

"I see." Here we are. Two magical creatures just shooting the shit.

"You a mermaid?"

"Yup."

"I like mermaids."

"I like fairies."

"Your tail's pretty."

"Thank you." I strain to look down the dock, to see if her parents are near. "Your wings are pretty, too."

She smiles wide and twirls around, letting her wings flutter behind.

"Tallulah! Tallulah! Come here." A man's voice. Footsteps beating down the dock. My heart is racing.

"Well . . . bye-bye," she says, then little Tallulah waves again, turns, and runs away.

I lie breathless in the doorway, waiting for the father to show up, find me, report me. Or murder me right on the spot. Any second he will peek inside the *Jennie B* and get the shock of his life when he finds that his daughter isn't the only mythical being on Ne'Hwas today. But he doesn't come. A few minutes go by, then a car starts up and drives away, down the crushed stone lot of Lobster Cove.

Tallulah, of the pigtails and fairy wings, has kept my secret safe.

Inside the wheelhouse, I begin drying off with the towel I stashed earlier. My tail itches like mad, worse than before, probably because there's so much more of it. I rub the towel into my scales, but my legs don't appear. I keep rubbing and rubbing. Scales fly off, cascading to the floor in prisms of color. Soon there's a pile of incandescent scales shimmering in the drab wheelhouse.

I wrap the towel around my tail. Hours go by, but the transition to human doesn't come. Finally I fall asleep on the gritty floor of the *Jennie B,* dreaming about the white shark and vanishing into the abyss.

~~~~

When I wake up, my legs are back. I throw on some shorts and a flannel from my reentry bag, then head out. On the dock, I stand and stretch. I let the air fill my lungs.

I wiggle my toes and rub the toughened skin of my soles against the splintered wood. My legs feel small, and walking is painfully slow compared to my underwater speed.

Gravity weighs on me. My body feels heavy and awkward in its humanness. This must be how astronauts feel when they return to Earth, when the atmosphere takes away their ability to float, free and weightless.

I gaze at the moon. Orion stands guard beside the waxing crescent. Five more days and it will be the full moon.

Five more days.

I know what I am. And now I know I won't be alone.

I am a mermaid.

My mind is set, but my heart is another matter.

I don't know what time it is when I turn right, down the dark road out of the cove. Instead of heading home, I walk all the way to Kotoki-Pun Point, knowing that each step will be among my last on land.

As I get close to the lighthouse, I smell wildflowers. Salt drifts on wind currents up the cliffs. I smell everything. The invisible microcosms in these meadows. I smell voles scampering in scrub grass. Foxes hunting. Bats circling the air above. I smell the difference between hiding and hunting, predator and prey.

By the time I get to the lighthouse keeper's cottage, I'm overcome by a devouring, ecstatic hunger. But not for food. I need Matthew.

The front door is locked. I walk around back to the wall of windows, open to the cool night breeze. I slide in through the lowest window.

Matthew is asleep as I climb into his bed. I smell vanilla, almond, and honey, as my animal brain processes notes of pleasure, love, lust, passion. I pull back the light blanket covering him and let my hands move across his chest, feeling the solid lines of his body. His skin is hot against mine.

I feel the deep need to possess him. I don't think I could pull myself away if the house were on fire. I kiss his neck, tasting the salt of his skin.

He responds slowly at first, lost in a dream. Then he bolts into consciousness. I can smell the sudden explosion of adrenaline in his veins.

"Creary." His voice is groggy.

I kiss his neck and the tender spot above his collarbone.

"How did you get in?"

I move to his lips and he gives over to my kisses. His hands run down my back.

"Through the window."

"What are you doing?"

I don't answer.

"Where were you today?" he whispers.

"In the sea," I whisper back. My hands continue moving down his stomach, to his thighs, feeling the muscles along his body. I close my eyes and imagine the sheer power hidden beneath the swift lines of the white shark.

"It's thrilling there," I say. I think about how, every time I'm in the sea, I walk the line between life and death. Life is bigger down there. And it makes me feel completely alive. Completely in the moment.

"Still with the mermaid fantasy?"

"It's real," I whisper. "It's more real than anything here."

I touch his lips and he moans.

"I don't want to lose you," I say.

"I'm not going anywhere."

"That's the problem." I straddle him, and he wraps his hands around my waist. I want to touch every inch of his body. I want to feel my skin on his, his lips on mine.

I look into his eyes, willing him to understand, but he is only a man. He only knows one kind of reality.

He kisses me again, and touches me gently, as if I'm a porcelain doll that might break.

But I am not fragile. I faced off with the deadliest animal on earth, and I survived. I have the courage of Ne'Hwas. I have the strength of the Passamaquoddy. I am warm-blooded and cold-blooded. Just out those windows, beyond the wild meadow and the rugged cliffs, lies the cold, dark freedom of the sea. The weightless world. My world.

I want him to understand what I am. To believe.

I pull myself away from him and stand at the foot of his bed. He sits up and gazes at me.

Moonlight bathes the room in a pale glow.

I strip naked in front of him.

A small grunt escapes through his parted lips. His eyes take me in, missing nothing.

I catch a glimpse of myself in the mirror over his bureau and gasp. Muscle ripples down my legs in smooth waves. My hips flare out from my narrow waist, my stomach is a topographic map of hills and valleys, exuding strength. My ripe breasts rise with every savage breath of my lungs. I am a vision of strength.

I can smell Matthew's arousal, the rumbling musk of desire. His brain shuts down. He, too, listens to his body.

He throws off the blanket and reaches for me, erupting with passion.

I take him as a predator takes her prey.

TWENTY-FOUR

Leave it to me to hit my sexual stride days before I turn in my legs for a tail.

Matthew rolls over and pulls me close. He wears his happiness all over, grinning ear to ear. "Good morning."

"Good morning."

"Last night was . . ." he whispers.

"What?"

"I think I'm the luckiest guy on earth." His eyes reflect the glint of the rising sun.

I press my nose against his chest and breathe in his smell. Like honey and vanilla. I run a finger over his crescent scar. When he smiles, I watch how the scar disappears into the laugh lines below his eye. "Let's stay here all day," I say.

A moan escapes from his lips. "I have a boat to drive."

"Screw work."

"I don't think Harold would appreciate that."

"Screw Harold."

He laughs. "I'm going to try to unhear that."

"Well, I'm not going in today. Let them get their own Snickers bars," I say.

"He'll fire you."

"I'm okay with that."

"I won't be able to save your job this time."

I smile. "I don't need a job."

He kisses my forehead. "Because you're a mermaid?"

"Yup."

"And you're going to leave Ne'Hwas and live in ocean."

"Yup."

"So mermaids don't need jobs? They just float around the ocean, riding seahorses?" It's not quite acceptance I hear in his voice, but he's not running for the hills, either.

He kisses me again and doesn't make any movement away from the bed.

"Skip work," I say. "Just today."

Matthew looks at me silently, the SparkNotes of his personality contained in those steady eyes. Loyal. Responsible. Full of integrity. Captain Matthew. "I can't. We'll have tonight, though," he says.

With a mighty effort he uproots himself from the bed. I watch him get dressed. It's almost as sexy as watching him undress. "Matthew?"

"Yeah?"

"If it turns out that you're wrong, and I actually am a mermaid, would you consider coming with me when I leave?"

He crawls across the bed and meets my lips with a kiss. "I'll go with you anywhere."

~~~~

Once Matthew leaves for work, I get dressed and call Sheriff. I need to tell him about Mom. He has a right to know. Losing someone you love is the worst thing in the world. But it can't be worse than losing someone and not knowing where or why they've gone. At least I can bring him some relief.

The part I'm seriously dreading is telling him that I'll be leaving, too. Mom and I will be together, but he'll be all alone. I don't even want to think about what this will do to him.

There's a hollow pit in my stomach as I dial his number.

Sheriff's phone goes straight to voice mail, so I call the station. His friend Sheila answers and tells me he's on patrol. Morning shift.

Sheila's the best dispatcher on the force, Sheriff always says. She's the one who broke the news that Kay's body had been found. She's the one who came around to the house when Sheriff was put on administrative leave during the investigation. Brought us casseroles nonstop. "Heart of gold, that Sheila," Sheriff would always say after she left, and my mother and I would listen to him talk about the importance of a good dispatcher on the force who can anticipate trouble by the tone of an officer's voice. We would listen and listen, because it was a relief to hear about *anyone* in those dreadful weeks other than Trip Sinclair.

Sheila is super chatty with me. She tells me just how darn happy she is to hear my voice and wants to know all about what I'm doing these days, and whether I'm planning on going back to school in the fall, which means Sheriff obviously has been talking to her about me, as well as lying to himself about my prospects for the future.

"Where is he on patrol?" I ask her.

"Honey, you know I can't say. You want me to call him on the radio?"

"No," I say. "I'll just drive around looking for him. It'll only take a few hours. I'll find him." For effect, I add, "Eventually."

"Oh, sweetie." Sheila sighs, the pity almost audible. "All right, I'll tell you where he is."

Sheila, heart of gold, arms of rubber.

"He's running a speed trap out on Ocean Road. He's parked at the bend by Sweet Water Tavern. You can find him there."

"Thanks, Sheila."

"You take care, honey."

~~~~

I open the passenger door of the cruiser and hop in.

"Is everything all right?" Sheriff asks, looking nervous.

"I need to talk to you about Mom."

He sighs deeply and puts his hands on the steering wheel. "Jess,

I know you want to believe that she's coming back, but we've got to face the facts. She's cut off all communication. She doesn't want to be found."

"I know where she is," I blurt out.

He turns to face me. "What? Did she contact you? Is she all right?"

"She's good."

"Where is she?"

My stomach turns in knots. This is going to be even harder than I thought. "It's complicated. I'll tell you where she is. But first, I need to tell you how I know."

"So, tell me."

Suddenly, the radio crackles and Sheila's voice is on. "Unit ninety-nine."

Sheriff pauses. He wants answers. But he's a cop first. "Go ahead," he says into the radio receiver.

"Report of a B and E, fourteen Magnolia Court at Smith's Point. Witness says property stolen. No suspicious cars reported in area."

"Copy that," he says into the radio. Then to me, "Where's Barbara?"

"It's a long story."

He rubs the bridge of his nose. "Fine. We'll talk later. Right now you've got to get out of the car. I need to respond to this call."

"But I need to talk to you." I have four days left. I can't waste any more time.

He glares at me as he presses the radio button, "Proceeding to Magnolia." He releases the button. "Get out of the car, Jess. I'll swing by later."

"No," I say. "I'll wait in the car. Then we need to talk."

The veins on his temple throb. "Well, then, buckle up."

I buckle my seat belt and Sheriff does about ten things all at the same time. He puts the lights on, hits the siren, hangs up the radio, punches something into a computer, pulls a U-turn, and heads down Ocean Road toward Smith's Point.

Lights flashing, we race down the middle of the road.

~~~

Fourteen Magnolia is a grand stone house on Smith's Point, a few doors down from the Sinclair mansion. It fits in with its elite neighbors, shielded from the outside world by iron gates and old money. Sheriff keeps the blue lights on and checks his belt—firearm, cuffs, pepper spray.

He opens the cruiser door. "Come with me," he says. "I want you to see this."

I follow Sheriff to the house. He bangs the brass lion door knocker, but no one answers. He knocks again.

When the door opens, an old woman is standing in a satin dressing robe. She wears heavy makeup that gathers in the wrinkles of her face.

"Officer Creary," she says in a frail brittle voice. "I was hoping it'd be you. Come in."

"Mrs. Peterson, this is my daughter, Jess. She's helping me out today."

"Hi," I say, a little uncertain.

"How lovely," Mrs. Peterson says, her cloudy eyes fixed on me.

We walk through the marble foyer into the cluttered living room. It smells of mildew and cats. The velvet couche sags and water stains spread across the ceiling.

Sheriff walks around, inspecting. "No shattered glass anywhere, Mrs. Peterson. That's a good sign. What makes you think you had a breaking and entering this time?"

She pulls her robe tight across her neck. It's got a hole in the sleeve and the hem is frayed. "It's the sterling, Officer Creary." She leads us into the kitchen. Her hands shake as she shows us the evidence—an empty silverware case opened on the old wood table. Forks, spoons, and knives laid out in pairs across the worn surface. "Two dessert spoons are gone," she says.

"Two dessert spoons?" Sheriff repeats.

"The entire set is ruined now."

I pick up a fork, turn it over. Tiffany stamp on the back.

"When did you get to the island, Mrs. Peterson?"

"Last week."

"Anyone here to help you?"

Her mouth quivers. "Oh no. Everyone is positively over-burdened. Mary is in the city and her children are in camps. Dennis and William are busy at the firm. I'm out alone this summer, I'm afraid."

"Have you noticed anything else missing?"

She thinks, her mind drifting. "One of the fitted sheets to the east guest room. The flat sheet is here, but the fitted sheet is gone. At least they didn't get the flat sheet. Do you think the thieves are still here? In the house?"

Sheriff puts a hand on her shoulder. He helps her to the living room.

"Have a seat. I'll check it out. Jess will keep you company."

I glare at him, shoot him a look that says, *We've got more important things to do.* I need to tell him about his wife who's missing for real, unlike the silver spoons and fitted sheet, which the old woman has obviously misplaced.

He returns my look. "We need to take care of Mrs. Peterson right now."

Sheriff disappears up the stairs and I sit nervously across from the old woman, fidgeting.

"Your father is a good man," she says.

I smile and look at the pictures of yachts on the wall. Another rich yachting family. Another thing I won't miss about Ne'Hwas when I'm gone.

Mrs. Peterson smiles. "He saved my son, you know."

"Who did?"

"Your father. Back when he was lifeguard all those years ago. I remember it well, indeed. I always felt comfortable letting the little ones swim with him in the chair. My William got caught in the rip current one summer. I was terribly frightened. Your father saved him. He would have drowned otherwise."

I think about the time I was five and Kay was eight and I got pulled out in the rip. "He saved me from a rip, too," I say, although I was never close to drowning. I remember how it felt, like the sea had cradled me. Like I was a dolphin crossing the ocean, and how I felt safe the entire time.

She crosses her frail legs. "I would have lost William that day. He's a real hero."

"I guess so."

She smiles and stares at me some more. "Are you training to be a police officer, too, then?"

I laugh. It sounds snarky and I wish I could take it back. "No. I'm not cop material."

"Oh. I assumed you were in training."

"I'm just along for the ride today."

"That's too bad. I bet your father would enjoy working with you. I miss having my children around me."

I look away, not sure what to say. I notice the photos of kids and grandkids cluttering the shelves and tables, lining the grand piano. All those privileged people with lives somewhere else, while Mrs. Peterson is here, alone, in this decaying mansion that's crumbling around her. I feel her loneliness like a shot in the arm.

Am I doing the same thing to Sheriff? Will he be just as help-less when I leave? What makes me think I'm any better than her absentee kids?

After a while, Sheriff returns. "Everything looks shipshape, Mrs. Peterson. I'm sure those missing items will turn up."

She takes his hand. "Thank you, Officer Creary. Can't you stay a little longer?"

"I guess we could have some tea," Sheriff says.

Mrs. Peterson leaps out of her chair with surprising agility, to get a kettle boiling.

~~~

Once we're back in the cruiser, after a cup of tea and some long, boring stories about all of Mrs. Peterson's grandchildren, I turn to Sheriff. "Why did you bother checking out the house? Obviously she made up the burglary."

Sheriff puts the cruiser in gear and pulls out of the circular drive. "She's lonely."

"No kidding."

"Husband left her years ago for a younger woman. Her kids are too busy to help her out. In the end, she's all alone."

"But it's not your job to babysit. She's got a family, and plenty of money."

"It's my job to make her feel safe, Jess. Loneliness can be the most terrifying thing of all for some people."

I twist my hair. How lonely will Sheriff be when I leave?

"So, tell me. What did you find out about Barbara?" Sheriff says.

I take a deep breath. "Did Mom ever tell you about the legend of Ne'Hwas?"

He furrows his eyebrows. "I know the legend. Two sisters. They become mermaids. You said yourself I'm more interested in your Native American roots than you are."

"But did Mom ever talk to you about it?"

He pauses, thinking. "Once. When we first met. She said there were lots of legends from the Passamaquoddy." He half smiles, his memory racing.

"What did she say about Ne'Hwas?" I ask, twisting my hair into a knot.

"She said it was a legend. Said she didn't hold with that sort of thing."

I look into his eyes. "Well, I think it's fair to say that she holds with that sort of thing now."

TWENTY-FIVE

I've been here before," Sheriff says.

We're standing at the heavy wooden door, the TRUTH WITHIN sign dangling precariously on its nail.

"I bought your birthday present here. Remember it? The comb made out of sperm whalebone. The Passamaquoddy symbol for strength. It's from this shop. The owner picked it out for me. Told me you'd like it. Insisted on selling it to me."

It's the most Sheriff has said since I started telling him the unbelievable story of my summer. I talked, and he listened. He didn't tell me I was crazy. He didn't think I was making up some fantasy, the way Matthew does. He asked a few questions. He wanted to know about Barbara. How she was acting, when was she planning on returning? Mostly, though, he listened.

Of all people, I never expected Sheriff to be the easy one to convince. Even Sammy doubted it, and she believed in the tooth fairy until she was nine.

But Sheriff believed me. He accepted the legend of Ne'Hwas as truth. Maybe it's because he's always celebrated that part of me and Kay that belonged to my mother. Our native heritage. And maybe because that part of me belonged to my mother, he cherished it even more.

"The comb is at the bottom of the ocean right now. I used it to fight off a shark the first time I transformed. I probably would have died without it."

Sheriff exhales deeply, shakes his head. "I don't think I want to hear the details of that one."

"Fair enough."

"And you think the woman in this shop knows why this is happening to you? She can help you stop it?" Sheriff asks, jerking his chin toward the TRUTH WITHIN sign.

My stomach drops. In all the confusion, I realize I still haven't actually told Sheriff that I'm leaving for good. That I'm choosing fins over legs; the sea over him.

"I don't know. She's the one who told me about Ne'Hwas. And I get the feeling that she knows a lot more."

Sheriff straightens his stance. "Maybe she'll be able to sort this out for us."

"Maybe," I say, feeling less certain.

"We'll see what we see," Sheriff says.

I nod.

"Do you think she can help us get Barbara back?" he asks.

His optimism spears me with guilt. I pull a creeper off the vine and tear it into shreds. "I don't think Mom *wants* to come back, Sheriff."

~~~~

The old woman is sitting in the bent-hickory chair by the window, hunched over a pair of knitting needles, when Sheriff and I walk in. She looks up from her work and peers at us with those hazel-rimmed eyes.

"Would you like some tea?" she asks calmly.

"This is my father, Jim Creary."

The metal needles clink softly as she knits. "I know who you are."

"We've met," Sheriff says. "I bought the comb from you a couple weeks ago. It was a present for Jess."

The woman is silent, and Sheriff and I exchange a glance. He continues. "I appreciate the recommendation. Apparently, that comb came in very handy. Isn't that right, Jess?"

"Yeah."

"You're Barbara's husband," the woman says abruptly.

"I'm sorry, I didn't catch your name." Sheriff advances toward her with an outstretched hand.

She laughs, and keeps knitting.

Sheriff puts his hand down, unperturbed. "Jess says you're a seer of sorts."

"Sit down. Tell me what it is you seek."

I take a seat on the low stool next to the old woman. Sheriff remains standing, stiff in his uniform, hands resting on the belt of tools and weapons.

"Last time I was here, I told you I was a mermaid, and you told me the legend of Ne'Hwas. Do you remember?" I start.

Click, click, click go her needles. I look at the tattered maps on the walls. The Maine and New Brunswick coasts. Cape Cod. Islands I cannot place. In a dark corner of the wall is a map of Ne'Hwas that I hadn't noticed last time I was here. There's an X has been marked in black pen, at Tutatquin Point. Is it new? Added since my last visit?

I turn back to the seer. "My mother is out there. She found me. She's a mermaid, too. I think she's been watching me the whole time. Did you already know that?"

She nods in time with her needles and the rocking of the hickory chair. "Of course I did." She looks up. "A mother always knows where her daughter is."

〰〰〰

Sheriff and I both gasp out loud.

"Barbara is your daughter?" Sheriff asks, his voice gruff.

"You're my grandmother?" Part of me feels like hugging the old woman, but another part of me feels betrayed. "Why didn't you tell me that before? Why didn't you reach out years ago?"

"You didn't need to know then. Now you do."

I can sense that Sheriff is skeptical. "Why didn't Barbara ever tell me about you? Why would she keep that from all of us?"

"Aren't there things about Barbara that have always eluded you?"

Sheriff looks down. "She was always a very private person. Kept a part of herself hidden away. Always has. All those times she disappeared. Her spirit journeys. I never knew what that was all about. But this . . . You. I'd like to think she would have shared this with me. Maybe she didn't know you were here."

"She knew," I say, feeling suddenly protective of Sheriff. "When I was little, Mom told me to stay away from here. She said that no one can tell you your destiny. I asked if the woman in the shop was Passamaquoddy and Mom said, 'Not our kind.'" I turn to the seer. "If you're my grandmother, why would she forbid me to see you?"

The old woman smiles. I study her eyes, her skin, her cheekbones, and I can see my mother.

"Barbara has made mistakes in her life."

"Now hold on. That's my wife you're talking about."

"Sit. I will tell you the things that you don't know about your wife." She peers at me. "And your mother."

Reluctantly, Sheriff sits on the edge of the other hickory chair.

"When Barbara was young, she was very brave, like you. She loved the water. She would spend hours swimming in the ocean, diving for shells, playing in waves. She could hold her breath for many minutes and swim a mile without stopping. She was born to be in the water. It was a wonder to watch her."

"No," I say. "My mother was terrified of the ocean."

"That wasn't until much later, when the ocean was a dark temptation to her. When Barbara was about thirteen years old, we took a trip up the coast of New Brunswick. There are sea caves up there, full of precious minerals and exotic rock formations. But at high tide the caves flood.

"There was a big group of us walking the beach that day, clamming in the mud, picking up crabs and fish caught in a weir.

One of the families with us had a young boy who went to explore the sea caves. As the tide came in, we all moved to the safety of the cliff. But the boy could not be found. His little brother told the group that he had never left the cave."

She puts down her knitting. "All we could do was stand on the edge of that cliff and watch as the dark mouth of the cave disappeared under the water, knowing the boy was inside.

I think about the Bay of Fundy tidal range and how it's the highest in the world, how we all have our stories of when the tide almost took us.

"I hadn't even realized Barbara was gone, when I saw her swimming toward the cave. I screamed for her to come back. I was so worried for her. But she dove under the water, right into that cave. She didn't come out for many minutes. When she finally emerged, she had the boy with her. She swam him over to the cliffs and set him on a rock. I stood on the edge of that cliff, feeling as proud as any mother has ever felt. By then, the water had turned brown from the rushing tide, and I could not see below her neck. But I saw into her eyes, and I knew that she had changed."

I look out the window. High tide. All the boats in White's Wharf afloat. In six hours they'll be resting in the mud, along with the crabs and bottom-feeders. "You mean she was a mermaid?"

"Yes. She had found a way into the Ne'Hwas legend."

"Did she know what was happening?"

"Of course! She knew the legend well."

The old woman takes my hands in hers. "You see, we were there because we were searching for the place where Ne'Hwas jumped into the pool. We were always searching for it. I've searched for it my whole life."

"You *wanted* her to be a mermaid?" I ask.

"Oh yes! She had brought great honor to our family. She would spend her life as a goddess. That day, I learned that where there are great acts of courage, there are doors into the other realm. When Barbara came out of that cave, I knew she had fulfilled the legacy of Ne'Hwas. Her destiny had found her."

Sheriff clears his throat. "Are you saying she's been a mermaid all these years? That she can be human one day and mermaid the next? And she kept it secret from me all this time?"

"She didn't choose one over the other." My grandmother swallows hard. Her lips turn into a frown. "She did not appreciate what a rare and beautiful thing it is to be possessed by the sea. She wasn't the brave girl I thought she was. She chose land over sea."

"But Mom went back."

The seer tilts her head. "I suspect she went back a few times."

I think about the time I was five and Kay was eight and I got caught in the rip current, and instead of drowning, it felt like the ocean lifted me up. How it felt like the ocean had hands that cradled me from below. And it hits me: it was my mother who saved me that day. She didn't disappear to get help. She wasn't back at the car, looking for a shovel to build my moat. She dove in and rescued me, without anyone knowing.

"What about this time?" Sheriff asks. "When is she coming home?"

"Grief will drive a person deep inside of themselves. It drove her back to the sea. The ocean will drown all sorrow. And once the sea takes hold of you, there is no turning back."

Sheriff looks deflated. "There must be a way to bring her back."

"I'm afraid not."

"If I can just talk to her," Sheriff says. "Reason with her."

"I am sorry. But Barbara has chosen her destiny."

"I can't just give up."

The seer looks out the window. "I only worry that it is too late for her. Ne'Hwas was a girl, with a girl's heart and a girl's passion. I don't know if the sea will be kind to a broken old woman."

"So you think she's in danger?" Sheriff asks.

I think of my mother swimming toward me, looking more beautiful and radiant than I've ever seen her. And I think of the shark swimming right past her, coming after me.

"I don't think she's in danger," I say. "When I was down there, a white shark tried to attack me. But it completely ignored my mother. Why?"

My grandmother turns her piercing eyes on me. "Sharks keep the balance in the oceans. They thin the herd, kill the sick and weak. You are neither fish nor human at the moment. You don't belong there yet. You are upsetting the natural order. Not until you decide what you are can you be safe. The shark was only doing its job."

"So, once I choose the sea, the sharks won't hunt me?"

Sheriff leaps to his feet. "What do you mean, 'once you choose the sea'?"

I stand, too, and look him in the eyes. I can feel the tears rising. "I'm a mermaid. It's my destiny."

"You aren't serious, are you?" Sheriff asks.

"I'm so sorry, Dad, but I am."

He hugs me so hard I can't breathe. "Oh, Jess."

"Can you forgive me?"

He lets me out of the hug but keeps his hands on my arms. "Of course I forgive you. You have to do what's right for you. That's all I've ever wanted for you. At least you'll have your mother. You'll have to take care of each other."

I wipe my running nose. "I'll come visit you all the time. We'll find a spot, and you can meet me there. I'll bring Mom. You won't be alone, Sheriff."

He hugs me again, and when I look down at the seer, a curious smile crosses her lips. Her expression is so familiar, so much like my mother's the day at the ferry station when she hugged me good-bye. Telling me she would see me soon, when really she knew otherwise.

TWENTY-SIX

It's a little like planning your own death, with the added bonus of knowing when and how you'll go. You can be picky about how you spend your final hours. And you get to plan your good-byes.

Sammy opens the door to her room, rubbing the sleep out of eyes. Her ability to nap at any time of day has always astounded me.

"What?" she snaps. I can see by the set of her jaw that she's still mad at me over beating up Spencer.

"I'm leaving, Sammy."

"Okay." She tugs on her slouchy Victoria's Secret pajama pants with the holes in the knees, which she's had since high school. "Good-bye."

She doesn't get it. I hug her. She hugs me back, reluctantly, and then like my best friend.

"I'm really leaving," I say. "In two days, it's a full moon."

"What, like, *leaving* leaving? Like, for good? Are you saying you're going to be a mermaid? Forever? You're never going to live on land? You're not going to have legs anymore? You won't walk ever again? You're just going to swim around the ocean all day? Jess, you can't do that. What about your family? What about us? Our friendship?" She adds, "What about the apartment?"

"You've seen what's happening to me, what I'm becoming. I belong out there." I nod seaward.

"But . . . but . . ." She breaks into hiccuped cries.

"It's the right thing for me to do."

She wipes her nose on the hem of her ragged T-shirt. "Promise me I'll still see you. I'll get in a boat if I have to, and you know how much I hate boats. I get seasick just standing on the dock." She hugs me again. "You can't just disappear out of my life forever."

"I promise."

"Pinkie swear?"

We make our secret sign. "I only have two days left, Sammy. I want to spend time with you," I say. "Our last hurrah."

She nods through her cries. And then she says, "Does this mean I can keep that crocheted dress I borrowed without asking?"

I smile "It's all yours. All of it."

~~~~

It's one of those spontaneous summer days where we don't plan anything or worry about what's next. We hang out at the apartment all morning, drinking coffee and playing rummy, like we used to when we first moved in and didn't have enough money to go out because first, last, and security ate up every last dollar.

"Can you ever come back?" Sammy asks, laying down three aces. "I mean, for special occasions? Weddings, funerals, that sort of stuff? I would just die if you weren't at my wedding. Or the birth of my children. Don't get me wrong—I don't want you down below the curtain! You can be standing near my head. You know, cheering me on."

I laugh. "I don't think I will have legs ever again. You'll have to bring the spawn of Spencer out to sea to visit."

"I didn't say they would be Spencer's kids."

"Okay. Then, the spawn of Leonardo DiCaprio."

"That's more like it." She laughs. "Does Matthew know?"

I stare at my cards. A pair of twos, a jack, a nine, and a three. Trash. "I've tried to tell him, but he's going to have to see to believe."

"Dude, I have it so much simpler with Spencer."

"It helps to be the same species."

By lunchtime, we're ready to get out, so we head down to Spinnaker Street. Every restaurant has lines out the door, but the hostess at the Crab Shack owes Sammy a favor and manages to squeeze us in at a high-top table on the water.

"You're going to miss all this," Sammy says.

I stretch out my legs, letting the sun bake my skin.

Our waiter, a white guy with dreadlocks, brings us beers on the house. Fringe benefits of being a townie.

"To friendship," we toast.

"You ladies hitting any of the Regatta pre-parties this week?" the waiter asks.

"Are there any we should know about?" Sammy asks.

One local to another, he says in a whisper, "I hear there's one down at Galleon Marina. Big yacht. Can't miss it. Some bigwig has his entourage up for Regatta."

"Who?" Sammy says, practically bouncing off her stool.

He squints, thinking about it. "Can't remember. One of those old industrialist names. Forbes. Rockefeller. Vanderbilt. Something like that. But the guy is some young hotshot entrepreneur. My roommate's girlfriend's cousin texted from the yacht and said it was off the hook. Two hotties like you could slip in there no problemo."

Sammy's eyes sparkle with the thought of it.

"I thought you hated boats," I say.

"Boats, yeah. Yachts, now that's a different story."

"We're not crashing a yacht party," I say, but the wheels are already turning in Sammy's brain.

"Bring us one more round," she tells dreadlock dude. "We're going."

"No," I say.

"Come on. This is my last request."

"We'll never get in," I say.

"Nonsense. It's all in the attitude. Fake it 'til you make it," Sammy says, slugging her Corona.

"I'm going to miss your nuggets of wisdom."

⌁⌁⌁

We make our way down to the Galleon Marina, where mega yachts fill the dock slips like a strand of pearls. The party of the hotshot entrepreneur (with the old industrialist's name) is impossible to miss. Hip-hop music rings out from the upper deck of the yacht, and beautiful people adorn it like Christmas ornaments.

"Follow me," Sammy says. Chin lifted, she swaggers to the gangplank. Two bouncers stand guard, one pierced and tattooed, the other with muscles like a bodybuilder.

I stand back and let Sammy do the talking. Any second the bouncer is going to tell us to buzz off, it's a private party. That would be fine with me, because Sammy and I will be able to continue our last hurrah alone. Instead, he nods us through.

Two hotties like us.

On board, it's packed. Beautiful people, dressed in clothes as shimmery as sardines, cluster in small groups. They seem immune to the luxury surrounding them, but I've never seen such a fancy yacht.

Feeling nervous and out of place, I follow Sammy down to a set of stairs.

"Let's get out of here," I say, but Sammy is in her element.

She grabs my hands. "Just relax. This is the last time you'll ever set foot on a boat like this. Like, literally."

I'd rather be back at the apartment, just the two of us, or alone with Matthew. But this is Sammy's dream come true, and the least I can do is be her wingman.

On the upper deck, more beautiful people cram into the space, which is sweltering with body heat and baking in the glaring sun.

They crane their heads like flamingos, looking past each other, jockeying for position near the center of the action.

A thousand scents ride on the hot air into my overdeveloped sensory receptors. Body odor and perfume. Sunburned skin. Diesel slick on water. Champagne. Silicone implants. A spike in adrenaline. The bass of hip-hop music beats in solar plexus and throat. The smell of blood from the fishing boats. The grinding of engines in the marina. The grinding of pelvises on the dance floor.

Within minutes, I lose Sammy. Her arms are swinging overhead, hips swaying. It doesn't matter that she doesn't know anyone here. She is the master of fitting in, as skilled as a skate hiding in the sand.

Sammy waves me over to dance with her, but I've never been a dancer. Don't see the point in learning now. This isn't my scene. I stand miserably against the starboard railing, watching.

A waiter walks by and I grab a crab cake off his tray. I swallow it, thinking about how food tastes under water. How much more precious it is. How much harder to come by. How much more satisfying when you eat it.

Below deck, there's a scuffle. I can hear anger in men's voices and the movement of bodies. I can taste the testosterone on my tongue. I lean over the rail, but I can't see the fight.

"Beat it," the bouncer says.

"Get your fucking hands off me."

"I'll make you leave."

"I'm skipper of the *Sea Nymphe,* dipshit. I was invited." Skipper of the *Sea Nymphe.* Trip Sinclair. This island is getting too small for the both of us.

Trip staggers up the stairs on the port side of the yacht. The girl on his arm is as drunk as he is, and she trips over the last step.

"We're here," Trip announces. That smile across his face.

The girl stands up, snaps her gum.

The hotshot entrepreneur with the industrialist last name walks over and greets Trip with a fist bump. My view is obscured by the heads and shoulders on the dance floor bobbing up and down to the music. I can't hear what the two are saying, but everyone on the yacht is suddenly interested in Trip Sinclair. Trip grabs a bottle of champagne from the bar and chugs. Then he shakes it and lifts his thumb off the end, showering the dancers.

This is his crowd, his people.

The injustice of it pierces me. He should be in jail, not partying on a lavish yacht. He inserts himself into a circle of women, who dance around him, grinding up against him. The smile painted on his face. The smile Kay loved.

He looks up from the women and his eyes fall on me. The smile disappears.

I tense up. My muscles tighten. My palms sweat.

Now he's walking over to me. Stumbling, I should say. He steadies himself on the railing and turns his head to me.

"Something tells me you crashed this party," he says.

I don't answer.

"I could have you arrested for trespassing."

"Go ahead."

He yells over to the yacht owner, "Hey Maxwell, you got a stowaway here."

Maxwell, young entrepreneur yacht owner and first-class douche, can't hear him over the music. He gives Trip a thumbs-up.

"You obsessed with me or something? You want a piece of this?" He taps his crotch with the backs of his hands like he's some kind of rap star. "You've been showing up everywhere I am this summer."

"You may have fooled my sister, but you don't fool me. I know what kind of person you are. The kind of coward who runs away." Heat rises to my cheeks.

"Legally, I'm not allowed to talk about your sister." He laughs. "But, off the record, I talk about her *all the time* to my therapist. Almost as much as I talk about my grandfather. 'The traumatic episode you experienced contributes to your risk-seeking behavior, Trip.'" He laughs again. "People like me need to feel through our emotional numbness, you see."

My hands turn into fists.

"Alcoholism." He pulls a flask from his jacket and takes a sip. "Another side effect of being a Sinclair."

I feel the anger boiling inside of me. The unfairness of it is what kills me. And the waste. Kay was kind and smart and thoughtful. She wouldn't have turned her back on the person dying next to her. She took care of people. She took care of me. She was great. And she was ours.

I think about the great white shark—the balance-keeper of the ocean. Where's the balance-keeper in this world? How can he commit murder and walk free? How can Kay be dead while Trip lives a life of entitlement and booze? Where is the balance in that?

Trip's date has wandered off to the dance floor. He puts his champagne-soaked arms around me.

My ears are ringing.

"You want an apology?" he asks, his breath thick with whiskey and champagne. He chokes out a laugh. "I'm sorry I'm sorry I'm sorry I'm sorry I'm sorry I'm sorry I'm sorry I'm sorry I'm sorry . . ."

His laughter is like venom. His words, a pin in the balloon of everything I believe. I see red. My body is shaking. And then I lose myself. The animal takes over. The predator comes out.

My hands are on Trip's body. I lift him off his feet. Shock in his eyes. The sour smell of fear. The edges disappear. All I see is him. The look in his eyes. The smile, plastered to his face. He slaps at my hands.

I toss him over the railing.

He scrambles, reaching to get purchase on the slick yacht surface. He whacks the metal railing, the fiberglass hull, and splashes in the water.

Behind me, there are shrieks. Girls who got their hair wet. People yelling, "Man overboard!" Someone jumps in after him. The music stops.

The bouncer with the tattoos is running up the port stairs. Sammy has me by the hand. We are pushing through the crowd. We are running down the starboard stairs. We cross through the glittering saloon to the port side. We are running down the gangplank. We push past a throng of people standing at the entrance, waiting to get in. And we run through the marina, past the Schooner Wharf until we are on Spinnaker Street, and we keep running.

TWENTY-SEVEN

"Can I borrow some sugar, sugar?" Lady Victoria is at my door in a silk kimono, her hair wrapped in a turban. She jingles a measuring cup at me. "I'm making a cake."

"Seriously?"

I don't have time for this, I think to myself. Tomorrow is the new moon. I've got farewell letters to write and phone calls to make and bank accounts to close and my room to clean. No one wants to leave behind a pile of dirty underwear to be remembered by.

I've got to make sure I leave Sammy some money to help with rent, and instructions for Sheriff on how to find me. Giving up your life requires planning.

And then there's Matthew. The biggest loose end of all. I need to see him tonight to say good-bye.

Or ask him to join me.

I pause too long. Lady Victoria bats her cat eyes and brushes past me to the kitchen.

"Come on in," I say.

"My my. What a shame. This place has such potential. Just look at the view. It could be a private little Shangri-la. Instead, it looks like you girls plundered the Dumpster behind the Goodwill."

I sulk and rifle through cabinets, looking for sugar.

"Aw, don't be sore. I was just playing with you, kitten."

I find of box of brown sugar. "Here," I say, and toss it to her.

"This is hard as a brick. I almost broke a nail."

"Well it's all I've got."

"Candy yam, what's eating you? Talk to Lady Victoria. I'm a good listener."

I look out at White's Wharf and the sea beyond.

"It can't be all that bad," she says. "Take a load off and let me help you. It tears me up to see my little ray of sunshine so blue. I care about you, darling. I plan on lip synching at your wedding someday."

I plop down on the stool next to her. She folds her hands daintily in her lap.

"I'm . . . moving," I start.

"Where you moving?"

"I'd rather not say."

"I'm going to miss you, sweet cheeks." The thick outline of lip liner accentuates her frown. "Tell me, is it better than here, this mysterious new hideaway?"

"It's great," I say. "I'm excited to start a new life there."

"So what's the problem, then?"

I exhale sharply. "I'm having a hard time letting go."

"Sweet cheeks, leave the past where it belongs—behind."

"Wish I could. But this might be it. I might never see the people I love again. My dad, Sammy. And there's this guy."

She slaps her knee. "Ha! I knew it. You are too charming and positively too scrumptious to be unattached."

I smile.

"Have you asked this boy to move with you? Love is a powerful motivator."

"It's complicated," I say. "There's a chance he might come with me."

"Hallelujah."

"But there's another boy, too."

"A three-way! Ooh-la-la."

"No. This guy's a jerk. He did something terrible and I want him to pay for it. When I leave, no one is going to make it right."

I think about Trip Sinclair and his mock apology, his whiskey-breath slur. *I'm sorry I'm sorry I'm sorry I'm sorry I'm sorry.*

"Oh, honey. You got to let it go. I know of what I speak. Imagine how I was treated in middle school. A boy named Victor who preferred Jimmy Choos over Michael Jordans. Do you think I would have turned out to be the Incomparable Lady Victoria, queen of the stage, diva of the drag, if I carried their contempt in my heart? No, ma'am! I learned to let go and trust in the universal law of karma. Everyone gets theirs. What comes around goes around."

"I hope you're right," I say, though I have my doubts.

‹‹‹‹

When Lady Victoria leaves (without her sugar), I go through my room, seeing what I can take with me. I won't need clothes, towels, or sheets. Pictures will get destroyed. Phones are useless. I'll bring a knife, of course, a shucking tool, and a net. But what can a mermaid really possess?

I'm trying to figure out how to waterproof my flashlight and spare batteries when my phone buzzes.

"Hello."

"Jess. Where are you?" Sheriff, sounding tense.

"At my apartment. What's wrong?"

"Trip Sinclair came to the station. Sheila called to let me know." There's a pause, and I can hear him breathing heavily, like he's been running.

"Did he turn himself in? Is he going to go to jail?" Maybe karma is at work after all.

"He's filing charges against you. Says you assaulted him."

"*He's* filing charges against *me*?"

"There are witnesses. Lots of witnesses. Plus the other incidents over the summer. He wants you for assault and stalking."

"He's the one who needs to be arrested for assault!"

"Don't you think I know that?"

"It's so unfair!"

"This is serious, Jess. They're taking a statement from him right now. That damn lawyer is involved, Grant le Carre. He wants to get a restraining order so you can't come near him during Regatta. He'll get it, too."

"Well, they can't arrest me where I'm going."

Another long pause.

"Nomeha," his voice breaks. "They're going to come for you tonight. They can hold you for forty-eight hours, until arraignment."

I look down the hall, half expecting to see the cops on the other side of the door with some kind of X-ray vision.

"But the full moon is tomorrow."

He takes a breath. "I know that."

"What are you saying, Sheriff?"

"You need to get out of here, now."

My father, the man who's dedicated his life to upholding the law, is telling me to run from it.

I think about the reputation he'll get after I leave. The cop whose daughter absconded. The Creary name forever tied to scandal.

"But *you're* the one who'll take the rap."

"I've been a cop my whole life," he whispers. "Right now I just have to be a father."

"Sheriff. Are you sure?"

"You know how these people are. They always get what they want. They always win."

"But I need more time. I have to find Matthew and say good-bye."

"Cops'll be there soon, Jess."

This is it, I think. There will be no more good-byes. No more last hurrahs. No more tying up loose ends. "I won't get to see you again," I say, choking back a cry.

"I know." He tries to sound strong, but I can hear right through it. "Maybe you can come visit me when I'm on harbor patrol. Maybe you, your mother, and I can figure out a way."

"I'll do my best."

"I know you will. It's time for you to leave."

"I love you so much, Dad."

He cries. I can feel his pain, as fresh as the day he stood in our living room listening to the news that Kay's body had been found on the rocks. As fresh as finding out that his wife left him to fulfill a different type of destiny.

"You two take care of each other," he says. "Promise me."

"I promise." I hang up the phone and grab my surfboard.

TWENTY-EIGHT

Crimson streaks are burning across the sky by the time I get to the gate at Wabanaki State Park. The first stars appear in the ink above. My mother loved this time of day. "This is when the Great Spirit tucks us into a blanket of stars, nomeha," she'd say.

She could make something as big as the night sky feel small and safe. And I would look up in the sky and let all my worries melt into darkness.

I park at the overgrown utility road, grab my board, and start walking, barefoot, through the pine needles. I think about Ne'Hwas when she was a girl. I think about her wildness, her courageous soul. Did she hurt the people she loved when she chose the river over them?

Was she scared? Did she have regrets? Did she ever find love?

It's too dark to paddle through the boneyard; I have to find another path into that dark, magical world below. I walk up the rock outcropping at Tutatquin Point to the top of the cliff where we used to picnic, where Kay and I once tested the laws of gravity dropping pine cones to the sea.

There's a low ledge that juts into the savage Atlantic midway down the cliff. Board under one arm, I climb down to the ledge, as waves clap against rock below, shooting white foam into the air.

Down here, the ledge is only a sliver wide. My breathing is hot and fast, but I can't hear it through the crashing waves. I curl my toes around the lip of slippery rock.

Eyes closed, I feel my feet on the cold stone. I wiggle my toes and silently thank them for their years of service. Will I miss them?

A wave explodes against the rocks. I have to time it just right, so I land in water.

All-in.

I jump.

My body hits the ocean with alarming force. Water churns all around me. I scramble onto my board and paddle hard to get away from the rock cliff before the next wave comes in.

The ocean is as black as obsidian now, except for the trail of moonlight all the way to the horizon. In the darkness, there is no warning. A wave is upon me.

I take a breath and paddle after it.

Surfing in the dark is an intense feeling. Without being able to see, I have to rely on my other senses—the sound of waves, the feel of water rushing against my board, the sensation of speed. As soon as the moment is right, I pop to my feet.

I don't know if I'm inside or outside of the sandbar. In the dark, there's no way of knowing how big this wave is. It might be too small. It might not curl. I'm riding blind, blind, blind. If the barrel is gone, and the sandbar is behind me, then I will end up on the rocks.

Suddenly the thunder of crashing waves is gone. There is only deafening silence. I am inside the barrel.

Time slows down. I'm floating on air. I will miss this rush, I think briefly. The hollow wave carries me all the way to shore. When the wave finally peels back I jump off my board and dive under water. My lungs fill with seawater. Almost instantly, my legs transform into a tail.

This is it. My new life. I'm a chameleon no longer.

Now what?

I decide I should find my mom before I do anything else. She can teach me how to survive here. We can be a family again. But how do you find a mermaid in the wide, wide ocean? Same way as on land, I suspect: follow their heart. I swim close to the shore, around Tutatquin Point, toward the rocks where Trip Sinclair ran his boat aground and where Kay's spirit dissolved into the sea.

Under the water, the waves pull me with a magnificent force, crashing like thunder above. As I kick out of the ground swell into deeper water, I think about how the ocean has pulled at all of us—my sister, my mother, me. Could any of us have resisted its deadly power? Or was it destiny that the three of us ended up in the sea?

When I get to a calm cove, around the point, I peek above the surface and see her silhouette against the pale horizon.

My mother is sitting on rock, above water, but sheltered from land. She looks so beautiful with the moon casting a silver sheen over her. Black hair cascades over her shoulders, down her back. She is the image of peace and tranquility.

She almost looks too lovely to disturb. I lift my head completely above water. "Mom."

She doesn't turn around.

"Mom. Over here."

She turns, startled. Her eyes find me.

I swim over to her rock and reach a hand to her. Her eyes dart left then right. She tilts her head to the side.

"Jess." Her voice is like a song. She smiles, and I feel a warm glow inside.

I pull myself onto the rock beside her, our tails dangling side by side in the water. "I'm coming with you, Mom. I'm choosing the life of Ne'Hwas. I talked to my grandmother. She told me all about it. She told me about you and the sea and rescuing that little boy. She told me how you gave it all up, but then, how your grief drove you back here. I'm going to be a mermaid, too. Just like you."

She smiles again.

"I told Sheriff where you are. He misses you, Mom. I wish you hadn't left us without saying good-bye, but he understands. He's happy that we'll be together."

She slaps the surface of the water with her tail, scattering all the small fish below.

She hugs me tightly, and I feel all the anger and resentment inside of me set free.

"It was you who saved me, wasn't it? That time I was caught in the rip current when I was five, and Sheriff found me doing the dead man's float. It was you all along. You jumped in after me, and no one saw. I thought the ocean was cradling me, but it was you. You held me afloat. And then you had to leave us after that, because the ocean was pulling you away and you weren't ready to leave yet. Kay and I were young and you wanted to stay with us."

She laughs and holds me close.

"Life got so unfair up there, Mom. Trip Sinclair took everything from us. He stole our chance at happiness. Now he's trying to get me arrested for harassment. Can you believe that? I want to be down here."

She smiles.

"Well, say something." I laugh. "Are you happy?"

"Jess."

"What do you think?"

She smiles. "Jess."

The smile on my face disappears.

"Mom. Talk to me. What's it like out here? Are you happy? Where do you sleep? Should we explore the ocean? Should we swim down to the Caribbean? Seems like there's more to see down there. I mean, it'll be like a vacation. We have to stay around here, of course. I told Sheriff and Sammy I'd visit them. And I'm really hoping Matthew will join me. Do you think he'll be able to transform like us?"

She smiles. "Jess."

I let go of her. A sick feeling comes over me. It starts in my gut and travels through me. "What is it? Why don't you talk to me?"

Her eyes are somewhere in the distance. She stares at the water. Then, with lightning speed, she reaches down and snatches a little fish out of the water. She holds it so expertly it doesn't even wriggle. Only its mouth moves, lips going up and down, gasping for water.

Then she bites the head off the fish. Blood drips down her chin. I stare in astonishment, the horror creeping in. "Mom. Why won't you talk to me? Can't you speak anymore?"

She smiles and rips off the fish's fins with her teeth, spitting them into the water. She devours the raw fish.

She's here. But she's long gone.

All the joy I felt a few minutes ago has vanished, replaced with a sick, scared sense that I've made the wrong choice. Has my mom lost her humanity? Does she have thoughts anymore? Is she able to think beyond her next meal?

Is she able to love? Or is survival the only thing driving her?

Am I looking at *my* future?

I watch her chew the fish. She smiles at me between bites. She smiles at the fish she ravages. She smiles at the moon. She smiles at the air. She smiles at everything and at nothing. And there is no one behind the smile.

"Are you the person you used to be? Are you still my mother?"

My words drift by her, and she doesn't catch them. She's more interested in eating than communicating. I look back at the island, wondering what I've done.

"I didn't know it would be like this," I say. I push down the lump in my throat. "I thought part of me would still be human, but it doesn't work that way, does it? I thought being a mermaid meant I could run away from all the suffering and pain. I was wrong. To live without sorrow isn't human." I understand it all now.

My mom picks fish bones out of her teeth.

"I love you, Mom. But I've made a mistake." And I leave her.

～～～～

I swim to the sandbar, then around the island toward Lobster Cove, listening for shark vibrations. I need to get home while there's still time.

As I let my senses guide me through the darkness, I run into a kelp bed that pops up before me. The ropelike strands wrap around my arms and I have to swim up to the surface to get untangled.

I'm about ten feet from the surface when something lashes across my neck. A sharp pain shoots through my neck and arms. It's hard to breathe. At first I think a shark has gotten me, but my eyes catch the flutter of a tentacle, lit up in bioluminescence like a blue flame. Bright neon illuminates the water. Pink, blue, green. Strings of Christmas lights pulsing brilliantly. A man-o'-war.

I dive down into the kelp to get away from the tentacles.

The initial pain is nothing compared to the hot white pain that consumes my body in the minutes that follow. It's like a thousand fire ants searing into my flesh at once. I sink to the bottom, lasagna strands of kelp weaving around me. I hit the soft bottom.

Pain racks my chest. It buzzes in my ears. I wait for it to go away.

But it doesn't. My throat is swollen shut. My skin burns and freezes at the same time. The pain travels from my neck, down my body, right into my tail. I try to kick, but there's no feeling. Even my gills hurt.

I stop breathing. A dark, panicky feeling comes over me. I'm drowning. Instinctively, I reach up, breaststroking toward the surface, but my arms are no use against the weight of my tail.

Breathe.

In.

Out.

In.

Out.

I drift down to the bottom again.

My hands are the only part of me that isn't searing with pain, so I flutter them in front of my gills to drive the water in. It seems to help, and it takes my mind off the pain. I curl into a ball on the seafloor and let my hands help me breathe. I flutter until my mind goes blank.

~~~

I'm dreaming about flying. My body soars through the air, wind in my hair. The sky is blue and I'm weightless and rising, up, up, up. Then I catapult back down. Like a slingshot, I hit the surface of the sea and dive into the frigid darkness. I can't stop falling. The bottomless ocean swallows me, my body sinking down.

I awake to a fresh new pain. The searing heat has moved into my muscles. They throb relentlessly.

I'm alive, I tell myself. *I'm breathing.*

My hands go to work fluttering water into my gills. I'm so tired that this tiny motion takes all my energy. I close my eyes, hoping that it will bring relief from pain. I try to hang on. My mind disappears.

All I can do is sleep. I go in and out of consciousness. For hours? Days? Have I slept past the full moon? Have I lost the window into the human world?

Pinprick dots of neon flash in the kelp, little creatures coming out to feed. The kelp sways in my vision, turning into eels and snakes. I try to get away from them, but I can't move. All I can do is sleep.

Finally, the lights come on. My eyes flicker open. Everything is dull gray. I am starving and spent and still in pain, but the initial shock of the sting has subsided. Welts circle around my neck, where the tentacles lashed me.

I look up. The surface is close. Maybe thirty feet. I can make it thirty feet. I try to swim, but my energy is gone.

The kelp sways in the current. I pull a leaf toward me and search it. Tiny worms cluster in the groove of a leaf. I pluck them off and into my mouth. They taste like pond scum. But I manage to swallow and eat some more. I find some translucent prawns and eat those—shells, eyeballs, and all.

It reminds me of fishing the mountain tarns for bullhead and trout with my mother in the spring. Kay came a few times, but she hated skipping school. She'd sit off to the side with a book. My mother and I would wade through the tarn, looking for creepers and scud to use as bait. The pond scum would get on our legs and hands and dry on our skin as we hiked home. That mother is gone now, I think, the sadness stabbing me fresh and new. She is devoid of emotion, suffering, love—and all those things that make us human.

I try to swim, but I can't.

I close my eyes again and drift into sleep. I dream I'm flying, but this time, when I open my eyes, I really am flying. My body is moving weightlessly through the water. Something is carrying me.

I'm so groggy I can't make sense of it. I look behind me and feel a wave of relief when I see my mother swimming above me, her arms wrapped under mine. My tail drags behind. We are moving very slowly and I can feel her heart beating against my back. I try to speak, but my voice is gone.

I hover in and out of consciousness as she carries me through the darkness along the coastline.

When I open my eyes this time, the sun has come up. The water has changed from clear, clean ocean blue to murky green. Engines roar around us. A prickly sensation pulses up and down

my sides and I taste the sour bite of fear on my tongue. Slowly,
I realize that the fear is coming from my mother.

It builds as we rise to the surface. She keeps hold of me as my
head breaks through to a blinding rain. Wind whips at my face.
I try to focus. There are boats, smells of fried food, the sound of
cars nearby. We're in Ne'Hwas Harbor.

I try swimming on my own, but my limbs ache. I barely have
enough energy to tread in place.

My mother's head breaks the surface next to mine. The smile
is gone and her eyes dart rapidly at all the human activity.

"Let's go home," I whisper.

Her heart beats faster. I can feel her anxiety in my chest, just
like I felt the anguish of the mother humpback. Slowly, I realize
that I am an injured animal. Predators can detect my distress
from miles away. I'm putting us both in danger. "Come home
with me," I repeat. "It's not too late."

She looks in my eyes. A tear escapes and quickly mingles with
the rain and sea and I know that she is not coming. This is as far
as she can go. It took every last shred of her humanity to bring
me this far.

A foghorn rings out from the ferry. Her eyes widen. She scur-
ries under the water, her hands still lifting me to the surface from
below, just like they did all those years ago when I felt like the
ocean would never let me drown, not realizing that it was her all
along. I think about the sacrifices that she must have made for
me and Kay. All those years when she resisted the tempting call
of the sea. The grief that she finally was able to submerge.

I slide my hands into hers and pull her up to face me. I want
to see her smile one last time. "I love you," I say, and hug her.
She smiles for me.

She hugs me again, and swims away.

Now I am alone, and I am injured. If I want to survive I need
to make my way to the *Dauntless,* to Matthew. I need to dig deep

and find that last bit of fight in me. I close my eyes and envision the Passamaquoddy symbol for strength—the four concentric circles—swirling around me. I lie on my back as rain pounds down. Staying on the surface, I swim on my back, making an S stroke with my hands. It's early still, and the rain has scared off the tourist boats, so I make it through the harbor undetected.

The white hull of the *Dauntless* is so close I can almost reach it. I inch my way over and reach for a blackened fray of rope hanging off the dock.

I close my eyes.

Matthew's voice comes to me through the haze. "Jess. *Jess!*"

There's a splash next to me. I open my eyes and see Matthew. His yellow raincoat spreads out behind him. His eyes are strange. Worried. Shocked.

"I tried to tell you," I say.

"It's okay. It's okay. It's okay. It's okay," he says, like he's trying to convince himself. He cradles my body in a lifeguard hold.

"I was stung by a man-o'-war."

"It's okay. It's okay. It's okay."

"Can you . . . get me . . . out of here?" my voice is starting to fail.

"I'll call someone." His voice is shaky. "We'll figure this out."

With my last reserve of energy, I turn my head to face him. "No. Don't tell anyone. Promise me."

And then I let the pain and fatigue take me.

TWENTY-NINE

A siren startles me out of my sleep.

I don't know where I am. My pillow is drenched. The smell of the sea hangs in the room, and I think, for a second, that I might be at Ne'Hwas County Hospital. The botched amputation that made national news flashes before me. What have they done to *me*? I look around, details seeping in—the beaded corners of the poster bed, the wall of windows looking out on a veil of fog and rain. Slowly, it comes back to me. Matthew pulling me into the Slack Tide skiff. My tail hanging over the side of the tiny boat. Everything slick with rain. Matthew asking me over and over if I am okay. The bleary light of Kotoki-Pun. Matthew carrying me over the rocks and into his house.

I remember the fever burning through me, my lungs adjusting to air. Feeling like I was drowning. Pain searing through me. Matthew at my side all night long, holding me.

Keeping his shock and horror to himself.

I remember him putting me in the bathtub, and how water was the only thing that could soothe me.

I whip off the sheet, not sure what I'll see.

My legs. Pale and unsteady. Little welts like braille on my skin.

I prop myself up and look out the window. The sky is thick with fog. Only the red stripes of Kotoki-Pun light are visible in the haze of gray. The cliffs are gone. The ocean has disappeared.

Matthew is asleep in the chair by the bed.

I hobble to the bathroom and flick on the light. The floor is shimmery with scales. Mine. What I must have put him through!

I wipe a cool washcloth across my face and neck. The T-shirt I'm wearing smells like Matthew, and I hold it against my nose, taking comfort in it. I feel lucky to be alive. And so terribly disappointed at the same time.

When I walk back into the bedroom, Matthew wakes up and stretches his arms. His blue eyes land on me.

"What day is it?" I ask.

He rubs his face. "Saturday."

"How long was I out?"

"All of yesterday and through last night." He twists his beard. "How do you feel?"

I look down at my legs. "Human."

He stands and takes me in his arms. "I'm sorry I didn't believe you."

"I wouldn't have believed, either."

"Coffee?"

I nod.

He leaves the room and I stand at the windows, staring out at where the ocean should be. I think about my mother and how the sea tugged at her until she couldn't ignore it. The animal in her has taken over, the human side almost gone. And yet, she rescued me. Was that the human or the animal?

Matthew comes back with the coffee in a dainty cup painted with yellow roses. Alice's teacups.

The coffee perks me up. I stretch out my legs and neck, cracking my joints.

Matthew sits on the edge of the bed. "Are you going back?"

I sit next to him. "No. It's over. Tonight's the full moon. My portal disappears."

"And all that talk about me going with you?"

"It was silly. I can't ask you to give up the life you know."

Matthew presses a hand to my heart.

"I want you to know that I would go anywhere with you."

"Really?"

"I'm all-in." The corners of his eyes turn upward in a smile.

I throw my arms around him and kiss him. But my body is still sore, and I slump into the bed.

"I'm going to run to the pharmacy and get you something for that pain," he says.

He kisses my forehead lightly and leaves the house.

Once I'm all alone, I get dressed and step outside. I walk over lichen-covered rocks and through wildflowers to the edge of the cliff. The pounding of waves echoes over the point. Fog is so thick it swallows everything—trees, cliffs, ocean. It's beautiful in an eerie sort of way. Alone, I stand at the edge of the island, churning through the possibilities in my mind. What do I do now? Go back to flipping burgers on a fishing boat, after all I've been through? Should I go through that barrel again and take Matthew with me? Can we be happy together in a place as alien as the sea? Will we just end up speaking in monosyllabic sentences to each other and staring off into space, like my mom?

Or was my grandmother right? Is it too late for my mom? Does a mermaid need the heart and passion of girl like Ne'Hwas?

As I head back to the front door I spot a newspaper in the pea gravel driveway. I walk across the wet stone and pick it up. I'll set it out for Matthew. We'll drink coffee and have pancakes and we'll talk about our future. And which animal kingdom we want to spend it in.

He's all-in. What more could I ask for?

I'm still smiling about a future with Matthew, when I look down and see Trip Sinclair's smug face on page one of the *Daily News.* He's standing on the bow of the *Sea Nymphe,* wind blowing his hair, looking like a model for men's cologne. The headline reads "Regatta Favorite Trip Sinclair Returns to the Circuit."

The article says that the race today is basically Trip's for the taking. Bennett Sinclair is quoted saying that he looks forward to his grandson's long-awaited return to the racing circuit. That the family looks forward to a bright future in sailing and to restoring their tattered legacy.

The anger is like lava in my veins. I need to let it out. I need to unleash the animal and let it do what the human in me can't.

I don't leave a note. I'm worried that just writing Matthew's name will make me change my mind.

〜〜〜

My legs are still wobbly as I bike down the driveway on an old cruiser I found in the garage. It must belong to Alice. A wicker basket with big plastic flowers bobs along on the handlebars. Steering with one hand, Matthew's board tucked under my other arm, I make my way out of Kotoki-Pun Point, past the diner, putting Matthew's house farther behind me. All I can think of is Trip Sinclair.

Wind whips up mini cyclones of trash on Barefoot Lane. It knocks down the LIVE LOBSTERS sign in front of the lobster pound.

The race will be getting under way any minute. And I will finally get the chance to get Kay the justice she deserves.

〜〜〜

The waves are sloppy. Double overhead at least. Closing out left and right. Bad conditions for Regatta. Worse conditions for surfing. No other surfers are out. Nipon Beach is empty. The fog has cleared out, and the ocean is in a fury.

And I'm in a fury, too. The fury attaches itself to me like a remora to a shark. I want blood.

I run into the water. Waves pummel me backwards with every stroke I take. I'm still weak from the fever and dehydration, and there's no lull between waves to catch my breath. It's a relentless force of water, determined to meet the shore.

Once I'm past the break, I don't rest. I spin around and paddle into a wave. It's an ugly one. Rough and frothy. Whitecaps on top of whitecaps. But I don't need pretty. I just need a barrel.

I paddle, paddle, paddle, the wave racing up behind me. I pop up to my feet. Nothing but air below the nose. I drop down the face, my legs wobbly, my heart racing, the cold spray of ocean in my face.

And I fall.

Headfirst, I plunge into the wave. A tornado of white water forces me downward, pushing me into the sand. My face scrapes the bottom. I cover my head with my hand as I somersault in the maelstrom.

When I come up for air, my board is gone, my leash detached. I look up just in time to see my board sailing over the waves in a gust of wind.

And the next wave is almost on top of me.

My strength is slipping. I struggle to keep my head above water. How am I going to surf a barrel without a board? It's like opening a locked door without a key.

I suck in a lungful of air and dive down, as far beneath the churning wash of the next wave as I can get. Sand grazes my belly. Thunder fills my ears.

My stomach aches, my muscles are weak. I should have eaten before I left Matthew's. Matthew will be wondering where I am now. What would he think of me if he knew what I was doing? Would he try to stop me? *Don't think about that now.* I push thoughts of Matthew deep down, away from the surface of my mind.

With my last reserve of strength, I swim seaward. Wind shaves off the top of the next wave, sending razor-sharp spray at me, burning my eyes.

I turn and see the next wave in front of me. It's as tall as a two-story building. A beast. A big, beautiful beast. I swim with it, feeling the energy behind it.

At the crest, I kick like hell and start moving down the face. I'm about to go under, so I thrust my head and shoulders down, adjusting my center of balance, forcing my hips to skim the surface. As I bodysurf down the face, racing to catch the barrel, speed is the only thing keeping me above water.

There's so much spray in my face, I don't even see the lip of the wave curl. This time, the transition is faster than ever. When I come out of the end of the barrel, I can already feel the tightening of my skin, my legs pressing together. My tail, my gills. That cold, delicious feeling of breathing water.

I dive under and swim to the racecourse.

I don't know exactly what I'm planning on doing with him, once I have him. Maybe I'll just scare him. Maybe I'll toy with him like a seal toys with its prey before it goes in for the kill. To do nothing seems like a disgrace. I want him to feel what Kay felt, the day that he crashed her into the rocks and then left her for dead.

I want him to be alone and desperate, slipping under the cold water, unable to swim. I want him to know the fear as urgently and acutely as she felt it. And I want him wondering if anyone is going to save him. If anyone cares about him.

Out here, Kay will finally have her justice because human rules don't apply in the wild. Animals aren't bound by any laws. We kill to eat. Kill to defend ourselves. Kill to keep the balance of the ocean.

I hear the siren under the water. Two short blasts. A pause. A long one. The five-minute warning signal. I need to get to the racecourse and get my hands on Trip Sinclair.

My head breaks the surface to a misty gray sky. A tall peak looms in the distance. Mount Wabanaki. I'm too far away. I dive again and swim parallel to shore, dolphin kicking with furious speed. I follow the north–south ridges in the sand, ignoring the electrical currents pulsing through my lateral line. *Prey nearby,* the electrical currents tell me. *Time to hunt,* my body says.

But it's not fish that I'm hunting today.

When I get to a long, shallow flat, I know I'm at North Beach. Noises come from every direction. Motorboats zip around like flies. Party voices ring out from the spectator boats. The race-course buoys are directly in front of the harbor, stretching between Kotoki-Pun light and Seal Point in a fifteen-mile loop.

The siren sounds again. A long, shrill blast. The race is on.

I sprint under water, below the great hulls that slice through the water above. I swim alongside the keel of one of them, and break the surface, just astern. I can hear the slashing of rain on sails, of men yelling commands. There are letters across the transom. I make out an *r.* An *o.* Wrong boat.

I dive again.

My human sickness is gone, replaced with animal strength and speed. My legs are not wobbly and weak. I don't feel pain. The shackles of fever from the last twenty-four hours have fallen away and something else in me roars to life. Like a majestic white shark, I swim beneath the boats, hunting for the black hull of *Sea Nymphe.*

These world-class racing yachts are no match for my speed. I pass two more boats, until I see the black hull leading the pack.

I swim up to it and peek above the surface in the trough of a wave. The water is a million shades of black and gray, mirroring the stormy sky. The words *Sea Nymphe* in gold cross the transom directly in front of me. The boat leans on its side. The men on deck work the winches. Vibrations run up and down my spine, sensing the stress of wind against canvas, halyards clanging on metal. The boom of the mainsail stretches across the width of the boat. A broad reach.

I can see him from behind. Trip Sinclair is standing at the big chrome wheel on the stern, commanding his boat. Enjoying his life. Winning his race. Winning everything. Getting away with murder.

Why does he get to live? Where is the justice in that? I let the rage rise up into my animal brain.

I hear Matthew's voice: *"Let it go, Creary."* I hear Sheriff's voice: *"Don't do anything stupid."*

And I push the voices away. I let my body do what it wants to do.

Attack.

The boat slows down as the crew prepares to tack. In teams of two, they crank the winches, man the lines, attend the sails. Like a hive of ants, everyone is busy with their task. The boat heels to starboard. All eyes are ahead; no one is looking astern. Now is my chance.

As the *Sea Nymphe* makes a hard turn, I speed up staying just below the surface. When I'm an arm's length away, I kick hard to catapult out of the water. I fly through the air and land with a thud against the sleek transom.

The yacht's high-tech design leaves nothing in the way of a barrier between the driver and the stern rail. All I need to do is grab him. I get one hand around his ankle, then the other. Startled, he looks behind and a split second later I pull him down.

In a heap, we roll off the transom. It happens so fast, no one notices. All hands are on deck.

Trip hits the water a second after me.

Clenching his ankles in my fist, I dive down.

He's wearing a thin flotation vest over his rain jacket—one of those high-tech gadgets that's more buoyant than it looks. He slips out of my hand and springs back up to the surface like a fishing bobber.

He claws at the surface, arms flailing. He tries to yell for help, but the *Sea Nymphe* sails ahead. A few seconds later, the cry "Man overboard!" sends the boat into a frenzy. In the water, I can hear every little sound. The mainsail is lowered. Someone takes the wheel. A voice hails an S.O.S. on the radio.

I break the surface next to him and quickly unbuckle his life vest. His eyes dart wildly, blind with panic. I yank the vest off him and toss it out of reach. Without it, he's mine.

I get him in a bear hug and dive under, putting as much distance between us and the *Sea Nymphe* as I can. Aware that every passing second is a cruel mix of panic and agony for Trip.

Just like it must have been for Kay as she crashed into the rocks of Tutatquin Point, wondering why she had ever trusted this man.

Under water, Trip tries to break free. His motions are clumsy. I can feel the erratic currents of his struggling body down my sides, in my spine. His vibrations mark him as easy prey—the type sharks go for. Thinning the herd. Keeping the balance in the ocean. Helping the species survive.

I let Trip go. He kicks to the surface, takes a breath, and I pull him down again. I swim him out to the open Atlantic, let him go, let him breathe, pull him down, swim, let him go, let him breathe, swim. Again and again. I let the fear burn deep inside of him.

Each cycle takes him farther from his boat, farther from his perfectly calculated racecourse, from the world where he's the master. This is my world now. Human rules don't apply.

I let him go again, and this time he doesn't scramble to the surface. He's suspended in the water, five feet below. I poke him in the ribs, but he doesn't respond. His eyes are closed, his skin pale. He's a limp rag doll.

I feel cold seawater rush through my gills. Around me, the ocean closes in, the edges of my vision turn bleak and murky. All is silent except for the thoughts in my head.

They are human thoughts. The kind that will escape me in my mermaid future. They are too loud to ignore: What have I done?

When did murder become so easy for me? Am I a monster? A human? Or am I simply an animal? Is it okay to kill if you're an animal? Does it give me the right to vengeance? No. Not even animals kill out of revenge. They kill to survive. This is murder. Is this who I am now? Is there any way back to humanity after this?

There are tears in my eyes that are quickly stolen by the sea. Off in the distance, I hear the rumble of an engine.

I grab Trip by the arm and lift him to the surface. His face is pale against the dark ripples of rain. My lungs fill with air as the water flushes out. I put my ear to his mouth, but he doesn't breathe.

I tilt Trip's head back, put my mouth over his, and blow. Rain beats against my neck and head. More boats are near. Their engines send roaring vibrations through the water.

It takes five breaths. Water gushes from his mouth and he coughs.

Through the fog, I spot the white hull of the police boat. I whistle the way Sheriff taught me and Kay if we were ever needed help. Those old police tricks ingrained in us.

I whistle again. This time the police boat kicks into idle. Trip coughs, still struggling to breathe. I whistle one last time. The police boat turns toward me and Trip. As it breaks through the fog, headed toward me, I dive under water.

From below I push Trip's body to the surface, cradling him in my hands, just as my mother did all those years ago when the rip tide took me to sea and I dreamed I was swimming with dolphins to their magical kingdom.

I stay completely submerged as the boat pulls alongside Trip's body. Someone reaches over the gunwale and lifts him inside. I can hear the clanging of the oxygen tank on board, another officer hailing headquarters on the radio, Trip coughing.

From under the water I see someone lean over the gunwale

again and peer down. Although the rain smears the surface of the water, obscuring the image above me, I know the slant of his shoulders, the gesture of a finger on the bridge of his nose.

Sheriff looks at me and I look at him. He blows me a kiss then disappears back into the boat.

I watch as the police boat cuts through the fog and rain toward home.

EPILOGUE

One year later

The surface of the ocean is like velvet today. Soft ripples spread across the Atlantic as the morning sun dances across the cerulean sky. This is a friendly sea. It will change again with the tide. An afternoon breeze will blow in. Waves will roar. Sharks will come out to feed.

I can feel a vibration pulsing through me now. A bass thump deep in my solar plexus.

Lady Gaga.

"Turn down the music," I yell to Toby, who's got his portable waterproof speakers on full blast again. He's a sophomore from some college in Wyoming who had never set foot on a boat until this month, when he flew to Cape Cod, slung his regulation rucksack over his shoulder, and boarded the SSV *Sipayik*. As a kid from Wyoming who grew up around cattle and mountains, he'd never been on a boat in the ocean before. He didn't even know that the SSV stands for Sailing School Vessel.

To be fair, neither did I, and I've been surrounded by ocean all my life.

Toby turns down the volume and gets to work labeling samples for the plankton splitter that we'll run in the wet lab later today.

Most of the kids on the boat don't know what to make of me. They call me the dolphin whisperer because every time I'm on bow watch, pods of dolphins appear out of nowhere. Whether it's four in the morning or eleven at night, the dolphins find me, leaping into the air, dazzling all on deck with their acrobatics. I don't tell anyone that I can feel the presence of all the life below; their hearts beat through me like the warm salt air.

How could a group of scientifically minded college students understand something as mystical as that? They've all taken the straight road here—high school, college, semester at sea, then on to graduate school for marine sciences. My road has veered and twisted like the bends of an ancient river.

I can't imagine my life any other way. It's my destiny to veer. To wander. To transform. It's what led me to my extraordinary summer. It's how I witnessed firsthand the majesty of the great white, and felt the bond between mother and baby humpback.

I wish I could use some of that magic to help me get through organic chemistry next semester, when we set sail for the Virgin Islands, but something tells me I'm going to have to rely on coffee and late-night study sessions instead.

It took some doing to get a spot on this boat. I'm paying my way on a special work-study program. I'm the steward, which is a fancy word for galley girl. They normally don't hire students as cooks, but they made an exception for me, thanks to a nudge from Trip Sinclair, who sits on the board of trustees for the Woods Hole Oceanographic Institution. After surviving a serious boating accident for the second time in his life, Trip felt that it was time to turn his life around. His encounter with the mysterious creature (was it rabid dolphin, he wondered?) made him take stock. Somehow he felt that what had happened to him during Regatta was karmic retribution. At least that's what he told Sheriff aboard the harbor police boat that day, when he finally acknowledged responsibility for Kay's death. He told Sheriff he was sorry. He told Sheriff Kay deserved better. And while he didn't go quite so far as to turn himself in on voluntary manslaughter charges, he promised to do right by our family. When my name came up on the sea semester program, I was even awarded a long-term contract to work on the boat and complete my missing college coursework through an independent study program.

Sammy thinks it's awesome. She made me promise to keep an eye out for any particularly tasty college guys who might be interested in spending their summer break on Ne'Hwas.

I look at my watch and see that it's time to get breakfast on the table, so I leave Toby to his specimens and head down to the galley.

First, I stop in the chart room.

Matthew is bent over the chart table with a kid named Rachel, from Virginia, who wants to earn her captain's license and run a boat of her own someday. He's teaching her how to plot a nautical course with a parallel plotter, compass, stopwatch, and number two pencil. The way sailors navigated the world long before electronics.

Matthew looks up and smiles at me, the lines around his eyes like those of a child's drawing depicting rays of sunshine. I smile back. We've gotten into a nice routine working on the boat. The captain and the galley girl.

At night, when homework is done and everyone has finished their stations for the day, and students are hanging out in the main saloon, playing cards or watching old movies on the VHS player, I tell them the legend from the Upriver People, about two sisters who had to make a choice: this world or the one below.

The older sister, Sipayik, was good and obedient and chose to climb out of the water with legs and live on land for the rest of her days. I tell them that I picture her as a bit of a nerd, always doing the right thing, like my sister. I bet Sipayik always had her nose in a book. She probably never snuck out of the tepee after dark or cheated on her vocabulary tests by writing the answers on her forearm. She probably won all the awards at school, dated the richest guy in the village, and planned to take the world by storm.

I hope she did.

I hope that Sipayik lived a full, happy life.

The younger sister, Ne'Hwas, was wild, and she couldn't ignore the wildness inside of her. She jumped into that cool, blue water and decided never to leave it.

I wonder what became of Ne'Hwas. I think about her often these days. Was she happy? Did she find love? Or did she lose herself to the wildness of the sea? I wonder, too, about my mother, and whether I'll ever get to see her again. I find myself searching. It might be a trick of the eyes, or a gust of wind on the water, but every once in a while I catch a flicker of purple, a flash of a smile.

~~~~

As I'm cracking the morning's eggs into a bowl, Toby sticks his head into the galley. "Jess, there are humpbacks! Come see!" I run up to the quarterdeck, where the entire crew and all the students are gathered. Cameras and binoculars are aimed out to sea.

A family of humpback whales breach in the distance.

"Do you think they're watching us, too?" Toby asks.

"Yes, I do," I say.

Matthew lifts his sunglasses over his forehead and gives me a wink.

"All right, everyone back to their stations," Matthew says, replacing the sunglasses. "This boat won't sail itself."

I linger by the railing. Matthew walks up and puts his arm around me. "Feeling homesick?"

I wonder, momentarily, which home he means. "No. We'll be back on Ne'Hwas for Thanksgiving. Sheriff's already texted me five times to make sure we're coming."

"Does this mean ham sandwiches for Thanksgiving dinner?" Matthew asks. The crescent scar below his eye disappears into his smile.

"Don't worry. Sheila's going to help him cook." The police dispatcher with the heart of gold has become a permanent fixture in his life. It makes me happy that he's not alone.

A gust of wind whistles through the shrouds of the ship. I can feel the salty air on my skin.

"Do you miss it, Creary?" Matthew asks, looking at the sea.

I look at the sea, too, and feel the savage pull of its depths in my veins. "Of course. It's part of me."

He kisses the top of my head and squeezes me close. "I'm glad you stayed."

"Me too," I whisper, though only time will tell.